I0747328

The Greater Light

The Greater Light

Lights of the Collapse
Book 2

Millie Copper

This is a work of fiction. All characters, places, and incidents are products of the author's imagination or are used fictitiously. Any resemblance to actual people, places, or events is entirely coincidental.

Technical information in the book is included to convey realism. The author shall assume no liability or responsibility to any person or entity with respond to any loss or damage caused, or allegedly caused, directly or indirectly by information contained in this book of fiction. Any reference to registered or trademarked brands is used simply to convey familiarity. This manuscript is in no way sponsored or endorsed by any brand mentioned.

Copyright © 2025 CU Publishing LLC
ISBN-13: 978-1-957088-35-8

All rights reserved.

No part of this publication may be reproduced, stored in a retrieval system, or transmitted in any form or by any means without the prior written permission of the author, except by a reviewer who may quote short passages in a review.

Written by Millie Copper

Edited by Ameryn Tucker

Proofread by MDC Proofreading

Cover design by Dauntless Cover Design

Also by Millie Copper

The Havoc in Wyoming Series

When a series of coordinated attacks devastate the United States, the people of Bakerville, Wyoming, must come together to survive. Unfortunately, not everyone has the town's best interest at heart. Some are striving for personal gain during the apocalypse.

The Montana Mayhem Series

A group from Bakerville, Wyoming strikes out on their own while searching for the desires of their heart. Unfortunately, the road will not be easy, and sometimes the heart is hardened and deceitful. When things don't work out as they hoped, will they become stranded in the wilderness? Or will each be able to find their way home?

The Dakota Destruction Series

After a series of coordinated attacks devastate the United States, Katie and Leo sacrifice everything to help their country. But some things aren't as they seem. Is it time to go home and start fresh, or can something good come out of this terrible situation?

Wyoming Fall Series (In The October Fall World)

In the blink of an eye, an EMP changed everything for Lauren and her family. Now they are in a fight for survival, trying to keep their loved ones alive as society collapses around them. Their once peaceful town of Cody, Wyoming has turned into a powder keg. And with law enforcement a thing of the past, evil lurks around every corner.

Nonfiction Books

Millie has penned seven nonfiction, traditional food focused books, sharing how, with a little creativity, anyone can transition to a real foods diet without overwhelming their food budget. Many of her books also include preparedness and food storage tips.

Find these titles at:
MillieCopper.com

Join My Reader's Club!

Receive a complimentary copy of *Starborn: A Lights of the Collapse Short Story Prequel*. As part of my reader's club, you'll be the first to know about new releases and specials. I also share info on books I'm reading, preparedness tips, and more. Please sign up at:

MillieCopper.com/Freebie

Chapter 1

The bells chimed softly as the door to Elle's Boutique swung open, the scent of jasmine wafting through the air. Alyson straightened a rack of dresses as her fingers brushed against the delicate fabrics. She glanced at her watch, noting the time. It was 12:15 p.m., the peak of the lunch hour rush.

"Hello!" she called out, her tone cheery and inviting. "Please let me know if I can set up a dressing room for you."

The two women dressed in business attire barely acknowledged her as they made a beeline for the sales rack at the back of the store. They were regulars, dropping in each week to not only check the latest deals but to see what was new.

Alyson suppressed a sigh. Some days, it felt like she was invisible, simply another fixture in the store. But she shook off the feeling and reminded herself that this job was a stepping stone, a means to an end. She was there to help pay her way through college, not to make lifelong friends with every customer who walked through the door.

"Hey, Aly, can you help me with this display?" her roommate and best friend, Jenna, called from across the store. She was struggling with a mannequin, trying to change its pose. Another shopper shook her head and moved away from Jenna and her struggles.

Alyson walked over, her movements precise and purposeful. "Jenna, you need to adjust the base first." She kneeled down to show her. "Once you've fixed the base, you can move the arms without it toppling over."

Jenna smiled sheepishly. "Thanks, Aly. I don't know what I'd do without you."

"Probably get fired," Alyson teased, but her tone was affectionate. She and Jenna had been friends since their first day of freshman year, when Jenna, teary-eyed and frazzled, had gotten turned around on campus. She wasn't completely lost, just close enough to the right area to miss it in her panic.

They had bonded quickly, both of them living in the dorms that year. Just a few weeks ago, as their first year wrapped up, they'd moved into an apartment with another friend. "And you'll have to beg your parents for rent money."

"Hey, speaking of the apartment . . ." Jenna whispered, glancing around to make sure there weren't any customers nearby. "Did you hear Megan last night? I swear, if she and that boyfriend of hers keep me up one more night with their video game marathons, I'm going to lose it."

Alyson nodded, and a spark of annoyance crossed her face. "I know. I thought about saying something, but . . ." She trailed off, not wanting to admit how confrontations made her uncomfortable. It was easier to put in her earbuds and drown out the noise so she could concentrate on her book. "It's Megan's apartment too. We all agreed we wouldn't nag at each other over little things."

"You're too nice." Jenna rolled her eyes. "This isn't a little thing. I need my sleep. One of these days, Aly, you're going to have to learn to stand up for yourself."

Alyson brushed off the comment, not wanting to dwell on it. She preferred to think of herself as diplomatic rather than passive. It wasn't like Jenna said anything either.

Alyson smiled as she glanced around. The boutique was bustling with activity. Women in tailored suits and chic dresses flitted from rack to rack, their conversations blending into a harmonious hum. Alyson loved this time of day—the energy of the shoppers, the satisfaction of a well-organized store. It gave her a sense of control, something she cherished deeply.

As she returned to the cash register, her thoughts wandered to her summer courses. Graduating on time was nonnegotiable, even if it meant tackling an extra workload. She'd finished high school a year early, skipping a grade in elementary school. While starting college younger than her peers might have been a hurdle, she turned it into a strength.

Organized and driven, she planned her days down to the minute, every hour accounted for. Jenna liked to tease her about being a control freak, but Alyson didn't care. She had a clear vision of her goals. And nothing was going to stop her.

"Can you grab another size for me?" a customer asked, holding up a sleek black dress. The woman's crisp suit and perfectly coiffed hair screamed "corporate executive," and Alyson felt a flutter of excitement. This was the kind of woman she aspired to be one day. Successful, confident, and in control.

"Of course. What size do you need?" Alyson replied, her smile warm and professional.

"An eight, please."

Alyson nodded and headed to the stockroom. She quickly found the dress and returned to the sales floor, handing it to the customer. As she scanned the room, her gaze landed on Jenna, who was chatting animatedly with a group of women by the accessory display. Jenna's outgoing personality naturally drew people in, a vibrant contrast to Alyson's quieter demeanor. They balanced each other well.

Watching Jenna effortlessly charm the customers, a flicker of envy stirred in Alyson. Social interactions never came naturally to her. She preferred the structure of numbers and the predictability of a well-planned schedule. Still, she reminded herself everyone brought their own strengths to the table, and hers held equal value.

Her finger hovered over the tablet screen, mid-tap, when a thunderous crash shattered the boutique's calm. The front window burst inward, and shards of glass spun through the air like jagged stars. A harsh, metallic screech tore through the space, drowning out the murmured conversations and the soft hum of music in the background.

Her chest tightened, and her pulse pounded in her ears. Her breath was caught somewhere between a gasp and a scream.

Time seemed to slow, the horrific scene unfolding in fragments before her eyes. An oversized SUV had careened halfway into the store, its front end crumpled against the display. Mannequins lay shattered on the floor, tangled with clothing and debris.

Alyson's mind raced as she took in the sight. Trembling, she pressed her hands to her mouth and leaned back on her heels, her legs unsteady as reality sank in.

Those weren't all mannequins.

People were lying on the floor. Their cries and screams left no doubt of their realism.

Her shaky legs were unable to support her, and she sank to her bottom.

The carefully ordered world Alyson had built for herself exploded along with the store's front window. The control she prided herself on slipped through her fingers like sand, leaving her grasping for something, anything, to anchor herself to reality.

Amid the frenzy, Alyson scanned the store, her eyes locking onto Jenna near the accessory display. Her friend stood frozen, eyes wide with terror.

Alyson swallowed hard and forced herself to focus. She couldn't afford to panic. Not when people needed her.

A voice in her mind, familiar and strong like her father's, cut through the noise. *You're a Reynolds, Alyson. And Reynolds don't fall apart when things get tough. We step up.* The words, ingrained in her since childhood, pushed her into action.

With a deep breath, she steadied herself. "Someone call 9-1-1!" she shouted, her voice cutting through the confusion. She grabbed Jenna, still paralyzed by fear, and pulled her toward the stockroom. "Jenna, we need to help them."

Jenna nodded. "Tell me what to do."

"If someone's bleeding, apply pressure. Use the clothes as bandages."

"The clothes? We can't—"

"Just do it. The owner will understand." Alyson moved swiftly, trusting her instinct about the owner understanding the use of the expensive clothing as bandages, as she turned her attention to the injured.

Her eyes landed on a woman with a deep gash on her leg, crimson pooling around her in a widening circle. "It's going to be okay," Alyson said, using a scarf from a nearby display to stanch the bleeding. "Help is on the way."

For the next woman she checked, help would never come. Her wide eyes stared unseeing at the ceiling.

A wave of nausea swept over Alyson, but she pushed it down. There was no time for weakness. Uninjured shoppers and people coming in off the street were doing all they could to help. As Alyson assisted a woman with an obviously broken arm who was having trouble breathing, someone checked the driver of the car.

"She's dead," the man said, shaking his head.

The minutes dragged on, each one feeling like an eternity. The sound of sirens in the distance was both a relief and a reminder of the severity of the situation. Alyson continued to move through the store, offering what help she could. She found a teenage girl, not much younger than herself, who'd been shopping with her mom, crying under a rack of clothes. She gently coaxed her out and held her close as she sobbed.

"It's okay," Alyson murmured. "You're safe now. Can you tell me your name?" The girl hiccupped and managed to whisper "Sophie" between sobs.

Alyson nodded, maintaining eye contact. "Okay, Sophie. I'm Alyson. Everything will be okay. You're safe. You'll be fine." As she spoke the words, she knew she was lying. The girl's mom was the one she'd found earlier. Dead. Sophie's life had changed forever in an instant. She wouldn't be fine.

Alyson's hands were steady, her mind focused. But she couldn't shake the dread that settled in her chest as she surveyed the damage.

Finally, the paramedics arrived and took over the scene with practiced efficiency. Alyson and Jenna stepped back, their adrenaline beginning to wear off. Jenna's face was pale, her eyes wide with shock.

"Alyson, what just happened?" she whispered, her voice barely audible.

"I don't know," Alyson replied, her own voice sounding distant in her ears. "But we're going to be okay. We did what we could."

As the paramedics worked, Alyson glanced around the store. The once-pristine boutique was now a scene of destruction, the normalcy of only minutes ago a distant memory.

A pang of sorrow gripped her for the lives lost, for the people who had been injured. Yet, beneath that sorrow, a quiet sense of strength emerged. In the face of disaster, she had uncovered a resilience she hadn't known she had. It was a disconcerting realization, one she wasn't quite ready to examine too closely.

Jenna clung to her, tears streaming down her face. "I'm so scared."

"We're okay, Jenna. We're okay," Alyson said, more to convince herself than to reassure her friend. "It's over now." But as the words left her mouth, doubt lingered. Was it really over?

Her carefully constructed world had shifted in an instant, and like her friend, she wasn't sure she'd ever be truly okay again. Something like this could break a person. Leave a mark that never faded.

Chapter 2

Alyson's walk home passed in a daze. Her fists were clenched tight, her knuckles pale as she hurried through unfamiliar-feeling streets. Walking became mechanical, her body on autopilot while her mind churned.

Beside her, Jenna stayed silent, her unfocused gaze fixed somewhere ahead. The police had questioned them for hours, their voices a distant murmur against the numbness pressing in.

The city's usual hum barely registered. She stole a glance at Jenna, noting the tight line of her lips and paleness of her face.

"We're almost home," Alyson said, her voice sounding hollow even to her own ears.

Jenna nodded absently, her arms wrapped tightly around her body as if trying to hold herself together. "I can't believe it," she whispered, more to herself than to Alyson. "It all happened so fast."

Alyson's jaw tightened. "I know. But we're okay. We're safe now." As she spoke, her mind replayed the scene in fragments. The shattering glass, the screams, the confusion. She shook her head, trying to clear the images.

"We need to keep moving," she said, more to break the silence than anything else.

Jenna's gaze shifted toward her, fear in her eyes. "Did you hear them? The police and paramedics? They said it was like the others. Here! In Portland. Did you hear about the traffic jam on I-205?"

Alyson gave a small nod. She'd overheard the conversations. In truth, she'd clung to every word. They said at least fifty cars were involved, with traffic backed up for miles. The entire interchange was frozen. But her thoughts weren't with the hundreds affected. Only one. Her dad.

He had called last night to tell her about a meeting with a client near Interstate 205 and Division Street. He thought he'd finish by four o'clock and asked if they could grab dinner afterward at the Moroccan place she loved. She'd turned him down, claiming she needed to study for an online class. It wasn't true. She didn't need to study; she hadn't wanted to see him.

Her last visit home for Memorial Day had made her feel like a kid again, a stark contrast to the independence she prided herself on in Portland. Sure, her parents and her roommates' parents chipped in for rent, but she still managed the apartment while juggling work and classes.

As soon as she heard about the mess on the interstate, she tried to call her dad. She needed to make sure he was okay and to tell him what happened. The call wouldn't go through.

She'd tried her mom next, figuring she'd be in her office at home in Astoria. The line rang endlessly before disconnecting. She called both of them every few minutes until the police interview began, and again afterward while she waited for Jenna to finish.

Now her phone was in her hand, ready to try again once they reached the apartment. For the moment, though, her focus was on getting them home. Jenna seemed too out of it to pay proper attention to where they were going.

"What if it happens again?" Jenna asked. "What if—"

"It won't," Alyson interrupted, her tone firm.

As they approached their apartment building, the familiar sight brought a small measure of comfort. Alyson reached for Jenna's hand and gave it a reassuring squeeze. "We're almost there."

Jenna squeezed back. Her grip was shaky at first and then became stronger. "Thanks, Aly. For everything."

Alyson managed a faint smile. "Let's get inside."

She unlocked the security door, and they climbed the stairs to their third-floor apartment, each step echoing in the industrial stairwell. The building had once been a factory, the brick exterior and tall windows a nod to its past. Now, it housed a mix of young professionals and students, the raw, exposed beams and ductwork lending it a modern, urban charm.

Alyson paused for a moment and glanced down the dimly lit hallway. The concrete walls were adorned with abstract murals, remnants of the building's artistic conversion. Normally, the eclectic decor appeared vibrant and alive, but this afternoon, it seemed cold and distant.

As Alyson unlocked the apartment door and stepped inside, the familiar creak of the heavy metal hinges sounded louder than usual. The apartment wasn't huge but had an open floor plan, making the most of the space. Large windows lined one wall, offering a view of the cityscape, and a small balcony extended out. It was usually a spot for morning coffee and late-night chats.

The industrial-chic decor, with its mix of modern accents and cast-off furniture from the roomies' parents, felt out of place, a stark contrast to the mess they'd left behind. Alyson took a deep breath, trying to anchor herself in what was familiar, but the dissonance was overwhelming.

Jenna followed her in, closing the door softly behind her. She leaned against it for a moment, eyes closed, as if gathering the strength to face the evening ahead.

Alyson watched her. Knowing that words wouldn't suffice, her heart ached for her friend.

"We're home," she said quietly, more to herself than to Jenna. The word *home* took on a different meaning now, reshaped by the day's events.

Jenna gave a weary nod. "We're home," she echoed, her voice barely above a whisper.

They stood there in silence for a moment, the apartment's familiar ambiance wrapping around them. It was a fragile comfort, but it was all they had. Alyson couldn't shake the sensation their world had irrevocably changed.

Their roommate, Megan, stood at the stove, spatula in hand. She turned, her smile fading as she took in their appearances. "Oh my goodness, what happened? Are you guys okay?"

Jenna burst into tears, the dam finally breaking.

Megan immediately abandoned her cooking and rushed over to envelop her in a hug.

Alyson stood frozen, unable to find the words to explain. "There was . . . an accident," she managed finally, her voice barely above a whisper. "At the store. A car . . ."

Understanding dawned on Megan's face. "I saw something on social media about accidents on the interstate, but I didn't realize . . ."

"Not the interstate." Alyson shook her head. "The boutique. A driver lost control and drove into the building."

"It was awful," Jenna added.

"Oh, no." Megan shook her head. "Come sit down."

She guided them to the couch, her arm still around Jenna's shoulders.

Alyson sank into the cushions, her body feeling every bruise and ache from the day's events.

"Ryan!" Megan called out toward the balcony. "Can you bring some water? And maybe some of those cookies from the top shelf?"

A tall, lanky guy with tousled brown hair appeared from the balcony, his expression shifting from confusion to concern as he took in the scene. He nodded, heading to the kitchen without a word.

"Do you want to talk about it?" Megan's hand rubbed soothing circles on Jenna's back.

Alyson shook her head. The words were there, pressing against her throat, but she couldn't bring herself to relive the horror just yet.

Jenna's sobs had quieted to hiccups, her face buried in Megan's shoulder.

Ryan returned with glasses of water and a package of chocolate chip cookies. He set them on the coffee table, hovering awkwardly for a moment before retreating to the balcony.

As Megan continued to murmur words of comfort, Alyson found her gaze drawn to the balcony door. Ryan stood with his back to them, his posture tense. There was something off about his stance, but exhaustion kept her from questioning it.

"You two should try to eat something," Megan said, breaking into Alyson's thoughts. "I made grilled cheese and soup for supper. Ryan and I were going to eat on the balcony. It's not much, but . . ."

"Thanks, Meg." Alyson managed a weak nod. "Maybe in a bit. I think we need some time to process."

Megan's expression softened with understanding. "Of course. I'm here if you need anything, okay? Anything at all. I can't imagine what you went through today. But you're safe now. You're home."

Alyson swallowed hard against the lump in her throat. She glanced toward the balcony, where Ryan still lingered. "I hope we didn't ruin your romantic evening."

Megan snorted and rolled her eyes. "Romantic? Hardly. He's going to take off after we eat. The last twenty-four hours have been the absolute opposite of romance. Unless you count staying up all night playing video games as romance."

Despite everything, a small grin tugged at Alyson's lips. "Not your idea of a fun night?"

"No, absolutely not." Megan sighed. "I mean, don't get me wrong, I like gaming as much as the next person. But all night? Every night? Whether he stays here or I go there, it's what we do. He never even wants to go out. Just play that stupid game. It's getting old."

Alyson raised an eyebrow. "Trouble in paradise?"

Megan shook her head, her expression a mixture of frustration and resignation. "There never was a paradise to begin with. I thought maybe things would get better, you know? But at this point . . ." She glanced toward the balcony. "I think it's time to cut my losses."

Alyson nodded sympathetically. "I'm sorry, Megan. Breakups are never easy."

"Yeah, well, it is what it is. I'm going to tell him tonight. No point in dragging it out."

Ryan's voice called from the balcony. "Hey, Meg? Can you come here for a sec?"

Megan rolled her eyes. "Duty calls," she said with a wry smile. "Maybe I'll do it now and get it over with."

As Megan stepped out onto the balcony, Alyson turned her attention to Jenna, who had fallen into a fitful sleep on the couch. She pulled a blanket over her friend, her mind still reeling from the day's events.

Raised voices from the balcony caught her attention. Alyson stared at the sliding glass door, concern growing as she heard the anger in Ryan's tone.

As soon as Alyson turned away, a piercing scream shattered the relative calm of the apartment. She whirled toward the balcony in time to see Megan's body sailing over the railing.

For a split second, Alyson froze, her mind struggling to process what she'd seen. She sprang into action. "Call 9-1-1!" she shouted—for the second time today—before racing toward the balcony, her screams pulling Jenna from her sleep.

Alyson spotted Ryan still on the balcony. When he turned to look at her, his eyes, usually warm and friendly, were empty. He hummed softly, the sound distant and mechanical, as if nothing had happened, as if he hadn't just thrown his girlfriend over the railing.

As Ryan rested his vacant gaze on her, a chill ran down her spine. The day's earlier tragedy seemed like a mere prelude to the terror now standing before her in her own home.

Chapter 3

Alyson's world narrowed to a single point: Ryan's vacant eyes. Time slowed. Her heart pounded. The balcony door stood ajar, the warm summer breeze carrying with it a cacophony of terrified screams and frantic cries from the street below.

"Call an ambulance!" someone yelled. The horrifying sounds of pandemonium erupting outside were a stark reminder of Megan's fate, while inside, an unnatural stillness had settled over the apartment. The normal world Alyson knew had shattered in an instant, replaced by a waking nightmare.

"Jenna, run!" she screamed, backing away from the balcony door. Her voice sounded foreign to her own ears, high-pitched and tinged with panic. The room seemed to tilt, reality bending at the edges.

Ryan lunged. Fast. Impossibly fast.

His eyes remained vacant, and a chilling grin twisted his lips as he continued to hum. His hands shot toward Alyson's throat, fingers splayed like talons.

She ducked, narrowly avoiding his grasp.

Ryan's momentum carried him past her, and he stumbled, fighting to regain his balance. His movements were jerky and uncoordinated, like a puppet with tangled strings. "Ryan! Ryan, stop!"

Jenna scrambled off the couch, disoriented. "What's happening?" Her voice was thick with confusion. The blanket Alyson had draped over her tangled around her legs, hindering her movements.

Ryan's head snapped toward Jenna. He changed direction, his strange tune growing louder and more intense as he rushed at her. His eyes locked onto her like an animal on its prey. The humming, combined with the wild look in his eyes, sent a jolt of terror through Alyson.

"No!" Alyson yelled, but it was too late. She lunged forward, fingers grasping at empty air as Ryan slipped past her. Time seemed to slow, each second stretching into eternity as she helplessly watched.

Ryan slammed into Jenna, sending them both crashing into the coffee table. The sound of breaking glass filled the air, mixing with Jenna's scream. Shards scattered across the floor, glinting in the sunlight streaming in from the balcony.

Weapon. She needed a weapon. Her room. The Taser. Images flashed through her mind. Her father's concerned face as he handed it to her, his warnings about the dangers of the city. She'd never imagined needing it like this, not here, not now.

She sprinted down the hall, Ryan's animalistic grunts echoing through the apartment. The short hallway seemed to stretch endlessly. The photos lining the walls blurred as she ran past, happy scenes at odds with the horror unfolding behind her. Her trembling hands fumbled with the doorknob.

Inside her room, Alyson yanked open her dresser drawer. Clothes flew as she searched frantically. There it is. "Just in case," her father had said. The small device was impossibly heavy in her hand. Her father's voice echoed in her head, "Remember, Alyson, this isn't a toy. It's for emergencies only."

Jenna screamed from the living room. The sound pierced through Alyson's thoughts, snapping her back to the present. Jenna needed her. Now.

Alyson gripped the Taser, her palms slick with sweat. She took a deep breath, steeling herself as she tried to recall her father's instructions, praying instinct would take over if needed.

The living room was a disaster. Overturned furniture. Broken glass. The room was unrecognizable, transformed from a cozy living space to a battlefield in minutes. The coppery scent of blood mingled with the familiar scent of home, creating a nauseating mixture. Jenna lay motionless by the couch, a gash on her forehead, her leg twisted at an awkward angle. Her face was pale. Too pale.

Ryan stood over her, his chest heaving. He turned at Alyson's approach, his eyes unfocused. His shirt was torn, smeared with blood—Jenna's blood. His hands curled into claws. A thin line of drool ran from the corner of his mouth. The humming had stopped, but the vacant look was still in place.

"Ryan, stop!" Alyson pleaded, her voice shaking. "This isn't you!"

A flash of something passed through Ryan's eyes. Recognition. Confusion. Fear. His rigid posture softened, and he blinked rapidly, as if waking from a dream.

"Aly?" he mumbled, his voice hoarse. "What's . . . what's going on?" He looked at Jenna, his eyes wide. "What happened?"

"Ryan, you're not well. We need to get help."

She took a cautious step forward, hand outstretched. Ryan's gaze followed her movement, still confused but less hostile.

"I . . . I don't . . ." Ryan started, before clutching his head, releasing a pained groan. When he looked up again, the vacancy was back in his eyes, all traces of recognition gone.

"Okay. Okay." A satisfied look crossed his face as he bobbed his head. "I understand. Yes. Yes. It is the way. The way of The One. I know what to do."

The humming returned a microsecond before he charged.

Alyson's finger found the trigger. She aimed and fired.

The Taser's prongs hit Ryan square in the chest. His body went rigid before he crumpled to the floor. Electricity arced between the prongs, the crackling sound filling the air. Ryan's body twitched and convulsed, a strangled cry escaping his lips before he fell silent.

Alyson didn't wait. She rushed to Jenna's side, her hands shaking as she checked for a pulse. Weak, but there. Jenna's skin was clammy under her fingers. The gash on her forehead was still bleeding, a thin trickle running down her temple. Glass shards glittered in her hair like a macabre tiara.

"Jenna? Can you hear me?" Alyson's voice cracked. She gently tapped Jenna's cheek, silently pleading for any sign of consciousness. "Please, Jenna. Wake up. I need you to wake up. We have to go. It's not safe here."

A groan came from behind her. Ryan was stirring.

The sound sent a jolt of fear through Alyson. She whirled around, eyes wide, to see Ryan's fingers twitching, his chest beginning to rise and fall more rapidly.

Panic rose in Alyson's throat. The Taser hadn't stopped him. At least not for long. Her father's warning echoed in her ears. "It'll buy you time, but it's not foolproof. Always have a backup plan."

Her eyes darted around the room, landing on the kitchen. Knives. The thought turned her stomach, but she shoved it aside. Survival first. Morality later.

She sprinted to the kitchen, yanking open drawers. Where were they? There. She grabbed the largest knife. The blade glinted in the light, sharp and menacing. Alyson had used this knife countless times to prepare meals. Now, it might be the only thing standing between her and death.

Ryan was on his feet, swaying slightly. His gaze locked onto Alyson. He started forward. His movements were more fluid now, less jerky. Whatever had taken hold of him seemed to be gaining strength.

"Stay back!" Alyson warned, brandishing the knife. Her hands trembled. She tried to make her voice sound commanding, but it came out as more of a plea. "I don't want to hurt you, Ryan. Please, please stay where you are!"

Ryan didn't slow. Didn't even blink. He lunged. His face was a mask of inhuman rage, all traces of the Ryan she knew gone. At that moment, Alyson realized she was no longer facing her roommate's boyfriend, but a predator intent on her destruction.

Her body moved on instinct. The knife plunged forward. A sickening resistance, then give. The sound it made would haunt her dreams for years to come.

Ryan's momentum carried them both to the floor. His weight crushed her. Hot, sticky wetness spread across her shirt. Time seemed to slow.

For a moment, there was silence. A rattling breath from Ryan followed. His eyes cleared, and confusion replaced the vacancy.

"Aly?" he whispered. "What . . . what happened?" His voice was weak, tinged with pain and confusion. His eyes now held fear and dawning realization.

Alyson stared, holding his gaze as the light faded from Ryan's eyes. "I'm sorry," she whispered.

His body went limp. She knew the exact moment the life left him, a subtle shift changing everything. The heaviness on her chest became oppressive, crushing the air from her lungs. Ryan's body, once animated by whatever psychotic force had possessed him, was now a dead weight pinning her to the floor.

Panic constricted her throat, making each breath a struggle. With desperate force, she shoved against Ryan's shoulders, her muscles screaming in protest. Every movement was a battle, like trying to shift a boulder that was wedged tight. Inch by agonizing inch, she managed to shift his weight, finally breaking free enough to squirm out from beneath him.

Gasping for air, she scrambled backward, her movements frantic and uncoordinated. Alyson's gaze fixed on her hands, trembling and slick with red. So much red. She stared, unable to process the sight of them covered in blood. Ryan's blood.

Reality crashed down on her. Megan. Jenna. Ryan. The apartment. A crime scene. Her crime scene. The full understanding of what happened threatened to crush her. Lives forever altered in the span of minutes. And she was the only one left standing.

Alyson's breath came in short gasps. She forced herself to move. To think. She jumped from one thought to another. *What will my parents say? Will I go to jail? Is Jenna going to be okay?*

Phone. Call for help. Check on Jenna. The tasks seemed monumental, but she clung to them like a lifeline. Action was better than paralysis.

As she dialed 9-1-1, Alyson's gaze swept the apartment. The life she knew lay shattered around her, as broken as the furniture and her sense of safety.

A recording came on, asking her to please stay on the line and her call would be answered as soon as possible. Alyson realized she was standing on the brink of a new reality. One where the world was darker, more dangerous, and she was forever changed. Nothing would ever be the same.

Chapter 4

The wail of sirens grew louder, a promise of help coming too late. She was kept on hold by emergency services for what seemed like forever as she cradled Jenna's head in her lap, her friend's breathing shallow and erratic.

They hadn't even asked her to hold the line or offered any sort of instructions. Only promised to send help as soon as possible. The help was coming quicker than expected. Alyson realized it was probably because of Megan, crumbled on the pavement below. Surely someone had reached 9-1-1 for her. Would it do any good? Could her friend have survived the fall?

"Stay with me, Jen," she whispered, her voice cracking. "Help is coming. Hold on."

Jenna's eyelids fluttered, a ghost of a smile touching her lips. "Aly . . ." she breathed, the word barely audible. "I'm sorry . . ."

"Don't," Alyson choked out, tears blurring her vision. "You have nothing to be sorry for. We're going to get through this, okay? Remember our plans? Three more years at Portland State, then law school for you, and a Master of Business for me. We're going to change the world, remember?"

But Jenna's eyes were losing focus, her breath coming in shorter gasps. A cold dread settled in Alyson's stomach, a terrible certainty she wasn't ready to face.

"Jenna, please," she begged, her words tumbling out in a desperate rush. "You can't leave me. Not like this. Not after everything. I promise I'll be a better friend. I'll make time for those stupid rom-coms you love. I'll even go to that yoga class you've been bugging me about. Please, please stay with me."

Jenna's hand twitched, her fingers weakly grasping at Alyson's. For a moment, her eyes cleared, locking onto Alyson's with an intensity that took her breath away.

"Thanks, Aly." Jenna's voice was barely a whisper, her words slurring. Her eyes fluttered closed, and her breath faded away.

The hand in Alyson's went limp, the warmth fading with each passing second.

"No." The word was a denial, a prayer, and a scream all at once. "No, no, no. Jenna!"

She shook Jenna gently, increasing the force with each movement, as if she could shake the life back into her. But Jenna's eyes remained fixed and unseeing, her chest motionless. CPR. She needed to do CPR.

The sound of splintering wood cut through Alyson's grief as the apartment door burst open. Paramedics came through the door, their voices sharp and frantic, filled with quick instructions and questions. But it was all background noise to Alyson, white static that couldn't penetrate the bubble of loss surrounding her.

Hands grasped her shoulders, trying to pull her away from Jenna. Alyson resisted, clinging to her friend with a strength born of desperation.

"Miss, you need to let go," a voice penetrated the fog. "We need to help your friend."

"Okay, yes," Alyson whispered, her voice hollow. "Please. Please help her."

She released Jenna and allowed the paramedics to take over. As they worked on her friend, a wave of emotion crashed over her. She stepped back, her hands shaking, as tears streamed down her face.

Time seemed to blur. She was only vaguely aware. Somebody took her arm and led her toward a chair. A blanket slowly covered her shoulders. People asked her questions, but she could only respond in single words, her mind still focused on Jenna.

As the paramedics worked, Alyson's gaze drifted to the open balcony door. Beyond it, flashing lights illuminated the street below. *Are they gathered around Megan's broken body?* The thought made her stomach curdle.

Her eyes fell on Ryan's lifeless form, still sprawled on the floor where she left him. The knife protruded from his chest, a grotesque reminder of what she'd done. Bile rose in her throat, and she swallowed hard, fighting the urge to be sick.

A paramedic approached. "Miss, we need to check you for injuries. Are you hurt anywhere?"

Alyson shook her head numbly. "No, I . . . I'm fine. It's not my blood." The words were hollow, detached. Was she actually fine? Would she ever be fine again?

It wasn't until a familiar voice cut through the haze that she snapped back to the present.

"Alyson? Alyson!"

She looked up to see her father pushing past the police officer, his face a mask of worry and relief. In three long strides, he was at her side, pulling her into a crushing embrace.

"Dad?" Her voice cracked, childlike in its vulnerability. "How did you . . .?"

"I was stuck on I-205 when everything went crazy," he explained, his words muffled against her hair. "I heard about the car driving through the boutique. I couldn't reach you by phone. Thank God you're okay. I . . . I knew I had to get here." He glanced around at the turmoil surrounding them, his eyes widening as he took in the full extent of the carnage. "Oh, Alyson . . . what happened here?"

Alyson clung to him, inhaling the familiar scent of his aftershave mixed with sweat and fear. For a moment, she was transported back to childhood, safe in her father's arms. But the illusion shattered as her gaze fell on the sheet-covered form on the floor. Jenna.

"She's dead, Dad," Alyson whispered, the words tearing at her throat. "Jenna's dead. And Megan. Ryan . . . I couldn't . . . I didn't . . ."

Her father held her tighter, his hand stroking her hair. "Shh, it's okay. You're safe now. That's what matters."

She shook her head and pulled back to look at him. "No, you don't understand. I . . . I killed him. Ryan. He was going to kill me, and I . . . Oh, Dad, what's happening? What's wrong with everyone?"

Her father's face tightened, and a mixture of anger and fear flashed in his eyes. "I don't know, sweetheart. But you did what you had to do. You survived. That's all that matters right now."

The police officer approached, his expression grave. "Miss Reynolds? I'm sorry, but I need to ask you some questions about what happened here."

Glancing around, Alyson realized the apartment was strangely quiet. The paramedics were gone and only the single officer remained. "Where is everyone?"

"Things are happening all over the city. Please, let me ask you a few questions. I need to go as well."

"But . . . but Jenna." She pointed to her best friend's body still lying in the same place. "What about Ryan?"

"Someone will be here to take them as soon as they can. Really, Miss—"

Her dad straightened, his arm still around her shoulders. "Can't this wait? My daughter's been through the wringer. She needs rest, not an interrogation."

"I understand, sir. But with everything that's happening in the city, we need to get statements as quickly as possible. I promise we'll keep it brief."

Alyson nodded, trying to pull herself together. "It's okay, Dad. I can do this."

As she described the afternoon, she had the sense of relaying a movie about someone else's life. The words came out mechanically, detached, as if she was reading from a script. She described the incident at the boutique, Megan's fall, Ryan's sudden change, and the desperate struggle that followed.

The officer listened intently, his pen scratching across his notepad. When Alyson finished, he looked up, his expression unreadable.

"You've been through a lot today, Miss Reynolds," he said, his tone softer than before. "What you've described . . . it's not an isolated incident. We're seeing similar reports all over the city. All over the country. The world, even."

Alyson's breath caught in her throat. "What? What do you mean?"

The officer ran a hand through his hair. "It's chaos out there. Traffic jams, explosions, seemingly random acts of violence. Reports of people snapping and attacking others without warning or reason. It's like nothing we've ever seen before."

She tried to process the information. "But why? What's causing it?"

"We don't know," the officer admitted. "But right now, we're trying to contain the situation as best we can."

Alyson's father spoke up, his voice tight with concern. "Is it safe to leave? I want to get my daughter out of here. We live in Astoria. I'm taking her home."

The officer shrugged. "I don't know. Things are a mess. There're looters and . . . other troubles. We're advising people to stay put if they're in a safe location. Plus . . ." He hesitated, glancing at Alyson. "We may need to speak with your daughter again as the investigation progresses."

Investigation. The word hung in the air, a reminder that despite the mess unfolding outside, what had happened in this apartment couldn't be ignored.

"Am I . . . am I in trouble?" she asked, her voice small.

The officer's expression softened. "From what you've told us, and given the circumstances, this appears to be a clear case of self-defense. But we'll need to conduct a full investigation to confirm that. For now, stay available in case we need to contact you."

"You have her cell number," her dad said. "I'll give you mine, plus our Astoria address. My name is Rich Reynolds. I'm sure the department there can reach out if you need something."

"I guess that'll have to do. Watch yourself."

As the officer moved away, he radioed in, informing whoever was listening that he was leaving the scene.

Alyson collapsed against her father, the adrenaline that had carried her now fading, leaving only exhaustion behind.

"I want to go home, Dad," she whispered, feeling every bit the scared child she'd once been.

He nodded, his arm tightening around her. "I know, sweetheart. We will. Let's get a bag packed. Only take what you absolutely need. You still have things at the house."

She glanced at Jenna, still on the floor. "I shouldn't leave her."

"They'll be here soon," her dad said. "We need to go now. It's not safe in the city."

Alyson moved through her room in a daze, pulling open drawers and grabbing clothes at random. Her hands shook as she stuffed items into an overnight bag. A photo on her nightstand caught her eye—Jenna, Megan, and her skiing at Timberline Lodge, with smiles and wind-kissed noses. She stared at it for a long moment before gently wrapping it in a soft sweater and placing it in the bag.

As she packed, her mind raced. *Will I ever come back here? Will there even be a "here" to come back to?* The world she knew was crumbling, and she was packing as if for a vacation. The absurdity of it all threatened to overwhelm her.

"Don't forget your laptop," her dad reminded her gently. "We don't know how long . . ." He trailed off, but Alyson understood. They didn't know how long it'd be until she could return to Portland.

She nodded and put the computer in a padded backpack. As she zipped her overnight bag closed, she sensed a finality to the action, as if she were zipping away her old life along with her belongings.

Her dad took her larger bag and placed the strap over his shoulder as he gave her a nod. "Put the backpack on and let's go."

As they made their way out of the apartment, Alyson paused at the threshold. She looked back at the place that had only recently become her home, now transformed into a crime scene. Yellow tape crisscrossed the doorway, and evidence markers dotted the floor like morbid confetti.

At that moment, the reality of what had happened hit her all at once. Jenna was gone. Megan was gone. She'd killed Ryan. The life she'd known, the future she'd planned, it had all evaporated in the span of a few horrific minutes. Could she ever get it back?

Alyson turned to her father, her eyes brimming with tears. "What do I do now, Dad? How do I . . . how do I go on after this?"

He cupped her face in his hands, his eyes fierce with love and determination. "You survive, Alyson. You keep going, one day at a time. And you remember that you're not alone. Your mom and I will help you. So will Eddie." Her dad raised his eyebrows at the mention of her younger brother.

She let out a small laugh as her dad said, "We'll get through this together, I promise."

As they stepped into the hallway, the sounds of sirens and distant explosions filtered through the building. The world outside was descending into anarchy, but Alyson clung to her father's words like a lifeline.

Survive. Keep going. One day at a time.

As they stepped onto the sidewalk, Alyson steeled herself. Whatever was going on, she would face it. She had to. For Jenna, for Megan, for herself. Because in the end, that's what it meant to survive. And if nothing else, Alyson Reynolds was determined to be a survivor.

Chapter 5

The streets of Portland had transformed into an apocalyptic nightmare. As Alyson and her father navigated through the confusion, the city she once knew seemed like a distant memory. Smoke billowed from several buildings, casting a haze over the skyline. The acrid smell burned her nostrils, a constant reminder of the world falling apart around them.

"Stay close," her dad urged, his hand firmly grasping her arm as they weaved through abandoned cars and trash. His eyes darted constantly, scanning for potential threats. "With all the emergency vehicles and people around, I couldn't find a close place to park."

Alyson nodded, her mind flashing back to the news reports she'd seen over the past few years. "It's like those riots during the pandemic summer, isn't it?" she whispered. "Only worse."

Her dad's jaw tightened. "I'm afraid so. Portland's always had its share of troublemakers. Rioters, anarchists, looters . . . they're probably seeing this as an opportunity. We need to be extra careful."

Her dad had opposed her decision to attend Portland State, and for good reason. The family used to love visiting Portland—walking downtown, enjoying the waterfront, attending events, or spending Saturdays at the Market.

But things had changed in recent years. They rarely ventured into downtown anymore. Her dad said it was different now. Alyson's mom still insisted it was the same Portland they'd always loved, but even she had tried to convince Alyson to consider colleges in Eugene or Corvallis instead.

They were barely two blocks from Alyson's apartment when a group of looters caught sight of them. The pack of men, their faces contorted with a mix of desperation and malice, started moving in their direction.

"Run!" her dad shouted, pulling Alyson along as they sprinted down a side street.

Alyson's heart pounded, her legs burning as they ran. The sound of pursuing footsteps echoed behind them, spurring them on. They turned corner after corner, the once-familiar streets blurring together in a maze of fear and adrenaline.

"Here!" He gripped her arm and pulled her into an alley where they crouched behind a dumpster. Alyson struggled to catch her breath, her father's arm wrapped protectively around her shoulders.

"I think we lost them," he whispered, peering cautiously around the edge of the dumpster.

Alyson nodded, unable to speak. The reality of their situation was sinking in. This wasn't only a localized incident; the entire city seemed to be descending into lawlessness.

The scenes unfolding around her were hauntingly familiar, reminiscent of the footage she'd seen of riots in years past. But this was different, more primal somehow. The violence seemed random and senseless, driven by something beyond mere opportunism or political anger.

"Dad," she managed between gasps, "what's happening? Why is everyone . . . like this?"

He shook his head, his expression grim. "I don't know, sweetheart. But we can't stay here. We need to get to the car and get out of the city."

As they caught their breath, a scream pierced the air, followed by the sound of shattering glass. She flinched and instinctively pressed closer to her father.

"It's okay," he soothed, though the tension in his voice gave away his own fear. "We're going to be okay. We need to stay calm and think this through."

She tried to steady her breathing. She closed her eyes and focused on the warmth of her father's embrace, the familiar scent of his cologne. When she opened them again, a sense of steadiness returned.

"Okay," she said, her voice barely above a whisper. "What's the plan?"

Her dad peered out of the alley again, his brow furrowed in concentration. "The car's parked about three blocks from here. Are you ready?"

They emerged from their hiding spot cautiously, every sense on high alert. The city seemed to have grown even more chaotic in the short time they'd been hidden. Distant explosions punctuated the air, and the wail of sirens created a constant, unsettling backdrop.

As they moved through the streets, she took in the details around them. Garbage cans lay toppled, discarded in the street. A mannequin, stripped of its clothes, stared blankly from a shattered shop window, reminding Alyson of the disaster at her workplace. These once-ordinary objects now seemed to mock the normalcy that had existed only hours before.

They were about halfway to the car when a woman stumbled out of a doorway, her movements jerky and unsteady. When her eyes met Alyson's, they held the same vacant, feral look Alyson had seen in Ryan's. The woman began to sing a verse from "The Star-Spangled Banner," her eyes never leaving Alyson's.

"Dad," she whispered, her voice tight with fear.

"I see her," he replied, slowly backing away. "Stay calm and don't make any sudden moves."

The woman's head tilted to one side, an unnatural angle that made Alyson's skin crawl. She repeated the same line again, singing at the top of her lungs. "Whose broad stripes and bright stars." She lowered her head and charged toward them.

Her dad reacted instantly, pushing Alyson behind him and snatching up a nearby trashcan lid from the ground. He swung it forcefully, striking the woman in the face. She crumpled, and her head hit the pavement with a sickening thud.

"Let's go!" He grabbed Alyson's hand and pulled her along.

"She's acting like Ryan. Why?" she asked, looking back over her shoulder.

"I don't know, and we're not sticking around to find out."

They sprinted down the street, the woman's inhuman shrieks fading behind them. Alyson's lungs burned, her legs as heavy as stone, yet fear drove her to keep moving. They didn't stop until they had put considerable distance between them and the woman.

As they paused to catch their breath, she looked at her father with newfound respect. She had never seen him like that—fierce, protective, almost primal in his instinct to keep her safe.

"Are you okay?" His eyes scanned her for any signs of injury.

Alyson nodded, still too winded to speak. She glanced back the way they had come, half expecting to see the woman in pursuit. But the street behind them was empty, save for the remains of a city in turmoil.

"We're almost there," her dad said, his voice tight with determination. "Not much farther."

As they rounded the corner onto the street where he had parked, Alyson's heart sank. The area was a war zone. An overturned car blocked most of the road, and several buildings were engulfed in flames. In the distance, a group of people fought over what looked like a suitcase full of supplies.

"Dad, how are we going to get through that?"

His jaw clenched as he surveyed the scene. "We'll find a way. We have to."

They skirted the edge of the mess, keeping to the shadows as much as possible. Alyson's heart pounded so loudly she was sure everyone could hear it. Every scream, every crash, every fleeting motion triggered a rush of adrenaline.

She spotted her dad's car, miraculously untouched amid the destruction. It was tantalizingly close, across the street from where they stood.

"Okay," he said, his voice low and urgent. "Here's what we're going to do. When I say go, we run straight for the car. Don't stop for anything, understand?"

Alyson nodded, her mouth dry with fear.

"Ready?" His hand tightened around hers. "Go!"

They sprinted across the street, dodging rubbish and abandoned vehicles. Her focus narrowed on the car, her father's hand in hers, and the pounding of her feet against the pavement.

They were halfway there when a voice rang out. "Hey! Stop right there!"

Her head whipped around to see a man pointing a gun at them. His eyes were wild, reflecting the bedlam around them. His appearance screamed "gang member." Tattoos snaked up his neck, a bandanna was tied around his head, and his clothes seemed more about making a statement than providing protection.

"Keep going!" her dad shouted, pushing Alyson ahead of him.

The crack of a gunshot split the air. Alyson screamed, stumbling as her father's hand was torn from hers. She turned to see her dad on the ground, clutching his leg.

"Dad!" She dropped to her knees beside him.

"Go," he gasped through gritted teeth. "Get to the car."

"No!" Alyson sobbed, trying to help him up. "I'm not leaving you!"

The man with the gun was approaching, his weapon trained on them. "Drop the bags."

Her dad put the overnight bag on the ground and raised his hands. "Okay. No problem." He tilted his head slightly. Alyson shook her head. "Go ahead," her dad said. "Take off the backpack."

With a sigh, she shimmied out of the pack, setting it on the ground next to her.

"Now give me the keys," the thug demanded, his voice shaking almost as much as his hand.

Her dad fumbled in his pocket, producing the car keys. "Take them." He tossed them toward the man. "Take the car and let us go."

The man snatched the keys from the ground, his eyes darting between them and the car. For a moment, Alyson thought he might walk away, but his expression turned cold.

"Can't leave any witnesses." He raised the gun again.

Time seemed to slow. Her father's eyes widened in fear. Not for himself, she realized, but for her. The gunman smirked. And at that moment, something inside her snapped.

With a cry that was part fear and part rage, she launched herself at him. The sudden movement caught him off guard, and they both went down in a tangle of limbs. The gun went off, the bullet ricocheting harmlessly off the pavement.

Alyson fought with a desperation she didn't know she possessed. She clawed, bit, and struck out with every ounce of strength she had. The man, caught off guard by her ferocity, struggled to fend her off.

In the scuffle, her hand closed around a piece of broken concrete. Without hesitation, she brought it down hard on the man's head. Once, twice, three times. Finally, he went still.

Panting, covered in blood and grime, she scrambled off the unconscious man. She stared at her hands in shock, barely recognizing them as her own.

"Alyson," her father's voice cut through her daze. "Alyson, look at me."

She turned to see her dad dragging himself toward her, his face pale with pain and worry.

"Are you hurt?" His eyes scanned her for injuries.

She shook her head, still too stunned to speak.

He pulled her into a tight embrace. "We need to go," he said after a moment, his voice hoarse. "Can you help me up?"

Alyson nodded, forcing herself to focus. She helped her father to his feet, supporting his weight as they limped to the car. The keys lay where they had fallen, forgotten in the struggle.

As Alyson helped him into the passenger seat, the reality of what happened hit her. She nearly lost her father. She nearly died. She might have killed a man. *Again.* The emotions washed over her in a dizzying wave, threatening to overwhelm her.

"Alyson," her dad's voice cut through her spiraling thoughts. "We need to go. Now."

She moved quickly to the back of the car, grabbed the overnight bag and backpack, and tossed them into the backseat.

When she slid into the driver's seat, her gaze caught the reflection of her own face in the rearview mirror. It was almost unrecognizable. Streaked with dirt and blood, eyes wide with fear and determination.

"You can do this," her dad said softly, reaching out to squeeze her hand. "I'm right here with you."

Alyson nodded and started the car. As they pulled away from the curb, leaving the man and the scene of their near-death experience behind, a sense lingered, a feeling that they were driving away from more than simply a dangerous situation. They were leaving behind the last traces of the world they had known, heading into an uncertain future where the rules had shifted, and survival was the only goal that mattered.

The city of Portland, once familiar, now appeared foreign as they moved through its streets. Her knuckles were white on the steering wheel, her eyes constantly darting between the road and the rearview mirror, half expecting pursuit at any moment.

As they finally reached the outskirts of the city, she let out a breath. "I'm going to pull over and check your leg."

"It's fine. Little more than a scratch. The bullet ricocheted off the pavement." Her dad was examining the wound.

She hazarded a glance to see there was very little blood.

"I've got a first aid kit in the trunk. Wait until we're outside of town and then find a wide spot on Highway 30 to pull over." He opened the glove box and took out a stack of paper napkins. "You're doing great, sweetheart. Keep going. We're going to make it."

She gave a nod, but she knew their journey was far from over. The road to Astoria stretched out before them, a hundred miles of uncertainty and potential danger.

She blinked back tears. As the lights of Portland faded behind them, she steeled herself for whatever lay ahead. They had survived the city. Now, they only had to make it home.

Chapter 6

The setting sun blazed directly ahead, forcing Alyson to squint as she guided the car onto the wide shoulder of Highway 30. The intense glare reflecting off the windshield made it difficult to see, adding another layer of stress to their already tense journey.

They had put some distance between themselves and Portland, but the day's events still weighed heavily on her. Her dad pressed a wad of napkins against his leg wound, his jaw clenched against the pain he was clearly trying to hide.

"Dad, we need to take care of that properly." She put the car in park and reached for the sun visor in a futile attempt to block out the blinding light.

Her dad grimaced as he shifted in his seat. "The first aid kit is in the trunk. Be quick about it." He glanced in the side-view mirror. "We're sitting ducks here."

She hurried to retrieve the kit, her eyes constantly scanning their surroundings. Traffic was heavy, with cars bumper to bumper as far as she could see. Horns blared impatiently, and the smell of exhaust filled the air. In the distance, a plume of smoke rose against the evening sky, a grisly reminder of what they had escaped. Could Portland come back from this? They had before, but Alyson didn't think it had been as bad.

Back in the car, she helped her father roll up his pant leg. "See? Nothing but a scratch," he said, though his clenched jaw betrayed the pain he was in.

Alyson cleaned the wound with antiseptic wipes, her hands shaking slightly. "Some scratch, Dad. You're lucky it wasn't worse." A chorus of car horns erupted nearby, making them both jump. "Here. Take these." She handed him a couple of over-the-counter painkillers. "Sorry, there's nothing stronger."

As she applied a proper bandage, her dad kept watch, his eyes darting between the rearview and side mirrors. "We need to keep moving," he said. "We're too exposed out here."

Alyson nodded, packing up the first aid kit. "Should I keep driving?"

"For now," he agreed. "Give me some time for the painkiller to start working. You're doing great, sweetheart."

She took a deep breath and prepared herself for the challenge of merging back onto the congested highway. Cars crept past in the right lane, leaving no room for entry. After several tense minutes, a sympathetic driver finally slowed, flashing their lights to let them in.

On the road again, a small wave of relief washed over Alyson. They had made it out of Portland, and her father's wound wasn't serious. But she knew they couldn't let their guard down. The world had changed in an instant, and danger could be lurking around any corner.

She hoped the farther they got from Portland, the more things would start to settle. To return to normal. She knew once they reached Astoria, they'd be fine. Life was always quiet in their small town. They didn't get the weirdness Portland was prone to experience.

As they approached Scappoose, she could see signs of unrest even from the highway. The parking lots of major stores visible from the road were chaotic, with people rushing in and out, arms full of supplies. A police car sped past them, sirens blaring.

"Keep moving," her dad instructed, his voice tense. "Don't stop unless we absolutely have to."

As they continued on, each small community they encountered told a similar story. St. Helens, Rainier, Clatskanie. Some showed more signs of disturbance than others, but all were far from their usual quiet selves. The sun had long set, but even in the dark, it was obvious things were not normal.

Between towns, the forested landscape of northwest Oregon flew by. Under different circumstances, it might have been a pleasant drive. Now, the dense trees along the highway loomed, hiding any number of potential threats.

As they approached Knappa, a figure on the roadside caught Alyson's attention. A man was waving his arms frantically beside a stalled car, a woman and two children huddled nearby.

Her foot instinctively moved to the brake. "Dad, should we— "

"No," he cut her off, his voice firm but not unkind. "We can't risk it, Aly. We don't know what's going on there."

Her grip tightened on the steering wheel as they drove past the stranded family. She caught a glimpse of the children's frightened faces in the rearview mirror, and it made her heart ache. "It doesn't feel right."

"I know, Alyson. But we have to think of our own safety first. We can't help anyone if we don't make it home ourselves."

As they approached the turnoff for Svensen, they could see increased activity. Cars were lined up near the old grocery market around what looked like a hastily assembled checkpoint.

Her dad smiled. "They might have the right idea."

Alyson clenched her jaw, her lips pressed together. "Yeah, great. Vigilantism is always smart."

"They're trying to protect their community, Alyson."

"And who's going to protect us from them?"

"It's not that simple." A sorrowful look crossed his face as he shook his head. "Sometimes you have to take matters into your own hands."

"I don't want us getting caught up in something else that's dangerous."

He glanced at her, his expression softening. "We'll be careful. I promise."

The next several miles passed in silence. "Almost there," her dad said as they approached the John Day River bridge. "We'll get through town and be home free."

Alyson allowed herself a small smile as she shifted her shoulders. Her arms ached from gripping the wheel much too tightly. After everything they'd been through, it seemed almost impossible they would finally be home.

Her stomach growled as a reminder of the time and that she hadn't eaten since breakfast. Would her mom still be up? Maybe she'd even held dinner. They'd tried to call, to tell her what was happening and that they were safe, but the calls wouldn't go through.

She was sure her mom had seen the news not only about the traffic trouble on I-205 but probably the problem at the boutique too. Would the deaths of Megan and Jenna make the news? Would the fact she killed Ryan be announced? What about the thug that attacked them? Had he been found and his injury—or death—made the news?

But as they rounded the bend past John Day County Park, about five miles east of Astoria, her hope crumbled. The road ahead was blocked by the twisted wreckage of metal and debris, stretching as far as she could see. A multicar pileup choked both lanes, flames licking from the wreckage. People scrambled over the mangled cars. Some attempted to help, while others seized the opportunity to loot whatever they could find in the confusion.

"Good grief." Alyson slowed the car.

"Don't stop," her dad warned. "Try to find a way around."

She guided the car onto the shoulder, trying to edge past the wreckage. They had almost made it when a loud bang startled them both. The car jolted and slowed.

Her dad cursed, a rarity reserved for the direst of circumstances. "A tire's blown. Probably ran over something."

She managed to maneuver the car off the road before it came to a complete stop. The smell of burning rubber filled the air.

"We can change it, right?" she asked, a note of desperation in her voice.

Her dad was already out of the car, assessing the damage. When he looked back at Alyson, his face was tense. "It's not only the tire. The axle's bent. We're not driving out of here."

The reality of their situation sank in. They were stranded, still several miles from home, in the middle of what was quickly becoming a war zone. Astoria shouldn't be like this. It didn't make sense. The crash site was drawing more attention, the crowd growing larger and more agitated by the minute.

"We need to move," her dad said urgently. "Grab anything useful from the car. We're going on foot."

"What about your leg?"

"I'll manage. Let's go."

Her hands shook as she gathered what she could—the first aid kit, a few bottles of water, and some energy bars from the glove compartment. She slung her backpack over her shoulder, her laptop a comforting familiarity, while her dad took the overnight bag.

As they prepared to leave, a group of men broke away from the crowd at the crash site, their attention now fixed on Alyson and her dad. Their intentions were clear in their predatory gazes and the crude weapons they carried . . . pipes, chains, and one even brandished a machete.

"Let's go," her dad said. "Into the woods. Now."

They took off, crashing through the underbrush. Her lungs burned as she ran, branches whipping at her face. Shouts rang out behind them, spurring them forward and pushing them deeper into the forest.

They ran until the sounds of pursuit faded into the distance, and every step became a battle to keep moving, her body heavy with exhaustion. Finally, her dad called a halt. They collapsed against a tree, gasping for air.

"I think . . . I think we lost them," Alyson panted between breaths.

He nodded, wincing as he stretched out his injured leg. "For now. Can you call your mom?"

She pulled out her phone, then shook her head. "No service."

"Okay. We'll try again in a bit. We can't stay here long. We need to keep moving."

As she caught her breath, the full reality of their situation crashed down on her. They were on foot, miles from home, with limited supplies and no way to call for help. The world had turned upside down, even Astoria, the town she'd always thought was immune to this madness, and now they were in the thick of it.

"Dad," she said, her voice small, "what are we going to do?"

His expression softened as he looked at her. Despite everything, he managed a reassuring smile, though it didn't quite reach his eyes. "We're going to do what Reynolds do best, Alyson. We're going to survive."

She swallowed, but the words didn't come as easily as she'd hoped. Instead, she gave a halfhearted nod.

"Okay," he said, his voice firm, grounding her again. "We know where we are. We need to be careful. Stick to the woods, avoid roads and open areas. It's going to be a long walk, but we can make it."

Alyson straightened her shoulders, drawing strength from his unwavering confidence. "Lead the way, Dad."

They set off through the woods, the familiar Columbia River close by. The going was slow. The underbrush was thick, and they had to constantly backtrack to avoid steep ravines or impenetrable thickets. Her dad's pace was slow as he favored his leg.

As they walked, her mind wandered to her mother and brother. Were they safe? Had the madness reached their quiet neighborhood overlooking the Astoria-Megler Bridge and the Columbia River? The thought of home being anything other than the safe haven she remembered was almost too much to bear.

"Dad," she said, her voice breaking the silence after endless walking, "do you think Mom and Eddie are okay?"

He was quiet for a moment before responding, "Your mother is one of the strongest people I know, Alyson. And Eddie . . . well, he's got more of your grandfather in him than anyone wants to admit." He chuckled. "Especially your mom. They'll be fine. They have to be."

They pressed on, the woods gradually thinning as they approached the outskirts of town. The sounds of the forest gave way to distant sirens and the occasional shout, reminders of the unrest that had taken over their world.

As midnight approached, fatigue began to set in. Alyson's feet ached, and she could see her father favoring his injured leg more and more. They rationed their water and energy bars carefully, knowing they had to make them last.

As they neared the edge of a neighborhood, not far from the city limits, the sound of voices carried on the wind. Her dad held up a hand, signaling Alyson to stop and be quiet.

The voices grew closer, accompanied by the crunch of leaves underfoot. Alyson's heart raced as she realized they were about to cross paths with whoever was approaching.

"Stay down." Her dad pulled her behind a large fallen tree.

They huddled there, barely daring to breathe, as a group of men passed only yards away. Through gaps in the foliage, she could see they were armed. Not with the improvised weapons of the looters, but with actual firearms.

" . . . telling you, I saw smoke from over this way," one of the men said. "Could be one of them setting up camp."

"Or it could be nothing," another replied. "We've been out here for hours. Maybe we should head back."

"Not yet," an authoritative voice cut in. "We keep searching. Mayor's orders. We need to secure the perimeter."

Alyson's dad tensed beside her, his hand instinctively tightening on her arm. She could see the conflict in his eyes. The desire to reveal themselves to potential allies warring with the need to protect his daughter.

"No, Dad," she mouthed, shaking her head.

With a nod, he moved his fingers to his lips.

The group moved on, their voices fading into the distance. Alyson and her dad remained hidden for several more minutes, ensuring the coast was clear before emerging.

"That was close," she whispered, her voice shaky.

He nodded. "We probably weren't in any danger, but it's best to be cautious. It does give us some valuable information. Sounds like Astoria's organizing some kind of defense. Same as Svensen. We need to be careful when approaching the town. They might shoot first and ask questions later."

The encounter had shaken them both, adding a new layer of caution to their journey. They moved more slowly now, constantly on alert for any sign of other people. As they entered the outskirts of Astoria, the familiar streets seemed alien in the dark, empty night.

"We're close now." Her dad's voice was heavy with exhaustion and pain. "Only a little farther."

Alyson nodded; her legs felt like lead, but determination was driving her forward. Home was so close. They were almost there.

As the first light of dawn painted a band across the horizon, they finally turned onto their street. The sight of their house, perched on the hill overlooking the river, brought tears to her eyes.

"We made it," she whispered, her voice choked with emotion.

"We did, sweetheart. We're home."

Together, they made their way up the driveway. As they reached the front door, it swung open, revealing Alyson's mother's worried face.

"You're here!" Beth Reynolds exclaimed, pulling them both into a tight embrace. "You're safe. You're finally home."

Chapter 7

The aroma of bacon and coffee wafted through the house, gently pulling Alyson from her dreamless sleep. For a moment, she lay still, her eyes closed, clinging to the illusion of normalcy. But as consciousness fully returned, so did the memories of the previous day's horrors. Her eyes snapped open, her heart racing as she took in the familiar surroundings.

She was at her childhood home in Astoria. Safe. The thought should've brought comfort, but it seemed almost unreal.

Alyson sat up slowly, her body protesting every movement. The events of yesterday crashed over her in a wave of grief and guilt. Jenna's face flashed in her mind. Her best friend's final moments, the life fading from her eyes. And Megan. Gone in an instant, without even a chance to say goodbye.

"Jenna . . . Megan . . ." she whispered, her voice breaking. Tears welled up in her eyes, spilling over before she could stop them. The reality of their loss hit her anew, a physical ache in her chest.

She sat there for several minutes, shoulders shaking with silent sobs. They had only known each other for a year, but in that time, Jenna and Megan had become like sisters to her. All their plans for the coming years—the classes they'd take together, the apartments they'd share, the life they would each build—now lay shattered, dreams turned to dust in the span of one horrific day.

When the tears finally subsided, Alyson was hollow and wrung out. She glanced at her phone, surprised to see it was nearly eleven in the morning. Despite sleeping for over five hours, she sensed she hadn't rested at all.

As she swung her legs over the side of the bed, her gaze fell on her hands. Clean now, but she could still see the blood that had stained them a few hours ago. Ryan's blood. And possibly the blood of the man who had tried to carjack them. Had she killed him too? The uncertainty gnawed at her.

She took a deep breath. She didn't want her family to see how shaken she was. They needed her to be strong, especially Eddie. Her little brother had always looked up to her, and she couldn't bear the thought of him seeing her fall apart.

She made her way downstairs, following the enticing smell of breakfast. In the kitchen, she found her mother at the stove, flipping pancakes with practiced ease.

"Morning, sweetheart," her mom said, her voice warm but tinged with concern. "How are you feeling?"

Alyson's mouth curved faintly, trying to reassure her mom. "I'm okay. A little sore, but not bad." It wasn't entirely a lie, but it wasn't the whole truth either. "How's Dad?"

"He's resting. I wanted to take him to the hospital when you got home, but . . ." She trailed off, shaking her head. "He insisted it wasn't necessary, and after what he told me about the situations you encountered last night, maybe he's right. Maybe we're better off staying put and not venturing out until things calm down."

Alyson nodded, relief washing over her. The thought of going anywhere, of facing the danger that had engulfed the world, was more than she could bear right now. "You're sure he doesn't need a doctor to check his leg? I cleaned it and put a bandage on it, but was that enough?"

"We cleaned and rebandaged it again before bed. Honestly, it didn't look too bad considering he was shot."

"He said it ricocheted off the pavement. Not a direct hit."

"Still. If the state would do something about all these guns— "

"Is that bacon I smell?" Eddie's voice preceded him into the kitchen. He bounded in, seemingly unaffected by the tension that hung in the air. "Morning, Aly! You missed all the excitement yesterday."

Alyson glanced at her mother, her eyes brimming with tears. A subtle shake of her mom's head signaled that Eddie didn't know the full story. They'd kept what happened in Portland from him. Though he'd stirred awake when she and her dad returned, they'd shielded him from the truth. "Yeah. I guess, maybe I did."

Eddie launched into an animated description of the previous day's events in Astoria—the sudden increase in police presence, the rumors spreading through social media, and the hastily organized town meeting.

As he talked, Alyson marveled at his ability to treat it all like some exciting adventure rather than the terrifying reality it was. If he knew what she'd been through, he'd probably lose that spark of excitement and see the world for the dangerous place it had become. It was probably good they were protecting him.

"Oh, and I talked to Maddie and Jackson last night," Eddie added, his mouth full of pancakes. "Things are pretty crazy in Casper, too, but they're okay."

Alyson leaned toward him at the mention of her cousins. "You were able to get through to them? I thought the phone lines were down."

Eddie shrugged. "Not by phone. Jackson was playing online, and Maddie sent me a message."

"The video game. What a surprise. Not." She gave her brother a mock-serious glare, crossing her eyes for good measure.

He stuck his tongue out at her before turning to their mom. "The internet's working great. All kinds of information and videos about the trouble happening. There's even a guy—some kind of doctor—saying it's a mass . . . um, I can't remember the word. But everyone's going crazy at once. He says it might be another pandemic."

"Enough, Eddie," their mom said, resting a hand on his shoulder. "Eat your food."

As they ate, Alyson found her gaze drawn to the large windows overlooking the Columbia River and the Astoria-Megler Bridge. The view had always been a source of comfort, a constant in her life. But now, it seemed to have changed.

The river, usually bustling with activity, was quiet. The absence of the merchant vessels and cruise ships that typically dotted the horizon was jarring, a visual reminder of how much the world had changed overnight.

"It's strange, isn't it?" her father's voice came from behind her. He made his way into the kitchen, moving slowly but steadily. "I've never seen the river so empty. I've been watching. There was a freighter this morning, as the sun was rising, but nothing since."

"Have you slept?"

"Some." He shrugged.

Her mom was immediately at his side, helping him to a chair. "You should be resting," she chided gently, but there was relief in her eyes at seeing him up and about.

He waved off her concern. "I've rested enough. We need to talk about what's happening and make a plan."

"Eddie's been keeping up on events happening around the world," her mom said. "Casper too. I know he's happy his sister is home and safe."

Even though her mom didn't say anything directly, the way her words came out and the tightness in her voice made it clear she intended to continue to shield Eddie from what Alyson went through for as long as possible. He asked about the cut she had along her jaw and the marks on her arms, but she explained them away, saying she'd fallen when riding her bike. He seemed to accept that as plausible.

As they sat around the table, the TV droned on in the background, a constant stream of news updates providing a depressing soundtrack to their meal. Alyson found herself torn between the desire to know what was happening and the urge to shut it all out.

"They're saying it's not only here," Eddie piped up, his eyes glued to his phone. "It's happening all over the world. Look at this video from London!"

Before Alyson could protest, he had already hit play, unleashing a storm of frantic voices and noise. Her chest tightened, and she hunched over slightly, gripping the edge of the table. The sound made her stomach churn, dragging her back to Portland. She stared at her plate, willing herself to focus on something, anything, that didn't remind her of the screams and panic she'd lived through.

"That's enough, Eddie," their dad said firmly, reaching over to lower the volume on Eddie's phone. "We don't need to see that right now."

Alyson gave a slight nod, her eyes still focused on her plate. The syrup pooling around the pancakes blurred in her vision, and her breathing hitched. She counted the ridges of the bacon and the yellow edges of the scrambled eggs, forcing herself to stay grounded. If she could focus on the details, she might hold back the rising tide threatening to drown her. As her breathing steadied, she lifted her gaze enough to meet her dad's.

His lips thinned into a firm line, his eyes glistening. Of all people, he understood what she'd endured, what she'd done.

"What we need," her dad said, holding her gaze, "is to focus on what we can control. We're safe here for now, but we need to be prepared for anything."

Her mom nodded, her face set with determination. "I've been taking inventory of our supplies. Hopefully, it won't be like it was last time during the pandemic, but we're fine for a couple of weeks if it is."

"Got toilet paper?" Eddie laughed, though he was too young to remember what it was like, having only heard the stories.

"Toilet paper is something we do have," their mom agreed. "We learned our lesson on that."

As her parents discussed plans to secure the house and contact the neighbors, Alyson's thoughts drifted. Jenna and Megan came to mind. She'd have to return to the apartment to clear it out. She should call their parents, somehow find the words to tell them how sorry she was. Her eyes welled with tears, and she absently dragged her fork through the syrup on her plate.

"Alyson?" Her mother's voice broke through her reverie. "What do you think about your father's plan?"

Alyson blinked, realizing she had missed part of the conversation. "I'm sorry, what plan?"

Her dad leaned forward, his expression serious. "I think we need to consider leaving for Wyoming. My parents' lodge near Yellowstone might be the safest place for us right now."

"And I think we're jumping the gun on this," her mom quickly insisted.

Alyson shook her head. "No. No way. Why would you want to do that?" She looked between her parents. Her mom was smiling and nodding in agreement while her dad sighed and dropped his shoulders.

"Because of the location," he finally said. "They're essentially in the middle of nowhere. It's almost an hour to the town of Cody. They're only a few miles from the East Gate of Yellowstone, which does have lots of tourists, but surely they'll be leaving to go home soon, right?"

"It'll probably be like before, Dad," Eddie said. "When the flu came through and they closed the national parks."

"That was more than the flu." Their mom shook her head. "That right there is another reason I don't want to go to your parents' house. Your dad puts ideas like that in his head. If you remember, we agreed we were going to limit our contact with your parents. I agreed to go visit them last summer, but there is no way I'm going to live with them. Their ideas are not okay."

"I know you and my dad have your differences— "

"Differences? He thinks it's okay to put children in cages. To separate them from their family."

"Not now, Beth. Now we need to focus on our family. On keeping our children safe. You weren't in Portland. You didn't see . . ." He glanced at Alyson, tears filling his eyes. "You didn't see the things we saw. Alyson . . . Me . . ."

"What happened in Portland?" Eddie asked, eyes wide.

"You, Dad?" Alyson asked around the lump in her throat. "What did you see?"

He shook his head. "That doesn't matter. You did what you had to do, and I did what I had to do. We both did what was necessary to get home to your mom and brother." He looked at Alyson's mom before extending his hand across the table.

She hesitated for only a moment before taking it.

"We did what we had to do to survive. And I'd do it all again. Going to Wyoming seems rather trivial in the scheme of things."

"Dad?" Eddie said, leaning forward. "What happened?"

Beth pursed her lips before releasing a breath through her nose. "I hear what you're saying. But there's no reason to leave our home. Our life. Yes, things are crazy right now, especially in Portland. They've had bumps like this before, and things always return to normal."

"Not this time, Beth. Not right away, anyway."

Eddie leaned back in his chair, crossing his arms with a quiet *humph*. "So, is anyone going to tell me what happened in Portland?"

The room seemed to close in on Alyson, the silence closing in like a trap. She understood about protecting Eddie, but something told her he knew more about what was going on than any of them, thanks to his constant connection to the internet.

Across the table, her little brother's expression shifted as he studied her face, his eyes lingering on the cut along her jaw before dropping to the marks on her arms. The casual acceptance on his features faded, replaced by something harder and more knowing.

She recognized that look. It was the same one she'd seen in the mirror this morning, the look of innocence slipping away. Eddie might be young, sheltered behind his video games and social media, but he wasn't stupid.

As his gaze moved between her and their father, and back to his phone, a sickening clarity washed over her. Their careful facade of protection was already cracking. Maybe it was time to stop shielding him from the truth, even if that truth would change him forever, just as Portland had changed her.

Chapter 8

Alyson straightened her shoulders, not daring to look in her mom's direction. "It was bad, Eddie. Beyond bad. My roommates— "

"Jenna and Megan?"

"Mm-hmm." Alyson swallowed hard, fighting the bile rising in her throat.

"Alyson," her mom said, her voice low and cautionary. "Eddie doesn't— "

"Let her talk," her dad urged. "Go ahead, Alyson."

"My roommates died. It was awful."

"Oh . . ." Eddie's eyes were wide as he shook his head. "Were they Star Brights?"

"Star Brights?" Their mom shook her head. "What does that mean?"

"It's what they call them. The people who freak out and kill people. They start— "

"Humming?" Alyson asked, her voice cracking. "Do they hum? Or sing?" Ryan had hummed. She couldn't remember the tune, but at the time she thought it was familiar. And the woman on the street, she kept singing the one line from "The Star-Spangled Banner" over and over. Both of them had the same vacant look in their eyes.

"Exactly. There's video." He thrust his phone toward Alyson.

She pushed it away. "I don't need to see it."

"That's why they think it's a sickness. Because people have the same symptoms. They think the explosions are coordinated, too, part of whatever is happening with the singing, with the Star Brights."

"Who's calling them Star Brights?" their dad asked, his own phone in his hand as he scrolled.

"Don't know who started it." Eddie shrugged. "But you can search for it and see all sorts of stuff about them."

"I don't want you doing that," their mom said, her voice firm. "You are not to go searching out videos of those awful events."

"But, Mom— "

"No. I mean it. I don't want you polluting your mind with those things. It's bad enough you spend all your free time in that video game, but this— "

"Enough, Beth." Their dad's voice was calm. "We're the ones who have given him the easy access. You can't expect him not to use the internet or play video games."

Her mom's flushed face told Alyson that she wanted to say more but would save it for later, probably when her parents were alone.

It was common for her mom to ground Eddie—and Alyson, too, before she turned eighteen—from the computer and game systems. Eventually, though, she would soften and allow them access again, rarely sticking to her original decision. Her mom had a tendency to fly off the handle, only to regret it later, often walking back her words once the anger cooled.

"They weren't Star Brights," Alyson said, staring at her hands. "Not Jenna and Megan. But Ryan . . ." She cleared her throat and lifted her chin. "Ryan was Megan's boyfriend, and I think he was one of them. He wasn't normal. I had to stop him." Her voice faded to a whisper. "He's dead too."

"You killed him?" Eddie's voice was laced with shock.

Alyson lifted one shoulder. "I didn't mean to. But I didn't have a choice."

The room was silent for many minutes until her dad cleared his throat. "Back to our discussion about Wyoming."

"No." Her mom's tone didn't allow room for argument. "We are not going to your parents' place."

"Why can't we go and pretend it's a vacation?" Eddie asked, looking around the table. "Like last year. I thought it was fun helping to feed the cows and chickens."

Alyson shot him a look. "They had way too many chickens." She made a face.

She had only visited her grandparents a few times in her life. Her mom didn't think they were a good influence. They had come to Oregon a few years ago after selling their business in Douglas, Wyoming, and buying the lodge outside Yellowstone. With six weeks between residences, they did a road trip.

They were supposed to stay with Alyson's family for a week, but they only lasted two days. Her mom and Grandpa Dick spent the whole time sniping at each other, while her dad did nothing about it. After they left, the tension lingered, with her mom questioning why her dad hadn't stuck up for her.

Last summer, Uncle Brian, who also worked at the lodge, invited them to visit. His children, Maddie and Jackson, were there too. Alyson and her family had their own cabin, thankfully one with electricity and running water, unlike the cabin where Uncle Brian, Maddie, and Jackson stayed. They were in a newly constructed cabin that was completely off the grid. Alyson couldn't believe people actually paid money to stay somewhere without electricity or running water, but they did.

Uncle Brian let them stay in the cabin he lived in. It was fine, especially since they had a flushing toilet, but it was definitely decorated by a man. Eddie might have loved the visit, helping with the cows and chickens and riding the horses, but Alyson hated it.

The lodge still had guests, and Grandma Ruth quickly enlisted Alyson and Maddie as free labor. When they weren't helping guests, they were weeding the garden or working in the greenhouse. They did get to do other things, like fishing and visiting Yellowstone, but it wasn't exactly Alyson's idea of a dream vacation. Not even close.

"I'm with Mom," Alyson said. "I don't want to go to Wyoming. It's true that Portland was awful. Beyond awful. But I'm sure it'll be fine soon. People were probably blowing off steam over . . . something. They'll get things back to normal in a day or so." Even as she spoke, she knew it wasn't true. The looting might be contained, but whatever else was happening was definitely more than just blowing off steam.

Eddie might be right. The doctors needed to figure out what was going on and why people were humming before freaking out and killing people.

Her mom's eyes softened, and she gave a slight motion of agreement.

Her dad shook his head. "I hope you're both right about this. No . . . that's not the right thing to say. I *pray* you're right. Because if you're not, we could have some serious trouble."

~~~~~

As the day wore on, they fell into a strange routine. Eddie retreated to his room, the sounds of him playing his video game and laughing in virtual reality with his friends
~~~~~

providing a bizarre counterpoint to the news reports that continued to play downstairs.

Her mom worked around the house, her motions more frantic than usual, as though keeping things in order could prevent the unfolding disaster.

Her dad alternated between making calls, most of which either didn't connect or went unanswered, and making lists of things they needed. He announced he was going to the store the next day. If they were going to stay in Astoria, he wanted to make sure they had plenty of food and other supplies.

Alyson logged into her online class, only to discover it'd been canceled. She soon found herself drifting from room to room, unable to settle, her mind a whirlwind of conflicting emotions.

In the early evening, she found herself once again drawn to the windows overlooking the river. The sun was still high in the sky, typical for early June in the Pacific Northwest. The landscape was bathed in a golden light, a beautiful sight that seemed at odds with the turmoil raging both within her and in the world beyond their walls.

"What're you thinking about?" Her father's voice startled her. She turned to find him standing in the doorway, leaning slightly on a cane her mom had insisted he use.

Alyson shrugged and turned back to the window. "Everything, I guess."

He made his way over to her and placed a comforting hand on her shoulder. "It's okay to be scared. Sad too. What we went through yesterday . . . it wasn't easy."

Tears pricked at her eyes. "I killed someone, Dad," she whispered, her voice breaking. "Maybe two people. How am I supposed to be okay with that? Not to mention my best friends are dead."

He pulled her into a tight embrace, and Alyson let the tears fall. She cried for Jenna and Megan, for Ryan, even for the rough-looking man who tried to steal their car. She cried for the world that seemed to be falling apart around them. She cried for herself. How would things ever go back to normal?

"You did what you had to do," he murmured, stroking her hair. "You saved us both. I'm so proud of you, Alyson. So proud."

They stood there for a long moment. When Alyson finally pulled away, a sense of lightness washed over her, as if sharing the burden of her actions had eased their weight.

"What do we do now?" she asked, wiping her eyes.

Her dad smiled softly. "We do what we've always done. We stick together, we adapt, and we survive. Whatever comes next, we'll face it as a family."

As if on cue, her mom called from the kitchen, announcing that dinner was ready. The normalcy of the moment, gathering for a family meal, was both comforting and surreal.

They ate in relative silence, the TV muted but still flickering with images of a world in chaos. Alyson found herself studying her family, committing every detail to memory. Her mother's determined expression as she ensured everyone had enough to eat. Her brother's animated gestures as he recounted some victory in his video game, the craziness of the world forgotten for the moment. Her father's watchful gaze, always alert, always protecting.

As they cleared the table after dinner, a sudden burst of static from the TV caught their attention. A grim-faced newscaster appeared on the screen, his voice tight with barely contained emotion.

"We interrupt this broadcast with breaking news. The president is strongly advising all citizens to stay in their homes if possible. I repeat, it is advised that you stay in your homes. The situation is being closely monitored, and further instructions will be provided as they become available."

"Does this sound like things are improving?" her dad asked.

Alyson's mom purposely avoided his gaze as she left the room.

As night fell, casting the world outside into darkness, Alyson found herself once again drawn to the window. The river stretched out before her, a ribbon of black water under the starlit sky. In the distance, the lights of the Astoria-Megler Bridge twinkled, a beacon of familiarity in a world turned upside down.

She thought of all the people out there, in Astoria, in Portland, across the country, and around the world. How many of them were huddled in their homes right now, same as her family? How many were scared, confused, and hoping for answers or salvation?

Alyson didn't have the answers. She had no idea what tomorrow would bring or the day after that. She hoped the president's warning would help get the crisis under control, but deep down, she knew it wouldn't. Somehow, she sensed this was merely the beginning.

Chapter 9

The living room was quiet as the CDC spokesperson finished the briefing. Alyson sat on the edge of the couch, her eyes fixed on the TV screen, absorbing every word. The gravity of the situation settled over her.

"A catatonic state?" Eddie whispered, breaking the silence. "What does that even mean?"

Their dad shook his head. "It means they're not in control of their actions, son. Like sleepwalking, but worse."

Alyson thought back to the incident in Portland. Ryan's vacant eyes, the humming, his sudden change in behavior . . . it all started to make a terrifying kind of sense. Even worse, what happened to Ryan was becoming common around the world.

As the president took the podium, Alyson found herself leaning forward, desperate for reassurance, for some sign that the authorities had this under control. With each new restriction announced, each measure taken, her hope dwindled.

"I told you they'd close the national parks," Eddie said. "But what about all the tourists?"

"They'll have to leave," their mom said softly, her voice tight with worry.

Alyson glanced at her mother, surprised by the concern etched on her face. It was a stark contrast to her usual calm demeanor and acceptance when it came to government decisions. Maybe she shouldn't be surprised. Things were different now. Life was different. Her gaze shifted to her dad, leaning back in the chair with his arms crossed, wearing a scowl.

The tension between her parents was uncomfortable, a lingering trace of yesterday's heated disagreement about whether or not to go to Wyoming. They were staying put for now. Her dad had conceded, and her mom had looked victorious earlier, but that didn't seem to be the case now.

As the president finished his address, the governor of Oregon appeared on screen. She listened intently as even stricter measures were outlined for their state. Part of her understood the necessity, but another part recoiled at the thought of such severe restrictions on their lives.

"This is ridiculous," her dad muttered, his jaw clenched. "It's worse than the pandemic. They're turning the entire state into a prison. I'll bet you a dollar Wyoming isn't being put under such tyrannical rule."

"Don't start, Rich. These measures are necessary. We need to follow the rules to keep everyone safe."

"Oh, come on, Beth. Can't you see they're overreaching? Acting without full information and stripping away our freedoms based on fear? Exactly like before."

"This isn't like before. People are turning violent without warning. We need to trust the experts."

Alyson watched the exchange, her stomach knotting. She'd never seen her parents so at odds, no matter the subject. "But, Dad, they're trying to keep everyone safe. The CDC doctor said they don't know how this thing spreads— "

"And that's exactly why these measures are too extreme," he cut her off.

"Really, Rich?" Alyson's mom shot him a look. "You need to let that go. What happened before isn't what's happening now."

"You sure about that?" he scoffed.

During the pandemic, her mom had been the voice of reason, always advocating for following the rules. Her dad had also done so, at first. But when days turned to weeks and weeks to months, with Oregon having many safety measures put in place that saved lives, her dad became angry. He insisted they were being denied privileges granted by the Constitution of the United States.

While Alyson understood safety protocols were important, it was also a difficult time for her. While some states, including Wyoming where her cousins lived, had gone back to school in the fall, only months after the pandemic began, she had online school for most of the year.

During the winter, they'd finally started a combination of in-person and online. The next fall, they returned to normal classes. Alyson had been concerned that the change in schooling would alter her plans for the future. As the youngest in her class, thanks to skipping from fifth grade into the seventh, she believed she had more to prove than the other students.

She'd carefully mapped out a plan to finish college in three years with her bachelor's degree in business and then planned to go on to get her MBA. With an MBA, she'd have opportunities galore for a fantastic and satisfying career. Her mom had encouraged Alyson to pursue a degree in business, just as she had.

Once a human resources manager in an office, her mom started a home-based business after Eddie was born. She offered similar services to a variety of clients with a much more flexible schedule. Despite her mom's thriving business, Alyson thought her education was going to waste. She had an MBA, but truthfully, anyone could do what she did, degree or no degree. Alyson planned on more. Much more.

She wanted to get a position where the sky was the limit. Maybe a CEO of a major corporation where she could travel the world. Of course, even when making a lot of money, she'd remember there were people less fortunate than her. That was the right thing to do.

Surprisingly, her dad, who had only an associate's degree from community college, ended up in a well-paying job. He traveled for work regularly, mostly along the West Coast since that was his sales territory. Alyson was surprised at how much an office furniture salesman could make. They lived a comfortable life. Their home was modest but still lovely, built in 1914 but updated to be fully modern.

Alyson's bedroom was a little on the small side, but it was the best room in the house, with a view of the Columbia River. Her parents didn't even have that view. Their bedroom and offices were in the fully finished walkout basement. While they could see the river from there, it wasn't the same.

Eddie had threatened to take Alyson's room when she left for college, but her parents reminded him since she was only an hour and a half away, she'd be coming home for holidays and long weekends. His room was at the back of the house. While he didn't have the view, the room was much larger and even had walk-in closets on either side of it. He used one for clothes and the other was his gaming room.

Alyson also had a lovely walk-in closet. Her closet even had a second door to a smaller hidden room. When she was a child, she played there often. She called it her dollhouse and had spent many hours in there, dreaming of the future she'd once have.

As the debate between her parents intensified, Alyson found herself torn. Part of her agreed with her mother, understanding the need for strict measures. But another part of her, the part that still saw the horror in Portland, wondered if her father might have a point.

"But . . . don't you think it's necessary?" she asked hesitantly. "I mean, after what happened in Portland— "

"What happened in Portland is exactly why we can't trust the government to handle this," her dad said, his voice rising. "They didn't prevent that, did they? And now they want us to believe they can keep us safe by locking us in our homes?"

"And what's your solution, Rich? Let everyone run around freely while people are turning violent without warning?"

Eddie nodded enthusiastically. "Yeah, it's like in that one game. When the authorities try to contain the zombie outbreak, it makes things worse."

"This isn't a game, Eddie," Alyson snapped, frustration bubbling up inside her. "People are dying."

A heavy silence fell over the room. Alyson immediately regretted her outburst, seeing the hurt look on her brother's face.

"I'm sorry," she said softly. "I didn't mean to— "

"It's okay, Alyson," her mom interjected, her voice gentler now. "We're all on edge. But that's why we need to follow the guidelines. They're there to protect us."

Her dad shook his head. "Protection at the cost of freedom isn't protection at all."

"You're starting to sound like your dad," her mom said through clenched teeth.

"My dad knows how to survive. A skill we desperately need."

As the minutes ticked away, the debate between her parents continued, their voices rising and falling in waves of frustration and concern.

Eddie retreated to his room, no doubt losing himself in a virtual world.

Alyson remained quiet, torn between her instinct to trust authority and the growing seed of doubt planted by her father's arguments.

Her dad stood. "I'm going to the store. We need to stock up before things get worse."

"Rich, no," Alyson's mom protested, her anger replaced by a tone of concern. "It's not safe. We have enough for now."

"I'm going," he said firmly. "And I'm going alone. It'll be quicker that way."

A knot of worry formed in Alyson's stomach. "Dad, please be careful," she pleaded.

His expression softened as he looked at his daughter. "I will, sweetheart. Don't worry."

As the door closed behind him, Alyson saw her mother's face tighten with concern, though she remained silent.

~~~~~

Hours later, her dad returned, his car loaded with supplies. It took the entire family working together to bring everything in. The kitchen counters were soon overflowing with canned goods, bags of rice and beans, and other nonperishables.
~~~~~

"Where are we going to put all of this?" her mom asked, surveying the abundance with a mixture of exasperation and grudging approval.

"We'll make room," her dad replied, determination in his voice. "Better to have too much than not enough. It's good I went today with the new shopping rules beginning tomorrow. I wasn't the only one with the idea of buying. The shelves are already low. I went to Costco, Fred Meyer, Safeway, and even Walmart." He widened his eyes in an exaggerated manner.

"Walmart?" her mom said in mock horror. "I didn't know we were that desperate."

Rich placed a hand on Beth's shoulder, their eyes locking in a quiet exchange of love and years of devotion. They may not always agree, but they were united in their commitment to each other and their family.

Later that night, as Alyson lay in bed with sleep eluding her, she could hear her parents' muffled voices from the kitchen. Unlike the united front they'd presented earlier, now their tones were clipped and tense, disagreement evident even through the walls.

She rolled over and pulled her pillow over her head to block out the noise. Part of her longed for the simplicity of the pandemic days, when the enemy was a virus they could fight with masks and distance. The new condition, which turned people into violent, unpredictable attackers, carried a far darker menace.

But how could it even be? How could something make people act like this on such a massive scale? Not just in Oregon and the United States, but the entire world was being affected.

She furrowed her brow. Was it the whole world? Eddie had shown them videos from different places, but she hadn't checked *all* the countries. Maybe tomorrow she'd do some research. She had a world map and could go country by country, checking online to see how many were affected.

It didn't matter much for her and her family in Astoria, Oregon, but knowledge was power, and she was certain that the more she knew, the better the outcome would be.

Alyson couldn't escape the sense that their world was teetering on the brink. The tension between her parents, the uncertainty of the situation, and the looming threat of violence all swirled in her mind. Whatever came next, she knew their family would never be the same. The only question was whether they would face the challenges united or divided.

Chapter 10

The morning sun filtered through the curtains, casting a deceptively cheerful glow across the room. Alyson lay in bed, staring at the ceiling, struggling to summon the energy for another day of uncertainty.

The muffled sounds of her parents' voices drifted up the stairs. They'd been arguing when she fell asleep. Had it gone on all night, or was it a new fight this morning?

With a sigh, Alyson shifted to the side of the bed and made her way to the window. The street below was quiet, devoid of the usual morning bustle. No kids riding bikes, no neighbors chatting over fences, not even the familiar sight of Mr. Verley walking his golden retriever. It was as if the entire neighborhood had collectively decided to hold its breath.

Her gaze shifted to the bridge. A lone car was traveling over it. Would there be any river traffic today? She doubted it.

As Alyson made her way downstairs, the voices grew clearer. Her parents were in the kitchen, their conversation halting abruptly as she entered.

"Morning, sweetheart," her mom said, forcing an overly cheerful tone. "Sleep okay?"

Alyson shrugged and reached for the coffee pot. "As well as can be expected, I guess. What's going on?"

Her parents locked eyes, a conversation passing between them. It was her dad who finally spoke. "I've been thinking about the neighborhood, about how isolated everyone's become. How it's only going to get worse."

Her mom's lips tightened into a thin line. "Rich, we talked about this— "

"I know, I know," he cut her off, holding up a placating hand. "But hear me out. We're all in this together, right? Is that what you like to say?"

"Don't twist my words."

"Wouldn't we be safer, stronger, if we actually acted like it? Acted like we're working together?"

Alyson looked at her parents, sensing the brewing argument. "What are you suggesting, Dad?"

He took a deep breath. "I think we should reach out to the neighbors. Organize some kind of . . . I don't know, community support system. Maybe regular meetings, check-ins, that sort of thing."

"That would violate the quarantine rules," Alyson's mom pointed out, her voice tight with disapproval.

"Sometimes rules need to be bent for the greater good," he countered.

A knot formed in Alyson's stomach, tightening with unease. She could see both sides of the argument, but the thought of breaking the rules, of potentially exposing themselves to danger, made her uneasy.

They'd gone through something similar before. During the pandemic, in the early days when the reports coming from other countries made it seem like the virus could kill instantly, everyone had locked themselves away. Eventually, the six-foot distancing guidelines allowed people to visit when outside.

As Mr. Verley walked his dog, he'd often chat with Alyson and her mom while they tended the rose bushes in the front yard. He stayed on the sidewalk, maintaining a distance of more than six feet from them.

"I don't know, Dad," she said hesitantly. "It seems risky."

His face softened as he looked at her. "I know it's scary, Alyson. But isolating ourselves completely, that's scary too. We need to stick together, now more than ever."

Before she could respond, Eddie came into the kitchen, his eyes glued to his phone. "Guys, you gotta see this! There's another video from London. It's crazy!"

"Not now, Eddie," their mom snapped, the sharpness in her voice disappearing as quickly as it had come. "Sorry, honey. We're having an important discussion right now."

He looked up, sensing the tension in the room. "What's going on?"

As their dad explained his idea, Alyson watched the emotions play across her brother's face—excitement, worry, hope. It was a reminder of how young he still was, how much he craved normalcy and connection. He didn't understand how dangerous things could truly be. To him, this was almost like one of his video games, a virtual world and not their current reality.

"I think it's a good idea," Eddie said finally. "It's boring being stuck inside all the time. And what if something happens and we need help?"

Their mom sighed. "I understand where you're both coming from, I do. But it's not only about us. What if one of us is infected and doesn't know it? We could be putting the entire neighborhood at risk."

"How could we be infected?" Alyson asked, shaking her head.

"She means you." Eddie pointed at her.

"Me? I— "

"No, no. That's not what I mean . . ." her mom stuttered. "Not exactly." She looked at Alyson's dad, her eyes silently pleading for his help.

He cleared his throat. "You see, Alyson, it's just . . . no one knows exactly how it's spreading. They don't even know what it is. It could be a virus or something bacterial. It may be spread in the air or by bodily fluids. There're some theories it affects the brain, or at least the part of the brain that controls decision-making."

"Okay? And? What does that have to do with . . . oh." Alyson's shoulders sagged. "Ryan. His blood. I had it on me." Tears filled her eyes. Was she infected? Had Ryan's blood mingled with her own somehow? Was she going to suddenly turn into a . . . whatever and kill her family?

"I'm sure you're fine, honey." Her mom pulled her close. "Nobody knows what is happening. Right now, it's all theory."

"That's why we'll be careful," her dad insisted, resting his hand on Alyson's back. "We'll be smart about everything. We'll meet outside and keep our distance. But at least we'll be facing this together."

"And if I have it? If I'm one of those . . . those . . ."

"Star Brights," Eddie offered. "That's what people call them, because they sing songs about stars. You know like— "

"Enough, Eddie," her dad said.

Alyson could see her mother's resolve wavering. "Maybe . . . maybe we could start small. Our immediate neighbors, see how it goes?"

"That's all I'm asking. I'll talk to a few people today, see who's interested. Only those on our street."

Their street was essentially a dead end, ending in a driveway at the final house on the block. Alyson had never taken the time to count, but she estimated there were about a dozen houses on their street. Her house was the second from the beginning where it met Lincoln Street. With a population of only ten thousand people, Astoria wasn't huge, but it was a bustling town, especially during the summer tourism season.

It was once well-known for the movies filmed there and in the nearby area. The cat house from the 1980s movie *Short Circuit* wasn't far from Alyson's home. Films like *The Goonies*, *Free Willy*, *Kindergarten Cop*, and *The Ring* were among the most famous, but even in recent years, lesser-known movies and documentaries had been made in Astoria.

Now, it seemed like things were so crazy she could be the star of her own horror flick. If Ryan's blood had been infected and she caught whatever he had, would she even know she was a killer before it was too late?

"I don't like it," her mom said. "But I know you're going to do what you do, whether I think it's a good idea or not."

Rich gave her a smile and leaned in to kiss her lips. Beth turned her head at the last minute so the kiss landed on her cheek. "This is the right thing to do. You'll see," he said.

With her dad leaving the house, clipboard and pen in hand, a sense of unease took root in Alyson. She hoped he was right, that coming together would make them stronger. But a small voice in the back of her mind whispered of danger, of the unpredictability of the situation that had turned their world upside down.

From the living room window, Alyson watched as her dad made his way down the street. He approached each house with a friendly wave, maintaining a respectable distance as he spoke with the neighbors. Some seemed receptive, nodding along as he talked. Others were more hesitant, their body language closed off and wary as they stepped even farther away.

"What do you think they're saying?" Eddie asked, pressing his face against the glass.

Alyson shrugged. "I don't know." She couldn't help but worry about how quickly things could go bad. If fear and suspicion took over, those hesitant neighbors might turn hostile. What if someone misinterpreted a gesture or a word from her dad? In tense times, even a friendly wave could be seen as a threat. This could escalate so easily, and they might find themselves facing more than wary glances.

As the morning wore on, Alyson tried to distract herself with household chores, but her eyes kept drifting to the window. While checking on her dad's progress, she noticed Mrs. Samms from across the street watching, too, her curtains twitching at regular intervals. Alyson could no longer see her dad; he was far enough up the street to be out of view. She doubted Mrs. Samms could see him either.

It was nearly lunchtime when he finally returned, his face flushed with excitement. "We're on!" he announced as he burst through the door. "Most of the neighbors are in. We're going to have the meeting in our backyard."

Her mom's forehead furrowed with concern. "Rich, are you sure about this? What about social distancing?"

"We'll spread out, use the whole yard," he assured her. "Everyone will bring their own chairs, stay in family groups. It'll be fine. We'll meet this evening. I thought we could keep it simple. It'll be after dinner, so we don't need to worry about food. Maybe iced tea? Lemonade?"

While her parents talked logistics, Alyson's thoughts swirled with both excitement and apprehension. The idea of visiting with their neighbors, of having some semblance of normalcy, was appealing. But the potential risks loomed large in her mind.

Hours slipped away in a rush of nonstop preparations. Her dad mowed the lawn while her mom deep cleaned the patio furniture. She and Eddie were tasked with creating signs to remind everyone about distancing. As she worked, unease crept in. Was this the right decision? What if someone out there was infected?

Or worse, what if it was her?

The thought lodged in her mind, refusing to leave. Could she already be a threat without even knowing it?

~~~~~

As Alyson finished hanging the last sign, directing people toward where the meeting would be held, her dad called her to the front yard. "Can you help me move these flowerpots?" He pointed to the large ceramic planters by the porch steps.

As they worked, Alyson noticed Mrs. Samms on her phone, pacing back and forth on her front porch, gesturing wildly.

"What do you think that's about?" Alyson asked, nodding toward their neighbor.

Her dad glanced over, his brow furrowing slightly. "Not sure. Probably nothing that concerns us. Don't worry."

But worry she did, as not ten minutes later a police car pulled up in front of their house, and two officers stepped out with strained expressions.

"Mr. Reynolds?" the younger of the two called as they approached. "We need to speak with you."
~~~~~

Alyson's heart raced as she watched her dad go to meet the officers. Were they here for her? For killing Ryan? Or maybe they found out she attacked the thug and left him for dead?

From her vantage point near the porch, she could see Mrs. Samms watching from behind her curtains, a satisfied look on her face.

"What's going on?" Alyson's mom asked, coming to stand beside her. Eddie stood behind them.

"I'm not sure," she replied, her voice barely above a whisper. "Maybe it's about Portland? What I did?"

Her mother took her hand as they watched in tense silence. Her dad spoke with the officers, his body language defensive at first, slowly easing as the conversation continued. After a stretch of endless seconds, the officers nodded and turned to leave.

"They're not here for me?" Alyson whispered.

Her mom squeezed her hand. "You're fine, honey."

Her dad made his way back to them, his face a mixture of frustration and relief. "Well, that was fun," he said sarcastically. "Apparently, our dear neighbor thought we were planning some kind of illegal gathering."

"Are we in trouble?" Eddie asked, his eyes wide with worry.

"No, no. They simply gave us a warning. Reminded us about the quarantine rules. I explained we were planning to follow all the guidelines and keep everyone distanced. They seemed satisfied with that."

"Maybe this isn't such a good idea after all, Rich. If people are this on edge— "

"No," he cut her off. "We need this, Beth. The whole neighborhood needs this. We can't let fear control us."

As they resumed their preparations, Alyson couldn't shake the sense that they were walking a dangerous line. Even though they weren't there for her, the police visit had shaken her more than she wanted to admit.

Chapter 11

By the time seven o'clock approached, neighbors trickled in, arriving in ones and twos. None brought their children. The air carried a quiet unease as they carefully spaced their chairs apart.

Eddie, annoyed to realize he was the youngest one there, muttered something about going inside to play his games. Alyson considered retreating, too, but not to game. She wanted to dive back into what she had started earlier. She had made some headway on the presence of the Star Brights, but the more she studied, the more questions she had. Curiosity won out. She stayed, eager to hear what plans her dad had in store.

Her dad stood at the center of the yard, beaming as he welcomed each new arrival. "Thank you all for coming," he began once everyone was settled. "I know these are scary times, but I believe that by coming together—safely, of course—we can support each other through this crisis."

As her dad spoke, Alyson scanned the faces of their neighbors. Most seemed cautiously optimistic, nodding along with his words. But a few looked distinctly uncomfortable, their eyes darting around as if expecting the police to burst in at any moment. It was no surprise that Mrs. Samms chose not to attend.

The meeting progressed, with people sharing concerns and suggestions. Ideas were floated about a neighborhood watch, a system for checking on elderly residents, and even a community garden to supplement their food supplies. Despite her initial reservations, Alyson found herself getting caught up in the spirit of cooperation.

The mood gradually lightened as the conversation flowed. A neighbor joked about their clumsy attempts at baking bread, sparking laughter. Another shared their efforts to transform canned beans into gourmet meals, earning more smiles. The backyard felt less tense as voices rose and fell in an uneven but warming rhythm. Alyson caught her dad standing a bit straighter, clearly buoyed by the increasing connection.

Bob, their typically quiet neighbor from two doors down, got to his feet. Usually reserved and meticulous in his mannerisms, he now seemed agitated. His face was flushed, his eyes unfocused. "This is not right for The One," he muttered, his voice rising. "There's no reason to resist."

A hush fell over the gathering as all eyes turned to Bob. Alyson's dad approached him slowly, hands raised in a calming gesture. "Bob, it's okay. Working together is the better choice. It doesn't mean we're resisting authority. Why don't you sit down and we can talk about— "

Before he could finish his sentence, Bob lunged forward with a guttural cry. His hands closed around her dad's throat as they both tumbled to the ground. A smile spread across Bob's face as he began to hum.

Panic spread instantly. People screamed, scattering in every direction. Alyson stood frozen in horror, watching as her father struggled against Bob's grip. It was as if she were suddenly back in her apartment. Bob's mannerisms uncannily mirrored Ryan's as he turned into a killer. Into a Star Bright.

"Dad!" she cried, snapping out of her paralysis and rushing forward. But strong arms held her back–her mother, pulling her away from the danger. A couple of neighbors managed to break up the brawl. Two people were now holding Bob as he glanced around, and another man was with her dad, asking if he was okay.

"Someone call 9-1-1!" her mom's voice cracked as she shouted.

"No, no. It's okay, Beth," Bob said, his hands raised partway. He and her mom both worked from home and had formed a small group of home-office workers who met every Wednesday morning at six for a walk. "I don't know what came over me. That was weird." He looked at Alyson's dad. "I'm sorry, Rich. Totally my bad."

Alyson huddled close to her mom, the horrors of that day in her apartment rushing back as Ryan's outburst replayed in her mind, the overwhelming memories triggered by the escalating tension with Bob.

Her breathing was uneven, and her chest tightened, the memory crashing over her like a wave she couldn't escape. She gripped her mom's arm, desperate for something solid, as the sounds around her blurred into a dull roar.

Sirens wailed in the distance, growing louder by the second. Even though Bob insisted he was fine, and he appeared to be, someone had already called the police. The two officers from earlier rushed into the backyard, their eyes scanning the scene.

"He's one of them!" someone in the crowd shouted. "A Star Bright!"

"I'm not!" Bob snapped, his frown deepening. "It was a misunderstanding. Tell them, Rich."

Alyson's dad raised his hands, signaling for calm. "I'm not sure what happened."

As everyone watched, Bob's face tightened, the smile creeping onto his lips again. His eyes went unfocused, as if something else was taking hold of him. "I see. Yes. I see now." He stared off into the distance. He blinked twice before lunging at the nearest police officer, catching everyone off guard.

The younger officer stumbled backward, his hand reaching for his weapon. But Bob was faster, fueled by an inhuman strength and the return of his humming. In a blur of motion, he wrenched the gun from the officer's holster.

"Stop!" the second officer shouted, drawing his own weapon.

Neighbors broke into a frenzy, their cries ringing out as they scrambled for cover.

Alyson's mother grabbed her, pulling her down behind an overturned lawn chair. The ground dug into her knees as she clung to her mother, her breath hitching with each sharp sound around them.

A shot rang out, echoing sharply across the backyard. Alyson's ears buzzed as she peered around the chair, her heart racing.

The first officer lay motionless on the ground, a dark stain spreading across his chest. Bob stood over him, the stolen gun now trained on the second officer.

"Drop the weapon!" the remaining officer commanded, his voice steady despite the situation.

Bob's eyes sparked with frantic energy, a crazed grin spreading across his face. "The stars are singing," he whispered, his finger tightening around the trigger. "Can't you hear them?" He tilted his head back, staring up at the sky, and burst into song, his voice rising to a wild, raw pitch.

"Oh, I'm chasing the star, burning bright in the sky, a beacon of dreams that won't let me say goodbye. Through the night, through the pain, I'll go wherever you are, forever chasing, chasing the star."

His eyes met those of the police officer, that creepy smile in place. "Soon, we'll be the greater light." Bob raised the gun.

Time seemed to slow. Alyson saw the second officer's finger move, heard the deafening crack of gunfire. Bob's body jerked, once, twice, three times, as bullets tore into him. But even as he fell, his own gun discharged, the shot going wide and splintering wood off the fence behind the officer.

Bob crumpled to the ground with the stolen gun still held in his lifeless hand. The backyard fell silent, save for the faint whimper of a neighbor and the heavy breathing of the remaining officer.

"Oh no," Alyson's mom whispered, her arms still wrapped protectively around her. "Oh no, oh no."

Her dad was the first to move, slowly rising from where he'd taken cover. "Is everyone okay?" he called out, his voice shaky but determined.

"Stay where you are!" the officer commanded. "All of you. Don't move."

Heads began to pop up from behind various pieces of lawn furniture and bushes. Shocked faces, tear-streaked cheeks, and wide eyes took in the carnage before them.

The police officer kept his eyes on the crowd as he spoke into his radio, moving toward his partner. "Officer down, suspect down. We need backup and medical assistance, now!" He moved toward Bob, his gun still drawn as he kicked the gun away.

A neighbor stepped forward, calling out that she knew CPR and could help. The officer rushed to his fallen partner's side as the woman moved in to assist. Another neighbor moved toward Bob, but the officer yelled out,

"Don't touch him! His blood. He might be contaminated. You could get it too."

Sirens wailed in the distance, growing louder by the second. Alyson's mind struggled to process what she'd witnessed. Bob, their quiet neighbor who she'd known for years, killed a police officer before being killed himself. And why? Because of some mysterious condition that caused ordinary people to turn violent.

As the memories from her apartment overwhelmed her, Alyson's lips turned numb. Her body wavered.

Her mom's faint voice told her to sit. "You're okay, honey. You're okay," she said as she helped Alyson to a chair. "Put your head between your knees."

Alyson closed her eyes for a moment, focusing on the steadying pressure of her head in her hands and her mom's soothing tone. The sound of sirens grew louder, and she became vaguely aware of the commotion in the backyard.

She tried to focus. Her heart still raced, but clarity began to break through the panic, pulling her attention to the officers, their grim faces, and the scene unfolding around her.

Paramedics rushed to the fallen officer, but it was clear from their actions it was too late. They were slower to check on Bob, first donning protective gear and thick gloves, even wearing face shields. Eventually, they confirmed what Alyson already knew. Bob was dead.

A senior officer approached her dad, his expression hard. "Sir, I need a full account of what happened here."

He nodded quickly. "Of course, of course."

"Are you okay, honey?" her mom whispered, her voice soft. "Okay enough for me to help your dad for a minute?"

"Mm-hmm. I'm okay."

Her mom squeezed her shoulder before moving to join her dad. With a heavy sigh, he started to speak. "We were having a neighborhood meeting, trying to figure out how we could support each other during these times. Bob . . . he seemed fine at first, but he . . . changed."

As her dad explained, Alyson noticed the neighbors pointing in their direction, whispering among themselves and making it clear who had organized the gathering. Several officers cast wary glances at her family, and one approached, notepad in hand, his eyes narrowing as he studied her.

"We're going to need statements from everyone here," he announced. "Nobody leaves until we've spoken to each of you."

The neighbors were questioned first. Alyson overheard the accusations, her dad being blamed for gathering everyone without considering their safety. Mr. Verley, however, made it clear that no one had been forced to attend and that coming together was the right thing to do.

The questioning stretched endlessly, each moment dragging by. Alyson recounted the same details again and again, her voice growing hoarse. She watched the strain deepen on her parents' faces as they, too, were interrogated relentlessly.

Even Eddie had been brought outside to tell what he knew. He'd been playing his game when he heard the ruckus and looked out the window, having witnessed the entire thing. Like Alyson, he was pale and shaky.

Finally, as the sky fully darkened, the police started to wrap up their investigation. The bodies had long since been removed, but dark stains on the grass served as a gruesome reminder of the evening's events.

The senior officer approached her dad one last time. "Mr. Reynolds, while we're not charging you with anything at this time, I want to make it clear that this gathering was a violation of current quarantine orders. I understand you were given permission earlier, but that was obviously a mistake. A fatal mistake.

"Consider this your final warning. Any further incidents will result in serious consequences. And, if I were you, I wouldn't consider myself innocent in this matter. I'll be taking this to the district attorney for consideration of charges. A police officer is dead, and it is your fault."

Her dad nodded, his shoulders drooping. As the last of the police cars pulled away, Alyson and her family stood alone in their backyard, the remnants of their failed community meeting scattered around them.

Her mom was the first to break the silence. "We need to leave," she said, her voice barely above a whisper. "We can't stay here anymore."

Alyson could see the surprise on her dad's face. "Beth, I thought you were against— "

"I know what I said before," she cut him off. "But after this . . . Rich, we're not safe here. None of us are safe anywhere. Maybe . . . maybe your parents' place in Wyoming is our best option after all."

Her mother's words brought a mix of relief and unease. The idea of leaving Astoria, abandoning the only home she'd ever known, sent a chill of fear through her. But after witnessing Bob's horrifying transformation and its deadly aftermath, the thought of staying was even harder to bear.

Her stomach tightened with nerves as she wondered if moving to Wyoming would change anything at all. She knew from her research the Star Brights were everywhere. In every state and every country, though, there were some places where the reports of infection were rare. Going to those places, obscure countries overseas, was not an option since travel by air or boat had been suspended.

"I don't know if they'll even let me leave." Her dad motioned in the direction of the final taillight. "It sounds like they're going to charge me. Put me in jail."

"All the more reason— "

"No, Beth. He was right. An officer is dead, and it's my fault. Let's get some sleep. We'll talk about this tomorrow. Hopefully, by that time, we'll know more."

As they made their way back into the house, Alyson cast one last look at their backyard. The place where she'd played as a child, where they'd had countless family barbecues, was now forever tainted by the memory of violence and death.

She realized that no matter what happened next, whether they stayed or left, nothing would ever be the same again. The world had changed, and they had no choice but to change with it.

Chapter 12

Alyson sat at her desk, staring blankly at the world map tacked to her wall, her mind a whirlwind of fear and uncertainty. Each tick of the clock seemed to echo the unstoppable march of time in a world spiraling out of control. She'd been up for hours, long before dawn, combing through reports of Star Brights from across the globe.

With the first light of day breaking, she tried to refocus on her project, but her mind kept drifting back to the events of the previous night. The image of Bob's face, contorted with rage and confusion, flashed before her eyes. The sound of gunshots echoed in her memory. Alyson shuddered, her fingers striking the keyboard by mistake.

"This is ridiculous," she muttered, shaking her head as if to clear the disturbing thoughts. But they clung stubbornly, dragging her back to that day in her apartment. Her chest tightened, her pulse quickening with the memory. She swiped at the tears clouding her vision, then stood and stretched, willing the tension from her limbs. The faint creak of movement sounded from downstairs, followed by the familiar scent of coffee drifting up to meet her.

She paused at the top of the stairs. She could hear her parents' voices, low and urgent. The news played in the background, a constant drone of updates and warnings.

". . . can't believe they're closing the state borders," her mother was saying. "How are we supposed to— "

"Shh," her father interrupted. "One of the children is coming down."

Forcing a neutral expression onto her face, Alyson descended the stairs. "Morning," she said, trying to keep her voice light. "What's going on?"

Her parents exchanged a look before her father spoke. "The governor announced additional restrictions. They're closing the state borders. No one in or out without permission. It's Martial Law, though they're not calling it that."

Alyson's pulse quickened. "But . . . what about leaving for Wyoming? What about your parents? If we did decide to go— "

"We don't know yet, honey." Her mother reached out to squeeze Alyson's hand. "They're setting up some kind of system for permissions and orders, but we don't have any details yet."

Silence stretched through the kitchen, thick and uncomfortable. The soft creak of the stairs broke the stillness, followed by Eddie's slow shuffle as he appeared in the doorway, his eyes still clouded with sleep. "Why does everyone look so serious?" he asked, stifling a yawn. "Did the police come back?"

"No, no," their dad assured him. "Nothing like that."

As her parents filled him in on the new restrictions, Alyson's mind raced. They were trapped here, in a town where their own neighbor had turned violent without warning. And what about her dad? Would he still face charges for organizing the meeting? For causing the death of a police officer?

A knock at the door startled them all. Beth's hands went to her mouth as her eyes widened.

"We're fine." Her dad touched her shoulder before he moved to answer it, his steps hesitant. Alyson followed, hanging back in the hallway.

"Morning, Rich," came the familiar voice of Mr. Verley. "Got a minute?"

Her dad stepped back, allowing Mr. Verley to enter.

"Where's your dog?" Eddie asked, glancing around the man to see if the dog was still on the porch.

"Steve is home. I already took him on his walk," the older man replied, nodding a greeting to Alyson and her mom before turning back to her dad. "Look, I know last night turned out . . . well, terrible is putting it mildly. But a few of us were talking on the way home, and we think your idea of working together is still smart."

Her dad's eyebrows shot up in surprise. "Really? I thought after what happened . . ."

Mr. Verley shook his head. "That's exactly why we need to stick together. None of us saw that coming with Bob. Who knows which of us might be next? We need to look out for each other. Plus, with the border closed, the additional restrictions, and them calling up the National Guard, things are going to get . . . interesting. Especially since the stores are closing too."

"I didn't hear that," her mom said, stepping forward.

"Yep. It was in the written statement that was released. Interestingly enough, it wasn't part of the press conference. The stores have until noon to lock their doors."

Mr. Verley pulled a folded paper from his pocket. "I've got a sign-up sheet here for patrols and neighborhood watch. We thought maybe we could take turns keeping an eye on things, watching for any . . . unusual behavior."

Alyson watched as her father's expression shifted from surprise to cautious hope. "That's . . . that's great, Jim. I honestly thought everyone would want nothing to do with me after last night."

Mr. Verley chuckled, though there was little humor in the sound. "Well, you might be surprised. Even Mrs. Samms is changing her tune."

"Mrs. Samms?" Alyson couldn't help but interject. "But she called the police on us!"

Mr. Verley nodded. "She did. But now she's scared of being a woman alone in all this chaos. Funny how quickly perspectives can change when fear sets in."

"But what about the no-gathering rules?" Eddie asked.

"Those are a concern," Mr. Verley admitted. "And we'll need to acknowledge them, but we'll figure out how to do what we need to keep people safe without breaking any of the current rules."

As her father and Mr. Verley exchanged a few words about the neighborhood watch, a glimmer of hope ignited in Alyson. Maybe this could work. Maybe they could protect each other.

After telling Mr. Verley goodbye, her dad grabbed his car keys.

"Where are you going?"

"To get more groceries. Supplies. I have a list. I have over two hours until they lock the doors. I'll get what I need and be back soon. Don't worry." He touched his wife's cheek.

She turned her head to kiss his fingertips. "I will worry."

The rest of the morning passed in a blur of activity. Neighbors dropped by, signing up for watch shifts and discussing plans to use a vacant lot at the end of the street for a community garden. The atmosphere was tense but determined, a far cry from the terror of the previous night.

When their dad returned home a few minutes after twelve, they ran outside to greet him.

"How was it?" her mom asked, peering into the car window.

"A madhouse. But it's done. Let's get it all inside."

They helped him unload the car, carrying bags and boxes into the house. Once everything was inside, they gathered at the kitchen table for simple tuna sandwiches and chips, a meal as familiar as it was easy.

It was shortly after lunch when another knock came at the door. This time, it wasn't a neighbor.

The senior officer from yesterday evening was on their porch, his expression cold and unyielding. "Mr. Reynolds," he said, his tone clipped. "A word?"

Her dad stepped outside, closing the door behind him. Alyson pressed her ear to the wood, straining to hear.

"The district attorney has decided not to press charges at this time," the officer said, his voice tight with barely contained anger. "But don't think this is over. When this crisis passes, that decision will be reevaluated."

"I understand," her father replied, his voice steady. "Thank you for letting me know."

"Don't thank me," the officer snapped. "You should be behind bars right now. A good man is dead because of your little 'community meeting.' His wife is a widow, and his children are without a father. That is on you. *You.*"

There was a pause, and when the officer spoke again, his voice was low and threatening. "Watch yourself, Reynolds. Because I'm watching you. One step out of line and you're mine."

Alyson stumbled back from the door as she heard her father's footsteps approaching. She tried to look nonchalant as he re-entered the house, but the worry must have shown on her face.

"It's okay, Alyson," he said, forcing a smile. "Everything's fine."

But she could see the strain in his eyes, the tension in his shoulders. Everything was far from fine.

As the day wore on, a strange rhythm began to establish itself. Neighbors came and went, sharing news and resources. Watch schedules were drawn up and distributed, being careful not to violate the rules for gathering in groups. Plans for the community garden began to take shape. They even came up with ways to tend to the garden while still adhering to the distancing guidelines.

Alyson threw herself into the activity, glad for the distraction from her racing thoughts. She planted seedlings in the freshly tilled garden beds and chatted with a former librarian working on the other side about setting up a neighborhood book exchange. She even managed to coax a small smile from Mrs. Samms when she waved as she passed by.

But underneath the bustle of activity, a current of fear ran deep. Every unexpected sound made people jump. Casual conversations were punctuated by nervous glances, as if at any moment, one of them might turn into a violent Star Bright without warning. Everyone made sure to keep their distance from each other, looking ready to escape at a moment's notice, and Alyson didn't dare to even think about humming.

She had noticed a few people were wearing long shirts or jackets, much too heavy for the heat of early June. As a man from the end of the block bent over to maneuver a wheelbarrow in the garden, Alyson caught a glimpse of a gun tucked at his hip. She'd seen guns before; last summer, she had even shot a few cans with a rifle at her grandparents' place. But in her everyday life, guns were a rare sight. Especially on the hip of a neighbor living in Oregon.

As evening approached, Alyson sat on the front porch, watching the neighborhood as the day's activities wound down. Mr. Verley waved as he came walking by with his golden retriever, the familiar sight comforting. The dog's ears perked up at every sound, mirroring the heightened alertness of the entire community.

Alyson's thoughts drifted to her father and the police officer's threat. Was her dad truly guilty of causing the officer's death? Alyson had killed Ryan, and maybe that second man, too, but she wasn't under threat of arrest. No one had even followed up with her about Ryan and the deaths of Jenna and Megan. The man on the street who tried to steal their car wasn't something she'd reported. Maybe she should have. Maybe that would've been the right thing to do.

As the sun began to set, casting long shadows across the street, Alyson couldn't shake the feeling that they were living on borrowed time. The fragile peace they'd established could shatter at any moment, as it had with Bob.

With a sigh, she stood up and stretched her stiff muscles. Inside, she found her parents and Eddie gathered around the kitchen table, poring over a map. "What's going on?" she asked, sliding into an empty chair.

Her mother looked up, determination clouded by worry. "We're trying to plan a route to Wyoming, in case we get permission to leave."

"But I thought the borders were closed," Alyson said, confusion coloring her voice.

"They are," her father replied. "But your grandfather has some connections. He's working on getting us clearance. Says he can have National Guard escorts meet us at key points along the way."

"You think leaving is the right thing to do? Everyone seems willing to work together."

Her parents exchanged a look. "Maybe," her mother said cautiously. "It's true, today has been okay . . . inspiring, even. I'll admit, I don't want to leave either, but we need to be prepared for anything. This situation is changing by the hour."

"Still, I don't think— "

"We won't make any rash decisions. But we will do everything we can to stay safe, and we will stay together." Her dad's tone left no room for disagreement.

Later that night, as Alyson lay in bed, she could hear the soft murmur of voices from the main level. Her parents' words were indistinct, but the tone was clear. Worry, fear, and underneath it all, a fierce determination. Unlike other times, they didn't seem to be arguing tonight but instead speaking with a shared purpose.

She thought about the day's events. The new restrictions, the community warily coming together, the lingering threat from the police officer. It was all so overwhelming, yet somehow, they were managing. Adapting. Surviving. Fine right where they were.

In the distance, a dog barked, breaking the unusual silence of the night. Alyson's eyes snapped open, instantly alert. Was it a normal bark, or was it a warning? In their new world, even the most mundane sounds could be a signal of impending danger.

She lay there, heart pounding, straining to hear any further disturbance. But the silence returned, and slowly her pulse began to ease. Finally, she drifted into a restless sleep, her dreams filled with Star Brights and long roads stretching toward an uncertain future.

Chapter 13

Alyson's fingers flew across the keyboard, her eyes fixed on the screen as she navigated through yet another online course. Although the instructor hadn't attended live, she'd left detailed instructions of what was to be completed before the next class.

The soft hum of her laptop mingled with the distant sound of her mother's voice, drifting up from the kitchen below. It was day ten of their new reality, and already a strange routine had begun to take shape.

Alyson glanced at the window, where thick curtains blocked most of the morning light. Her mom had sewn them from a couple of quilts they found in the linen closet. The curtains stayed closed most of the time now, a precaution against prying eyes or potential threats.

Down the street, the community garden project continued in the vacant lot. The garden wasn't currently essential for their survival—thanks to her dad's shopping and the state-arranged food drops—but it might be in the future. For now, the garden served as busy work, a way to keep idle hands occupied and worried minds focused on something tangible.

A knock on her bedroom door broke her concentration. "Come in," she called, minimizing her browser window.

Her mother entered, a basket of laundry balanced on her hip. "Hey, sweetie. How's the studying going?"

Alyson shrugged. "Fine, I guess. It's weird trying to focus on calculus when the world's falling apart."

Her mom set the basket down and perched on the edge of Alyson's bed. "I know it's hard, but keeping up with your studies is important. We don't know how long this situation will last, and when things get back to normal— "

"*If* they get back to normal," Alyson interjected.

Her mother's jaw clenched, but she pressed on. "When things get back to normal, you'll want to be caught up."

Alyson swiveled around in her chair to face her mother fully. "Mom, is that seriously what you expect to happen? We'll wake up one day and everything will be fine?"

Her mom was quiet for a moment as she pulled the laundry basket closer to her body. "I don't know, honey. But we have to hope, don't we? We haven't had any trouble lately, not since . . ."

She didn't finish her sentence, but Alyson knew she meant not since the terrible thing in the backyard with Bob. Even the local news seemed to have less to report on the Star Bright occurrences, though there were plenty of them online from various sources to prove they were still happening around the world.

Her mom took a pile of laundry from the basket and set it on her bed. "You can't give up, Alyson. You have to keep going. Keep doing what you know you need to do. Follow through with your plans in the hope things will soon be fine. They have to be fine. They have to be."

The uncertainty in her mother's voice sent a chill down her spine. Beth Reynolds had always been the voice of reason in their family, the steady presence that kept them grounded. Seeing her falter, even for a moment, was unsettling.

"Your father and I are still talking . . ." she continued, her tone cautious. "About leaving Oregon."

Alyson's stomach dropped. "But the borders are closed. It's illegal to leave." They'd discussed this ad nauseam. She was getting tired of the entire conversation.

"I know, I know. But your Grandpa Dick . . . he thinks he might be able to help us get out. Maybe arrange for some kind of escort. Find the right papers."

"An escort?" Her voice rose in disbelief. "Mom, that's crazy. It's too dangerous. What if we get caught with fake papers? Or we run into Star Brights on the way?"

"Who said anything about fake papers?" Her mom's expression hardened. "I said the right papers. I don't plan to do anything illegal. Not with that police officer always around."

The officer had stopped by several times since the shooting, and they'd seen him drive by nearly daily, slowing his car to a crawl as he looked over their yard and house. He'd even parked by the community garden, watching the workers, yelling more than once when he believed they were violating the proximity rules.

"Besides," her mom continued, "it might be more dangerous to stay. I'm not sure we're safe here."

"We're not safe anywhere," Alyson countered. "At least here we have a community, people looking out for each other. If we leave, we're on our own."

"Only until we reach the lodge. Your grandparents and your Uncle Brian are there."

"You don't even like Grandpa Dick," she shot back, her tone sharp with irritation.

Her mother raised an eyebrow in her direction as she lifted her chin. "Brian is hoping for Maddie, Jackson, and Heather to move up to the lodge." Her mom said *Heather* with more than a hint of disgust.

Her mom was not a fan of Brian's former wife. Heather Reynolds had issues, no doubt about it, and she wasn't a very good mom to Maddie and Jackson. If it wasn't for Heather's mom, Bea, the children would have been taken away from her and probably live in foster care. Brian had wanted full custody, but with his own issues, it was a battle for him too. Alyson's dad had suggested the children could live with them, but Beth said no, that it was too much.

"They have other people there too," her mom continued. "Friends of your grandpa. There's a girl around your age. His friend's granddaughter. Something . . . I'm not sure what happened, but something did. Anyway, they're building a little community at the lodge."

"Are they getting food drops?"

"In Wyoming? Yes, according to Jackson— "

"I don't mean Casper. I mean at the lodge."

"No. They're too far from town, an hour to Cody. It's only them and the nearby neighbors. You know, the other lodges in the area. But they're pretty isolated."

"Do you think that's safe? How will they eat?"

"I'm sure they're fine. Do you remember your grandma's garden and the greenhouse? The cows, plus all the wildlife?"

"You hated it there. You and Grandpa Dick argue all the time. You hate him."

"I don't hate him," she said, her voice quieter but firm.

She stared at her mother, her eyes searching for any sign of the truth behind her words. "Then why do you always avoid going there? We don't invite them to visit. And when they do visit, they leave early."

Her mother sighed, her shoulders slumping. "It's complicated, Alyson. There are things you don't understand."

"Like what?" Alyson pressed, frustration edging into her voice.

"Family stuff. Old arguments. Different values. But it doesn't mean I hate him." Her mother's eyes softened as she reached out to touch her arm. "He's still your grandfather, and they'll take good care of you. Of all of us."

Alyson paused, her thoughts tangled in confusion and concern. "Okay," she finally said, her voice uncertain.

Her mom smiled faintly, though it didn't reach her eyes. "You might even enjoy it."

She nodded slowly, though doubt still lingered in her mind. "Yeah, maybe. But I still don't see how we can go. If there are guards preventing people from leaving Oregon, it's going to be a problem—even if you do find the right papers. Can we even get to Wyoming? What about Idaho? Will they let us through?"

"We're working on the details." Her mother stood, pacing the small confines of the bedroom.

"And what about that cop?"

"That's such a sad situation. I can't blame the captain for coming by so often. He blames your dad for his officer's death. I get it. I do. Your father feels responsible for what happened too. That officer . . . he was doing his job, enforcing the rules. And now he's dead because he came to our house."

Alyson's protectiveness of her father flared. "That wasn't Dad's fault! He couldn't have known Bob would . . . would turn like that."

"I know, sweetie. But the guilt is eating him up. And that police supervisor, Captain Davis, the way he threatened your father . . . while I understand he's angry, I'm worried about what might happen if we stay."

An understanding of the situation settled over Alyson. She thought of her father, the strain evident in the lines of his face, the slump of his shoulders. She thought of the community garden, of Mr. Verley and his golden retriever, of everyone working together. Could they honestly leave all that behind?

"What does Eddie think about all this?" she asked, already suspecting the answer.

Her mom's lips quirked in a humorless smile. "Oh, you know your brother. He's all for it. Sees it as some grand adventure." She paused. "As long as he can take his VR set. Your brother does have his priorities." She chuckled.

Alyson shook her head. Of course Eddie would be excited. He'd probably imagined himself the hero in one of his video games, battling Star Brights across the country.

"I don't like it," Alyson said firmly. "The rules are in place for a reason. They're trying to keep us safe."

"Are they?" Her mom's voice was soft, but there was an edge to it. "The rules didn't keep that officer safe. They didn't stop Bob from killing him. Bob, who'd never hurt anyone." Her voice caught. She paused and turned away, staring at the pile of laundry. "Maybe . . . maybe we need to start thinking about our own safety, even if that means bending the rules a little."

Alyson stared at her mother, shocked. She had always been a stickler for following the rules, for doing things by the book. To hear her talk about "bending the rules" was almost as unsettling as the idea of fleeing the state.

"I need to think about this," Alyson said finally. "It's a lot to process."

Her mom nodded and reached out to squeeze Alyson's hand. "I know, sweetie. We're not making any decisions right away. There are still things to figure out. Keep an open mind, okay?"

As her mother left the room, Alyson turned back to her computer, but the screen now seemed meaningless. Her mind raced with the implications of what her mom had suggested: leaving Oregon, sneaking across state lines, and relying on her grandfather's mysterious "connections." It all seemed like a recipe for disaster.

But a small voice in the back of her mind whispered that maybe her mother had a point. The rules hadn't saved Bob. They hadn't protected that police officer. And they certainly weren't doing much to make Alyson secure in her own home.

While things had been quiet in their neighborhood, and she'd even enjoyed spending time in the community garden, there was always an undercurrent of fear. Fear someone would start humming or singing or fear the police would come banging on the door and drag her father away, charging him with murder.

She shook her head, trying to dispel the doubts. *No*, she decided. *Following the rules, maintaining order, that is the only way through this crisis. Isn't it?*

The rest of the day passed in a haze of online lectures and halfhearted attempts at homework. Alyson found herself constantly distracted, her attention drawn to the muffled conversations from downstairs or the occasional shouts from a neighbor outside.

Dinner was a stressful affair. Her dad picked at his food, his eyes distant. Her mom kept up a steady stream of forced cheerfulness, asking Eddie about his online gaming sessions and Alyson about her studies. Her brother, oblivious to the undercurrents of stress, chattered away about his latest virtual victories.

"So," he said between bites of lasagna, "when do you think we'll leave for Grandpa and Grandma's?"

The clatter of her dad's fork against his plate broke the sudden silence. "Eddie, we haven't made any decisions about that yet."

"But Mom said— "

"Your mother and I are still discussing our options. Nothing's been decided."

Alyson watched the exchange, noting the way her father's jaw clenched and the worried glances her mother kept shooting his way. The idea of leaving was clearly a source of conflict between them.

"I think we should stay," Alyson said, surprising herself with the firmness in her voice. "We have a support system here. People who depend on us. We can't abandon them."

Her dad's gaze held both pride and frustration. "It's not that simple, Alyson. The situation here . . . it's volatile. Unpredictable. We might be safer somewhere more isolated."

"Like Grandpa's place!" Eddie chimed in. "It'd be awesome. We could ride horses and help with the cows and— "

"Eddie, please," their mom interrupted. "This isn't a vacation we're talking about."

Alyson pushed her plate away, her appetite gone. "I don't understand how you can even consider this. It's dangerous. What if we get caught? It's illegal. What if . . ." she hesitated, not wanting to voice her other concern. "What if one of us turns into a Star Bright on the way?"

The table fell silent at her words. The possibility, though unspoken, had been on all their minds. Though it had been a week and a half since the incident with Ryan, when Alyson ended up covered in his blood, no one knew how long the incubation time might be. They still didn't even know what was causing people to turn violent. Not only did people attack individuals out of the blue, but there were still terrorist-style attacks where things were blown up or destroyed.

There had also been instances of the Star Brights working together. She'd seen videos where one person started singing, and others joined in before launching into some sort of coordinated attack. She didn't want them getting caught up in something like that.

"We don't even know how this thing spreads," Alyson continued, her voice rising. "What if I'm already infected? What if I'm putting all of you at risk by being here?"

"Alyson," her father said sharply, "don't talk like that. You are not infected."

"How do you know?" she challenged. "I had Ryan's blood on me. What if that's how it spreads? You saw how they were with Bob? How they put the protective gear on? What if I'm a ticking time bomb?"

Her mom reached across the table, grasping Alyson's hand. "Sweetheart, we can't think like that. We have to believe we're going to be okay."

Alyson pulled her hand away and stood abruptly. "But we're not okay, are we? None of this is okay. And running away to Wyoming isn't going to fix anything."

She stormed out of the kitchen and pounded up the stairs, ignoring her parents' calls to come back. In her room, she slammed the door and collapsed onto her bed, hot tears of frustration stinging her eyes.

The sound of raised voices drifted up from below. Her parents arguing, no doubt. Alyson buried her face in her pillow, trying to block it out. How had everything fallen apart so quickly? Two weeks ago, her biggest concern had been finishing her summer courses and planning for the fall semester. Now, she was worrying about turning into a violent, uncontrollable monster or being arrested for fleeing the state. Or worse, staying here and her dad being arrested.

A soft knock on her door roused her from her thoughts. "Aly?" It was Eddie. "Can I come in?"

She considered ignoring him but relented. "Fine."

He slipped into the room, closing the door behind him. He stood awkwardly for a moment before perching on the edge of her desk chair. "Are you okay?"

Alyson sat up and wiped her eyes. "No, Eddie. I'm not okay. Nothing about this is okay."

Her brother nodded, his usual exuberance dimmed. "I know. I think going to Grandpa and Grandma's would be better than staying here and being scared all the time."

The vulnerability in his voice tugged at Alyson's heart. Sometimes she forgot how young Eddie still was, how much he looked up to her and their parents for guidance and safety.

"I'm scared too," she admitted. "But running away isn't the answer. We have responsibilities here. People are counting on us. We're getting the garden going and the neighborhood watch."

He picked at a loose thread on his jeans. "But what if something happens? Like with Bob? What if someone else turns and hurts Mom or Dad?"

Alyson sighed. "That could happen anywhere, Eddie. Even at Grandpa's. We're not safe simply because we're family."

"What if that cop comes back and takes Dad away? He has it in for him, you know."

They sat in silence for a moment.

"I want things to go back to normal," Eddie said finally, his voice small.

Alyson moved to stand beside him, wrapping an arm around his shoulders. "I know. Me too. But we can't pretend that running away will fix everything. We have to face this, here and now."

As they sat there, the sound of their parents' argument faded, replaced by a tense silence. Alyson knew this wouldn't be the end of the discussion. The idea of leaving, of seeking safety in the isolation of their grandparents' property, would continue to tempt her parents.

But Alyson had made up her mind. She would stand firm in her belief that following the rules, maintaining order, and supporting their community was the right path forward. It might not be the easiest or the safest option, but it was the one she could live with.

Chapter 14

Later that night, as the house settled into an uneasy quiet, Alyson was unable to sleep. She tossed and turned, her mind replaying the day's events in an endless loop. The conversation with her mother, the tense family dinner, and Eddie's fears . . . it all swirled together in a confusing maelstrom of emotion.

She got up and quietly went to her desk. The soft glow of her computer screen illuminated the room as she pulled up news sites, searching for any updates on the Star Bright situation. The headlines were bleak. Outbreaks in major cities, governments struggling to contain the violence, theories about the cause ranging from the plausible to the absurd.

One article caught her eye, a piece about communities coming together in the face of the crisis. It highlighted neighborhoods that had formed support networks, sharing resources and watching out for each other. Though set in a different state, Alyson recognized her own street in the descriptions, and a spark of pride ignited within her. They were making a difference. They were changing things, even if it was only on a local level.

This was why they needed to stay—this sense of unity and shared purpose. It was something tangible, something real in a world that had become unpredictable and frightening. Running away might offer the illusion of safety, but at what cost?

A soft knock on her door startled her. "Alyson?" It was her father's voice, low and hesitant. "Can we talk?"

She hesitated for a moment before answering. "Come in."

Her dad entered, looking tired and drawn. He sat on the edge of her bed and ran a hand through his disheveled hair. "I couldn't sleep," he said by way of explanation.

"Me neither," she replied, turning her chair to face him.

He gave a nod. "I heard you moving around up here."

They sat in silence for a moment, unspoken words hanging between them.

"I understand what you were saying at dinner," he finally began. "About staying, about our responsibilities here."

Alyson nodded, waiting for him to continue.

"You remind me so much of your mother sometimes," he said with a sad smile. "Always the voice of reason, always thinking of others."

"But Mom is willing to leave," she pointed out.

"She's scared, Alyson. We all are. The idea of going somewhere isolated, somewhere we think we can control . . . it's tempting."

"But it's not realistic," Alyson insisted. "We can't abandon everything and everyone here. We're helping people. They need us. And what about the rules? The quarantine?"

Her father's expression tightened. "The rules . . . Sometimes I wonder if they're doing more harm than good."

As his words mirrored her own doubts, unease stirred within her. "But without rules, without order, what do we have? Chaos?"

"Maybe," he admitted. "But maybe we need to be flexible, to adapt to this new reality."

They lapsed into silence again, each lost in their own thoughts. Alyson glanced at her computer screen, at the article about communities coming together.

"Dad," she said slowly, "I know you feel guilty about what happened with Bob and the officer. But that wasn't your fault. You were trying to bring people together, to create exactly the kind of support network we need right now."

His eyes glistened with unshed tears. "Two men died, Alyson. Because of a meeting I organized."

"No," she said firmly. "Both died because of whatever this Star Bright thing is. Not because of you. And running away to Wyoming won't change that. It won't bring either back or erase what happened."

"When did you get so wise, huh?"

Alyson managed a small smile. "I had good teachers."

He reached out, squeezing her hand. "I can't promise we won't leave," he said softly. "Your mother and I, we need to do what we think is best for this family."

Irritation surged through her, and she almost had to bite her tongue to keep from reminding her dad that she was an adult. She could make her own decisions and even if they decided to go, that didn't mean she had to. Letting out a breath through her nose, she gave a nod.

"I hear you, sweetheart," he said softly. "I understand why you want to stay."

A glimmer of hope rose within her as her dad got up to leave. She might not have changed her parents' minds entirely, but at least she'd made them think. It was a start.

As the door closed behind him, she turned back to her computer. She had research to do, arguments to prepare. If they were going to stay, and she was more determined than ever to make that happen, they needed a plan—a way to not only survive in this new world but to thrive. She needed to prove to them that banding with the neighbors was the right thing to do.

She also needed to find a way to get Captain Davis off their backs. Surely, she could do something to convince the man that her dad wasn't at fault, that he wasn't to blame for the loss of the other officer.

She began to type, outlining ideas for strengthening their community bonds and creating a sustainable support system that could weather whatever storms lay ahead. It wouldn't be easy, and it certainly wouldn't be without risk. But as she worked, a sense of purpose settled over her.

This was her stand, her way of facing the turmoil and uncertainty head-on. And no matter what her parents ultimately decided, she would be ready to fight for what she believed in: the power of community, the importance of order, and the strength found in facing challenges together.

Even if they decided to leave, she'd put plans in place so she could stay behind. She'd continue working with the neighbors and make it through this. She'd be the adult in this situation.

As the first light of dawn crept through her curtains, Alyson's eyelids grew heavy. She saved her work and shut down her computer, crawling into bed for a few hours of much-needed sleep.

When she woke later that morning, the house was quiet. She found a note from her mother on the kitchen counter. "Gone to help with the community garden. Dad's at a neighborhood watch meeting. Eddie's in his room. Love you."

Alyson made herself a piece of toast, her mind still churning with the events of the previous night and her plans for the future. As she ate, she pulled up the local news on her phone, scanning for any updates on the Star Bright situation.

A knock at the door made her jump and drop the toast on the table. She approached cautiously and peered through the peephole. It was Mrs. Samms, shifting nervously from foot to foot.

Alyson opened the door, maintaining a safe distance. "Mrs. Samms? Is everything okay?"

The older woman wrung her hands. "I'm sorry to bother you, dear. I was hoping to speak with your father."

"He's at a neighborhood watch meeting. Can I help with something?"

Mrs. Samms hesitated before nodding. "I've been thinking about what your father said, about us all needing to work together. And I feel terrible about calling the police on you before. I know if I hadn't done so . . . maybe . . ." She shook her head as her eyes filled with tears.

Alyson's eyebrows rose in surprise. This was unexpected.

"I was wondering," Mrs. Samms continued, "if there might be something I could do to help. I used to be a nurse, you know. Before I retired."

A spark of inspiration hit. "Actually, Mrs. Samms, I think there might be. Would you like to come in? We can talk about it."

"Well, I'm not sure," the older woman hesitated.

"Or we could sit on the porch," Alyson offered.

"Yes," she agreed with a nod. "Let's sit on the porch."

After each taking a chair, Alyson outlined her ideas for strengthening the community. Mrs. Samms listened intently, occasionally offering suggestions based on her experiences.

"A first aid station," the older woman mused. "Yes, that could be very useful. The hospital has very strict rules for going to the emergency room. If we could treat people here, that'd be best. We'd need to use precautions. We still don't know how this spreads, and we can't risk contamination."

Alyson agreed, choosing not to tell Mrs. Samms about the situation with Ryan and how she may have already been contaminated by his blood. Surely, if she was, she'd know by now, right?

"I could help organize it," Mrs. Samms continued. "Perhaps teach some basic skills to the others."

Alyson nodded. "Exactly. And maybe we could set up a system for checking on the elderly or anyone living alone, make sure they have what they need."

The conversation reignited a sense of purpose in Alyson. This was what they needed. Not isolation, but connection. Not retreat, but engagement.

A noise from the sidewalk drew their attention. Her dad was returning home, looking tired but determined.

As he caught sight of them, he momentarily stopped moving before pasting a smile on his face. "Mrs. Samms," he said as he climbed the stairs. "Is everything all right?"

The older woman stood, smoothing her skirt. "Everything's fine, Mr. Reynolds. Your daughter and I were discussing some ideas for the neighborhood. She's quite the organizer, you know."

His eyes met Alyson's, a question in them. She nodded slightly, a silent reassurance.

"Well," Mrs. Samms said, moving toward the steps, "I should be going. Alyson, dear, let me know when you want to start on that first aid station." She paused and turned toward Alyson's dad. "I wanted to tell you how sorry I am. For phoning the police the other day. I was . . . this is a difficult situation."

Her dad gave a nod. "It is. And I do understand why you saw the need to call them. May I walk you home?"

"No, no. I'm fine."

As she walked down the sidewalk, he turned to Alyson. "First aid station?"

Alyson grinned. "It's part of the plan. Dad, I think I've figured out how we can make staying here work. How we can build something strong enough to withstand whatever comes next."

She launched into an explanation of her ideas, watching as her father's expression shifted from skepticism to interest to cautious hope.

"It won't be easy," she concluded. "And it won't guarantee our safety. But I think it's our best shot."

Her dad took a moment to think before giving a slow nod. "You might be right, Alyson. It's certainly worth a try. But I'm still going to keep trying to get us passes to go to Wyoming. That way we can leave if we need to."

"I understand, Dad," she said, choosing not to add that she'd be staying there no matter what the rest of them decided.

As they began to discuss the details, a weight lifted from Alyson's shoulders. They had a direction now, a purpose beyond mere survival. It wasn't a guarantee of safety, but it was a step toward something better.

The rest of the day passed in a flurry of activity. Alyson and her father called a meeting of the neighborhood watch, presenting their ideas for a more comprehensive community support system. To their surprise and relief, the response was overwhelmingly positive.

By evening, plans were in motion for the first aid station, a communal food pantry, and a buddy system to check on vulnerable residents. People volunteered skills and resources. All the way from one man offering to use walkie-talkies for emergency communications to a teenager down the street setting up a neighborhood intranet for secure local messaging. And everything was done with the proper cautions put into place.

Mrs. Samms made sure to tell everyone that, until they knew exactly how this outbreak was spreading, they needed to follow the distancing guidelines and universal precautions. "And wash your hands," she added. "People don't wash their hands enough. It's no wonder there are new viruses popping up."

"Man-made viruses," one of the neighbors muttered under his breath. "They aren't fooling me this time around."

Mrs. Samms pierced him with a look but said nothing more.

Later, as Alyson helped prepare dinner, her mother watched her. "You've thrown yourself into this, haven't you?" she observed.

She nodded, chopping vegetables with focused determination. "It feels right, Mom. Like we're actually doing something instead of waiting for the next disaster."

Her mom's voice was soft as she said, "You know, your father and I . . . we're still considering leaving. Just in case."

Alyson's knife paused mid-chop. She took a deep breath before responding. "I know. And I understand why. But, Mom, this could work. We're stronger together than we would be alone in Wyoming. I don't think there'd be enough people there to make it work. Not without the food drops and government help. We can't realistically survive on our own. At least here, we can all work together, plus we'll have food and people looking out for us."

"Maybe," her mom conceded. "But promise me something, Alyson. If things get worse, if we decide we need to go . . . promise me you'll come with us. Don't let your commitment to this community put you in danger."

Alyson met her mother's eyes, seeing the fear and love there. She wanted to promise she'd go, but she couldn't. Not without lying. "It'll be fine, Mom. You'll see."

As they sat down for dinner that night, the atmosphere was different. There was still tension and fear of the unknown future. But there was also a sense of purpose, of forward momentum.

Eddie regaled them with tales of his online gaming exploits, but this time, he also talked about how he and his friends, along with their cousin Jackson, were using their server to share information about the Star Bright situation across different states.

Her dad discussed the progress made with the neighborhood watch, the new protocols they were putting in place to keep everyone safe and informed.

As Alyson looked around at her family, a fierce love and determination surged within her. They were adapting, evolving to meet the challenges of this new world. It wasn't perfect, and the future was still uncertain. But they were facing it together, as a family and as part of a larger community. They would make a difference.

That night, as Alyson settled into bed, she recognized a genuine sense of hope for the first time since the crisis began. They had a long road ahead, full of unknown dangers and challenges. But they also had each other, and a growing network of support.

Chapter 15

As the sun edged above the horizon, Alyson dug her hands into the soil, dirt streaking her fingers. The rhythmic work of weeding and thinning provided a welcome distraction from the constant undercurrent of anxiety that had become their new normal.

"Looking good, Alyson!" Mr. Verley called from a few rows over where he was tending to a patch of tomatoes. His loyal golden retriever lay at the edge of the garden, keeping a watchful eye over the proceedings. "Those beans should be coming up nicely in no time."

Alyson brushed a stray hair from her face. "Thanks! I hope so. It'll be nice to have some fresh vegetables to add to our rations."

The mention of rations sobered her mood slightly. The weekly food drops had become a source of increasing concern. Last week's allocation had been noticeably smaller than the first week, and rumors were circulating about further restrictions.

As if reading her thoughts, Mrs. Samms approached, her gardening gloves caked with soil. "Did you hear about the new system they're implementing for the food distribution?" she asked, her voice low.

Alyson nodded. "Yeah, my dad told us last night. Starting next week, everyone has to go individually to get their own portions. No more picking up for the whole family."

Mrs. Samms clicked her tongue in disapproval. "It's going to be chaos. All those people crowding together?

What are they thinking? It's not safe. They're asking for trouble."

"Maybe," Alyson conceded, "but I guess they're trying to ensure fair distribution. Make sure nobody's claiming extra rations for nonexistent family members or anything."

The older woman huffed. "Well, I suppose. But it's not like they don't have public records to show who is in the family. Before, I was even able to send my info with Mr. Verley and he brought my groceries back. Now . . . I'm going to have to go on my own. It's risky for a woman on her own to be out and about, not to mention being so close to others. We need to maintain our distance. Oh, speaking of risks, how's that first aid station coming along?"

Alyson brightened at the change of subject. "It's going well! We've got a good stock of basic supplies, and your training sessions have been helpful. People are more prepared now, I think."

As the conversation went on, pride swelled within Alyson. Despite the challenges they faced, their neighborhood had come together in ways she never would have imagined only a few weeks ago.

Later that afternoon, she returned home to find her parents in deep discussion at the kitchen table. They fell silent as she entered, exchanging a look that sent a chill down her spine.

"What's going on?" she asked, trying to keep her voice casual as she poured herself a glass of water.

Her father cleared his throat. "We were discussing some . . . contingency plans. You know, in case things get worse."

Alyson's grip tightened on her glass. "You mean leaving for Wyoming."

Her mother placed a hand on her arm. "Honey, we know how you feel about staying. And we're so proud of everything you've done to help the community. But we have to be realistic. Things are getting worse, not better."

"But we're managing," Alyson protested. "The garden, the first aid station, the neighborhood watch. We're making it work."

Her dad sighed and ran a hand through his hair. "We are, for now. But the food situation is getting more precarious. And now, with the power outages starting . . ."

Alyson blinked in surprise. "Power outages? When?"

"There was one for about an hour while you were at the garden," her mom explained. "The internet's been spotty this morning, and the cell phones are acting up again. Your father couldn't reach your grandparents."

The implications of this new development hit Alyson like a punch to the gut. Without reliable power or communication, their carefully constructed support system could crumble.

If the internet went out, how would she continue her studies? Even though the instructors didn't always show up for the live-streamed classes, they were good about uploading the new assignments. She even had a meeting scheduled with her counselor regarding her fall schedule. While she knew it was unlikely she'd be returning to Portland for in-person classes, she relied on the university offering online ones.

"Have you heard anything from the university?" Alyson asked, trying to keep the worry from her voice. "About their plans for the fall semester?"

Her mom shook her head. "Nothing definitive. I imagine they're scrambling to figure things out, same as everyone else. But, Alyson, honey, we need to consider the possibility that continuing your education might not be possible right now."

The thought sent a wave of panic through Alyson. Her education had always been her top priority, her ticket to the future she'd dreamed of. Putting it on hold seemed like admitting defeat.

"We need to stay here and make this work," she argued. "If we leave, we're on our own. And I can't bear the thought of facing this alone."

Her father's expression softened. "I know it feels that way. But your grandparents' place is more self-sufficient. They have their own power supply and their own food sources. It might be safer in the long run."

Alyson shook her head, frustration building. "So, we abandon everyone here? After everything we've built?"

"We haven't made any decisions yet," her mother interjected, shooting a warning look at Alyson's dad. "We're continuing to explore our options, okay?"

Alyson nodded reluctantly, knowing further argument was pointless for now. But as she headed up to her room, her mind raced with counterarguments and plans to reinforce their community's resilience.

The garden was doing well. In a few weeks, they'd start harvesting things from it. Even with fewer rations, they'd be okay. They could figure out how to make this work.

They'd discussed sending groups out fishing from the jetty where the Columbia River met the Pacific Ocean. They could bring back enough fish to begin preserving. She knew there were rules in place for fishing, and new licenses weren't being issued, but several of the community people had bought annual licenses before things started happening. She thought those were still valid. Maybe Mr. Verley knew? She'd ask him the next time she saw him.

Later that afternoon, Alyson returned to the community garden for the evening watering. As she approached, she heard raised voices. Rounding the corner, she saw two neighbors who had never quite gotten along, facing off over a row of carrots.

"You're overwatering them!" the older man, around Alyson's dad's age, shouted, his face red with anger. "You're going to drown the whole crop!"

"I know what I'm doing," the younger man snapped back. "Maybe if you spent less time criticizing and more time actually helping, we'd have a better garden!"

Before anyone could intervene, the older man lunged forward, shoving the other man hard. The younger man stumbled back, retaliating with a wild swing that caught the man in the jaw.

"Stop it!" Alyson yelled, rushing forward. Other neighbors who had been working nearby hurried over and pulled the two men apart. "What are you doing? We're supposed to be working together!"

The two men struggled against those holding them back, their faces contorted with rage that seemed disproportionate to the argument about watering carrots.

"Let me go!" the younger man shouted, breaking free from the neighbor restraining him. He charged at the older man and tackled him to the ground. They rolled in the dirt, throwing punches and kicking wildly.

Alyson watched in horror as the fight escalated. "Someone do something!" she cried, feeling helpless as the violence unfolded before her.

A sickening crack echoed through the garden as the older man's head struck a nearby rock. He went limp instantly, and blood pooled beneath him.

The younger man scrambled back, his anger evaporating as he realized the severity of what happened. "I didn't mean to. Is he . . . is he okay?"

Alyson rushed to the fallen man's side, her first aid training kicking in. "He's unconscious. We need an ambulance, now! Call 9-1-1! And someone go get Mrs. Samms. She used to be a nurse."

As one neighbor ran to fetch Mrs. Samms and another called 9-1-1, Alyson checked the man's pulse and breathing. They were present but weak. She looked up at the gathered crowd, her voice shaking but firm. "I need clean cloths to stop the bleeding. And someone needs to go tell his wife what happened."

The community sprang into action, fetching supplies and comfort items. The younger man sat on the ground, head in his hands, muttering repeatedly, "I didn't mean for this to happen."

Mrs. Samms arrived, her face showing her concern as she assessed the situation. "Let me see him." She kneeled beside Alyson and put latex gloves on. She checked the man's vitals and examined the head wound. "We need to keep pressure on that wound and get him to the hospital as soon as possible."

"I tried calling for an ambulance," someone said. "But the line won't connect." Several others agreed they couldn't get through.

Alyson's father appeared, drawn by the commotion. "Alyson, what happened?" he asked, his eyes widening at the scene before him.

"Dad," she said, her voice cracking. She stood and moved into her father's embrace. "They were fighting, and he hit his head, and . . ."

Her dad held her close, stroking her hair. "It's okay, Alyson. You did good."

As they worked to stabilize the man, she couldn't help but think about how quickly things had spiraled out of control. What had started as a petty argument had turned into a potentially life-threatening situation.

"I finally got through to the 9-1-1 operator," a young neighbor said, holding her phone. "They can't send anyone. They said to drive him to the hospital."

"I'll take him," the young man responsible for the injury said. "I'll talk to the police, too, about what happened. Please, God, please let him be okay." With that, the man ran toward his house to get his car.

Mrs. Samms maintained her composure, her voice calm but authoritative. "We need to move him carefully. Don't jostle his head or neck."

Under Mrs. Samms's guidance, the neighbors worked together to gently move the injured man into the backseat of the car. "Someone needs to hold his head steady during the drive," she instructed. "I'll go with them to the hospital." She moved toward the front passenger's seat.

Alyson stepped back, her hands shaking. She watched as they loaded the still-unconscious man into the car, his wife climbing in beside him, her face pale with shock and worry as she held her husband for the ride to the hospital.

The car sped away, tires screeching as it went. The community garden, once a symbol of their unity and resilience, now stood marked by violence and fear.

Alyson walked home with her father, the events of the afternoon replaying in her mind.

Her dad kept a comforting arm around her shoulders. "You did well today," he said softly. "But I hope you can see why your mother and I are concerned about staying."

She nodded slowly, her certainty wavering. "I know, Dad. I thought we were better than this. I thought we could make it work. I don't even think he was a Star Bright or anything. They got into a fight. A stupid fight over watering carrots."

"Sometimes, no matter how hard we try, things are beyond our control. We have to think about what's best for our family."

Alyson wondered, as she had so many times since the crisis began, if staying was really the right choice. But she couldn't bear to leave. She couldn't bear to give up.

Chapter 16

The next few days passed in a blur of activity. The community was still reeling from the death of the older man who had been injured in the garden fight. His passing had cast a pall over the neighborhood, and the younger man's imprisonment at the county jail only added to the somber atmosphere.

The widow of the dead man had moved across town and was living with a friend. Captain Davis had increased his patrols of the neighborhood, driving through at all hours of the day and night, even shining a spotlight on their house the previous night, shortly before midnight. Alyson had already gone to bed, but the bright light woke her up and made her unsure of what was happening.

Despite the tragedy, or perhaps because of it, Alyson threw herself into community projects with renewed vigor, determined to prove that staying was the right choice. She organized a skill-sharing workshop, where neighbors taught each other everything from basic car maintenance to home-canning techniques. The first aid station expanded its services, offering regular health check-ins not only for the elderly on their street but for those in the immediate area.

Despite her best efforts, she couldn't ignore the signs of deterioration around them. The power flickered with increasing frequency, and the internet became frustratingly unreliable. Tempers flared at the new food distribution center, where long lines and strict rationing led to more than one heated argument. It was so bad there that her dad decided he'd go alone, even though it meant only getting enough food for one.

"It's better than nothing, and I worry about your safety," he'd said while holding his wife's hand and meeting the gazes of his children.

"I can go with you, Dad," Eddie had said, thrusting back his shoulders. "I can help."

"I know you can, but I'm still going alone. If things go bad, I'd . . ." He shook his head as tears filled his eyes. "No. I'll go alone and get what I can. It's better this way."

Alyson knew it wasn't only the volatile tempers at the ration centers that had her dad on edge. Violence had been rising across Clatsop County. Home invasions were becoming more frequent, and people were disappearing. Sometimes entire families, but more often only the women. The men were found dead.

The neighborhood watch patrols intensified, with residents taking shifts around the clock. Reports of break-ins and violence in nearby areas had everyone on edge. Alyson's father had taken to carrying a baseball bat during his patrols, a sight that both reassured and unsettled her.

She suspected that wasn't all he carried. Like some of the other neighbors, she'd noticed the telltale bulge at his waistline. Where he got the pistol, Alyson didn't know. They didn't have any guns in their house. She was especially concerned that Captain Davis was going to stop her dad while he was making his rounds, frisk him and haul him away for carrying an illegal weapon.

As Alyson sat in her room reading, her father and Eddie were at a neighborhood watch meeting, and her mother had retreated to her basement office to try and get some work done during a rare moment of stable internet connection.

Alyson didn't actually believe that her mom had clients any longer. She thought her mom needed a break from things, and work was a suitable excuse to check out for a bit. Alyson understood. She used the same excuse herself sometimes, saying she needed to study when she didn't.

Her calculus professor had not only failed to show up for class but hadn't loaded any assignments. There was no explanation as to why, but another professor announced she was done with classes for the summer session. She'd give everyone a passing grade, but classes were over.

The meeting Alyson was supposed to have with her guidance counselor was postponed. The counselor explained that fall semester plans were still undecided, making a meeting unnecessary.

Alyson sat cross-legged on her bed, a well-worn copy of *Pride and Prejudice* open in her lap. The familiar words provided a comforting escape from the stresses of their new reality. The sun hovered low on the horizon, with about an hour left before it dipped completely. The beauty of the sunset seemed out of place against the fractured streets and growing silence.

Somehow, she must have dozed off. She woke with a start, wiping the drool from the corner of her mouth. Outside, the sky had deepened into a dark navy. How long had she been asleep? She glanced at her watch. It was a few minutes before ten o'clock.

A faint noise drifted through the stillness, a soft, irregular tapping on the edge of her hearing. She froze, straining to place it, but the sound was gone as quickly as it had come. Were her dad and brother home? Tonight's meeting was supposed to run late. They weren't only discussing changes; they were expanding the perimeter to include the street to the north, bringing in more people and widening the patrol zones.

She settled back onto her bed, eager to get back to her reading. A sudden thud from downstairs snapped Alyson's attention away from the page. She froze, listening closely. It could have been nothing, the house settling or some other random noise. Another sound followed, unmistakable this time—the creak of the back door opening.

Her heart began to race. Her dad and Eddie would have come in through the front door. Her mom was still downstairs, in the daylight basement. Or had she gone outside from the lower level and come in the back door? And if so, why?

Another thud, followed by the murmur of low voices. Alyson froze, a chill running through her as fear gripped her. Someone was in the house. Someone who shouldn't be.

Taking a deep breath, she crept to her bedroom door and eased it open a crack. The voices became clearer, harsh whispers drifting up the stairs.

"Check upstairs. Find the women. I'll look down here. This place is supposed to be loaded with supplies. These people have been organizing the whole neighborhood. They've got to have a stockpile somewhere."

"What do we do with them when we find them?" came a second voice, sounding nervous.

"Really?" the first voice replied coldly. "Why do you think we're here? Let's do what we're hired to do. The supplies are a bonus."

Alyson clapped a hand over her mouth to stifle a gasp. This wasn't merely a burglary. These people were willing to kill her and her family. Not willing. Hired.

Find the women? Her mom was still in the basement. *Is she safe? Did she hear the intruders? And what about Dad and Eddie? What if they come home while these men are still here?* Memories of the stories she'd heard about other home invasions brought tears to her eyes.

The sound of heavy footsteps on the stairs snapped her back to the immediate danger. She had to hide, now.

Her eyes fell on her closet door, and a memory surfaced. The hidden room behind it, her childhood "dollhouse." Without hesitation, Alyson slipped into the closet, pressing the hidden latch that opened the secret door. She squeezed into the small space, pulling the door closed behind her as she heard her bedroom door open.

Heart pounding, Alyson pressed herself into the farthest corner of the hidden room. She could hear the intruder moving around her bedroom, opening drawers and muttering to himself.

"Looks empty," the man said quietly. "Good. I'd hate to have to— "

"Are we clear?" the man downstairs called out.

Another muffled voice said, "Basement's empty."

"Up here too," said the man who was leaving Alyson's bedroom.

"That's fine," came the reply from the hallway outside her bedroom door. "We'll find a place to wait for them to return. I found their pantry. It's packed. We'll do what we came to do and take what we want."

Alyson's fists clenched. They had indeed been storing extra supplies from her dad's early shopping trips. But they'd agreed the food and such were not only for themselves but for the entire neighborhood in case of emergencies.

She had to figure out something to do. A way to warn her dad and brother to stay away. And she needed to find her mom. Was she hiding too? The man said the basement was empty. Alyson shifted slightly, brushing against the edge of the wall.

"What was that?" one of the men asked.

"Thought you said there wasn't anyone here?" the other responded. "Go. See what it is."

She held her breath as the man's footsteps approached her closet. She heard hangers being pushed aside and boxes being moved. The hidden door vibrated slightly as something heavy bumped against it.

"Gabe! Get down here! I found one of the women."

The scream split the air, and Alyson's pulse quickened. Footsteps echoed down the stairs, heavy and fast, as the men made their way to the one who had found her mother.

Her whole body trembled. Sweat beaded on her forehead, and tears filled her eyes. The sound of her mother's voice, usually so strong and steady, now twisted into something raw and desperate, piercing through her like physical pain. Every instinct screamed at her to stay hidden, to stay safe, but the thought of what they might be doing to her mom made that impossible.

Alyson had to do something. She had to help her mom. She had to save her. Quietly, she slipped out of her hiding place and crept into Eddie's room. Her hands shook as she searched for anything she could use as a weapon. Finally, her fingers closed around the cool metal of his baseball bat, a replica of the one her dad had started carrying when out on neighborhood patrols.

Armed with the bat, Alyson inched toward the stairs. She could hear the intruders threatening her mother, demanding to know where the rest of the family was. Her mom's voice was trembling as she pleaded with them.

Taking a deep breath, she descended the stairs as quietly as she could. Peering around the hallway corner into the living room, she saw two men. One held her mother at knifepoint, while the other frantically shoved items into a duffel bag. She knew there was a third, but she had no idea where he might be. Maybe in the pantry off the kitchen. The two men in view, along with her mom, had their backs to her.

Alyson took a deep breath before rushing forward. The man holding her mom turned as she swung the bat with all her might. His sudden movement weakened her strike, but the blow still landed.

He cursed in pain, his grip tightening on her mother with his other arm.

The third guy came from the kitchen while the one who was stuffing the duffel bag lunged at Alyson.

She managed to dodge him, swinging the bat again and catching him in the ribs.

Through the noise of the struggle, she caught the unmistakable sound of the front door creaking open. Her father's voice called out, "Beth? Alyson? We're home! Put on the teakettle. We've got company."

The intruders cursed. "Grab her," the one holding her mom hissed. "We'll use her as a shield."

"Dad!" Alyson screamed. "Help!"

Her dad and Eddie burst into the room, followed by Mr. Verley and two others from the neighborhood watch. Alyson's dad tackled the man holding her mom, sending the knife skittering away while Eddie and Mr. Verley wrestled with another. The third man was pinned down by the remaining members of the watch.

Alyson grabbed her mom, pulling her to safety. The bat still in her hand, she stood in front of her, providing protection.

The fight was brutal and intense. Her father took a hard punch to the jaw, but he kept fighting. Eddie, despite his youth, was holding his own against the larger intruder with the help of Mr. Verley and the final man was on the ground, subdued by the neighborhood watch men.

Right as it seemed the intruders were going to be defeated, the man her dad was grappling with broke free and pulled out a gun. "Back off!" he shouted, waving the weapon wildly.

Her dad's hand moved to his waistband, where he kept his own gun. The intruder's finger tightened on the trigger. Without thinking, Alyson hurled the baseball bat at him with all her might.

The bat struck the intruder's hand as the gun went off. The shot went wild, shattering a window. In the moment of confusion, her dad drew his own weapon and fired. The intruder fell to the floor, clutching his leg and screaming in pain.

The man Eddie was holding had a burst of energy and tried to escape Eddie's and Mr. Verley's clutches, but they managed to get him to the floor where he started yelling, "Don't shoot me! Don't shoot!"

"No one's going to shoot you," Mr. Verley said, glancing at Alyson's dad, who still had his gun aimed at the man who was cradling his leg.

Once the fighting ceased, Alyson stood frozen, taking in the scene before her. The living room was in shambles, there was blood on the floor, and everyone was breathing heavily. But they were alive.

Her mom rested her hand on her shoulder. "Are you okay?" she asked, her voice trembling.

She turned to her, falling into her mother's arms.

Her dad quickly secured the intruders, using zip ties from their emergency kit. "Eddie, call the police," he ordered before turning to Beth and Alyson. "Are you okay?"

Her mom nodded, though she was shaking. "I'm . . . I'm all right. Shaken but fine."

Alyson lifted her head and gave her dad a slight nod. The adrenaline was fading and leaving her feeling weak. Her dad led them both to the couch. With her arm around her shoulders, her mom pulled her into a tight embrace. "You were so brave, Alyson," she whispered, her voice choked with emotion.

As they waited for the police to arrive, the reality of what had happened began to sink in. They'd been attacked in their own home, the place they'd thought was safe. They had fought for their lives and won, but at what cost?

Her dad's expression hardened as he took in the damage. "We need to talk," he said firmly. "As a family. This . . . this changes everything."

Chapter 17

The aftermath of the home invasion hung heavy in the air, a tension that seemed to vibrate through the household. Alyson sat on the couch, her mother's arm wrapped protectively around her shoulders, while her dad paced the living room, his jaw clenched tight. Eddie, still riding the adrenaline high, couldn't seem to sit still, alternating between peering out the window and checking on everyone.

Mr. Verley had brought Mrs. Samms over to tend to the wounded man, who insisted he was dying. Alyson's dad told him to stop his whining, but she could tell he wasn't entirely convinced the man wasn't seriously injured.

Mrs. Samms assured the man he would be okay, but there was a faint doubt in her voice. As she worked to stop the bleeding, Alyson watched her expression closely. Was he going to make it? She couldn't be sure. And if he didn't, what would that mean for her dad?

"Where are they?" Alyson's mom muttered, glancing at the clock for the hundredth time. "It's been over an hour."

Her dad paused his pacing. "They're probably overwhelmed. Who knows how many other incidents they're dealing with tonight. Every night."

Alyson shuddered, imagining similar scenes playing out across Astoria. How many other families were huddled in fear, waiting for help that might come too late? How many were not as fortunate as they'd been?

"They're here," Eddie announced as red and blue lights finally illuminated the street outside.

Their dad nodded. "About time."

"The ambulance?" Mrs. Samms asked.

"I don't think so," Eddie replied. "Just the cops."

"Figures," Mr. Verley mumbled.

Her family watched as two police cars pulled up, followed by an unmarked vehicle. Alyson's stomach dropped as she recognized the man stepping out of the unmarked car. Captain Davis.

"It's him," she whispered to her mother, whose arm tightened around her in response.

"Stay calm," her mom murmured, though Alyson could sense her mother's own tension. "Let your father handle this."

As the officers approached the house, her dad opened the door. "In here," he called out, leading them to where Mrs. Samms was tending to the wounded intruder.

"Where's the ambulance?" Mrs. Samms snapped.

"On its way. On its way." Davis waved his hand as if shooing a fly.

The living room grew cramped as the officers filed in. Alyson pressed herself further into the couch, trying to make herself as small as possible.

Captain Davis's eyes narrowed as he took in the scene. "Mr. Reynolds," he said, his voice dripping with disdain. "Why am I not surprised to find myself here again?"

Her dad bristled but kept his voice steady. "Captain Davis, I can explain— "

"Oh, I'm sure you can," Davis cut him off. He turned to one of his subordinates. "Secure the suspects. Tape their mouths. I'll get their statements at the station." To another, he barked, "Canvas the area and see if there are any other witnesses." He met her dad's gaze. "Impartial witnesses."

The officer's tone sparked a rush of indignation in Alyson. Didn't he understand they were the victims here?

As the other officers moved to comply, Davis turned back to her dad. "Now, Mr. Reynolds, why don't you tell me exactly what happened here?"

He took a deep breath and began recounting the events of the evening.

Alyson watched the officer's face, noting how his expression grew increasingly skeptical as her father spoke.

When he finished, Davis shook his head. "Once I saw the address, I had a feeling it would be you at fault."

"At fault?" Her dad shook his head.

"You're not getting away with it this time. By your own admission, you pulled the trigger. Do you even have a permit to conceal carry?"

"I was open carrying." Her dad's voice was tight with controlled anger, as he motioned to the holster clearly visible on his hip, his once-untucked shirt now neat and tidy. The pistol was on the dining room table, having already been cleared by the officers.

Davis scoffed. "There is no allowance for open carry under the current rules. Anyone with a firearm without proper training is considered outside the law. Amazing you happened to have the gun on you when these men broke in. How convenient."

"Convenient? You know there have been break-ins all over Astoria. Not only break-ins, but murders. I was protecting my family!"

"Are you suggesting my husband planned this?" Alyson's mom interjected, her voice sharp with disbelief.

"I'm not suggesting anything, ma'am," Davis replied coolly. "I'm trying to get to the truth. And the truth is, this house has a history of violence, and your husband always seems to be smack dab in the middle."

"That's not fair!" Alyson found herself on her feet, anger overwhelming her fear. "My dad was protecting us! Those men were here to kill us!"

Davis turned his cold gaze on her. "Young lady, this is an official police investigation. I suggest you sit down and be quiet unless you're spoken to."

Her face flushed with anger and embarrassment. She opened her mouth to argue further, but a sharp look from her father silenced her.

Her dad stepped between Davis and them. "That's enough. If you have any more questions for me or my family, you can ask them through our lawyer."

A tense silence fell over the room, broken only by the murmur of the other officers as they went about their duties.

Alyson watched as the officers photographed the scene, bagged evidence, and spoke in hushed tones. One of them helped Mrs. Samms and Mr. Verley with the injured, while the others seemed content to ignore them. It was almost like a crime show on TV, except this was her home, her life.

Finally, Davis spoke again, his voice low and menacing. "I will be taking your pistol and checking it to see what other crimes it's connected with."

"You will not take my sidearm."

"Oh, but I will. McCracken?" Davis called over his shoulder. "Write the man a receipt for the Glock." He turned back to Alyson's dad. "Let your lawyer know he can collect it in . . . oh, three or four months."

Her dad's face went pale, his fists clenching at his sides. "My gun hasn't been used in any crimes, and you know it," he said through gritted teeth.

"I don't know that, not by a long shot. And get this straight, Reynolds, I'd haul you off right now if I could. But since they broke into your home and threatened your wife, the useless district attorney has to make that decision. You can bet I'll remind him of your history and how you are responsible for the death of a police officer."

"Dad," Eddie whispered, his eyes wide with fear. "Are they going to arrest you?"

Their dad forced a smile. "No, buddy. It's going to be okay."

Before he could say more, one of the other officers approached. "Sir, we've finished processing the scene and taking statements. The ambulance should be here shortly."

Davis nodded curtly. "Mr. Reynolds, don't leave town. We'll be in touch."

As Davis turned to leave, he paused, his eyes sweeping over her family. "I hope for your sake, Reynolds, that this is the last time we meet under these circumstances. Next time, you might not be so lucky."

It was only a few minutes later when the paramedics arrived. Mrs. Samms gave her treatment report, and the police soon cleared out behind the ambulance. The neighbors who had gathered to help started to disperse as well. Mr. Verley and Mrs. Samms were the last to leave. Mrs. Samms hugged Alyson and her mom, while Mr. Verley gave her dad and Eddie reassuring pats on the shoulder.

"If you need anything, anything at all, you let us know," Mr. Verley said, his voice low and serious.

They shook hands. "Thank you, Jim. For everything."

The door closed behind them, leaving her family alone in the sudden quiet. The last of the adrenaline that had been sustaining Alyson began to ebb away, leaving behind a bone-deep exhaustion.

Her mom was the first to break the silence. "We need to leave," she said, her voice barely above a whisper. "We can't stay here anymore."

"The captain told Dad he couldn't leave town," Eddie stated.

Their mom shook her head. "I don't care."

"You're right." Their dad nodded, sinking into an armchair. "We need to go. But how? The borders are closed, and after tonight . . ." He ran a hand over his face.

"We'll figure it out," Alyson said, surprising herself with the determination in her voice. "We have to."

Eddie bounced to his feet. "What about Grandpa's connections? Didn't you say he might be able to help us get out?"

Their dad looked up, a spark of hope in his eyes. "He did, but nothing came of it. I'll check with him again and see if there have been any changes. If the phones are working."

"And if they're not?" their mom asked.

"We'll find another way. We can try texting. Email. Social media. We'll figure it out. We're leaving, one way or another. We can't risk staying here any longer."

"Wyoming?" Alyson asked.

"Yes, Wyoming," he said, his tone leaving no room for doubt. "To your grandparents' place. It's isolated and defensible. We'll be safe there."

A lump formed in Alyson's throat. Despite everything that had happened, the thought of leaving their home, their community, still seemed wrong. But as she looked at her family—her mother's bruised and battered face, her father's haunted eyes, and her brother's forced bravado—she knew they had no choice.

"When?" she asked, her voice barely above a whisper.

Her parents exchanged a look, then her mom said, "As soon as possible. Tomorrow, if we can manage it."

"Tomorrow?" Eddie's eyes widened. "But what about our stuff? Our— "

"We'll take what we can," their dad cut him off. "The essentials. Everything else . . . we'll have to leave behind."

The statement hung in the air. Leave behind. Their home, their possessions, their entire lives.

"We should try to get some sleep," Alyson's mom suggested, though she made no move to stand. "We'll need to be rested for whatever comes next."

Her dad nodded. "You're right. But I don't think any of us should be alone tonight. Why don't we all camp out here in the living room?"

No one argued. They spent the next few minutes gathering blankets and pillows. Her mom took the sofa and Alyson took the recliner, while her dad and Eddie made a spot on the floor.

As they settled in, Alyson couldn't help but think of all the times they'd done this before, during storms, on Christmas Eve, or simply for something different and fun. Now, huddled together in the aftermath of violence, she questioned whether this was their last desperate attempt to cling to normalcy.

The bat she'd used, plus the one her dad had carried on neighborhood watch patrols, sat in the corner. She hesitantly asked her dad about the pistol the police had taken, wondering who it belonged to.

With a raised eyebrow, her dad responded, "It's mine, of course."

"Yours? When— "

"I bought it a few years ago. When I started traveling so much."

"He bought it for me," her mom added. "Though he knew I never wanted one. Had never even thought of touching one."

"I told you we could get you lessons— "

Her mom raised her hand. "Anyway, your dad kept it in a safe in our room, but now . . ." She shook her head.

"I'll see about getting a replacement," he said.

Instead of arguing, as Alyson would have expected, her mom sighed. "I suppose you'd best."

Sleep was elusive, despite Alyson's exhaustion. Her mind raced with thoughts of what lay ahead. How would they get out of Oregon? What would they find in Wyoming? And what about their friends and neighbors here?

In the dark, Eddie whispered, "Aly? Are you awake?"

"Yeah," she murmured back.

"Are you scared?"

Alyson considered lying, but in the vulnerability of the moment, honesty won out. "Yeah, I am. But we'll be okay."

Eddie's hand reached up to find hers, squeezing tight. "You were pretty awesome tonight."

"You too, kid."

As she lay there, listening to the quiet breathing of her family, she tried to imagine what their lives would be like in Wyoming. Would they find peace there? Safety? Or were they merely trading one set of dangers for another?

She thought of her friends, of the community they'd built in Astoria. Of Mr. Verley and Mrs. Samms. Of the garden they'd all worked so hard on. Of her plans for college, now a seemingly impossible dream.

But the terror of hiding in her closet came rushing back, the sound of her mother's scream, the violence that had invaded their home. And she knew, deep down, that leaving was their only choice. She didn't have to like it, but she had to go.

As the first light of dawn began to creep through the windows, she made a silent promise to herself. Whatever came next, whatever challenges they faced, she would be strong. For her family and for herself. They would survive this, together.

With that thought, she finally drifted off into a fitful sleep, dreams of wide-open Wyoming skies mingling with nightmares of shadowy intruders and accusing police officers.

Chapter 18

The soft hum of the dryer was the only noise in the quiet early morning. Alyson shifted in the recliner, her body stiff and sore from too little sleep. She rubbed her eyes to clear the haze of uneasy dreams and was hit with the memory of the chaos that had happened mere hours before.

Her dad was already up, pacing the room with a cup of coffee in hand. The dark circles under his eyes suggested he wasn't in much better shape than her.

"Morning, sweetheart," he said softly. "How are you holding up?"

She stretched, wincing at the soreness in her limbs. "I'm okay, Dad. Processing everything, I guess."

"Same here. Exactly the same."

Her mom emerged from the laundry room and gave Alyson a tired smile. "I thought I'd better take advantage of the electricity while it's on and get as much laundry done as possible."

"How long have you been up?" Alyson asked.

"Oh, not long," her mother replied.

"Hours," her dad interjected. "She already had the washer going and was cleaning the kitchen when I got up."

"I have a lot on my mind," her mom gave him a sad smile.

Eddie began to stir as well, the entire family gradually coming to life in the quiet morning light.

"So," Eddie said, his voice still thick with sleep, "what's the plan? Are we leaving today? How are we getting to Wyoming?"

"That's the million-dollar question, isn't it?" their dad said. "I've been trying to figure it out."

"I checked the internet, which is up and running," their mom said. "They showed photos of different routes out of Oregon. We already know the Astoria-Megler Bridge is closed, passable by special permit only."

She waved in the general direction of the bridge visible from the front window. Alyson couldn't remember the last time she'd actually seen a car on it.

"Sometimes trucks go on it," Eddie said. "I guess they get special permission?"

"Yes," their mom agreed. "And the occasional car, but according to everything we've heard and what I've seen on the internet, they aren't letting anyone across without a pass."

"Going from here to Washington wouldn't solve our problem anyway," their dad added. "Washington has strict border restrictions too. California also, which means heading south wouldn't do us much good either. Our only option is to head east."

"The state line near Ontario is locked up tight too. Getting into Idaho would be as difficult as going over our bridge into Washington."

"But Idaho is okay, right?" Eddie asked. "It's not that they have the border closed to people entering, it's that Oregon doesn't let people leave?"

"Doesn't make much sense, does it?" their dad asked. "But that is what's happening."

"But if we get to Idaho, then we're fine?"

"At the moment, Idaho, Montana, and Wyoming all have open borders," their mom said. "Other states, like Colorado, have restrictions, but we don't need to go through there."

"We'll find a place to get across." Her dad sounded only partially confident.

"How?" Her mom pointed to the map. "It's not like we can walk across the Snake River."

"There's a bridge here," Eddie pointed at the map.

"That one's closed too," their dad said quietly. "Getting across the Snake River will complicate things."

"So, we go farther south. Avoid the river," Alyson traced the spot on the map where the river took a sharp turn to the east. "We could walk across there."

Her mom shook her head. "We can't walk. We have to be able to keep the car. There's no way— " A sob stopped her words as she covered her face with her hands.

Alyson's dad moved to comfort her, placing a reassuring hand on her shoulder. "We'll figure it out. We need a plan."

Eddie, eager to contribute, said, "What about finding a boat? We could cross the Snake River that way."

Alyson's mom considered the idea, nodding slowly. "It's possible, but we'd need to find one first, and it has to be big enough for all of us and our supplies."

"And we'd need to find a car on the other side," her dad said. "Buy one or . . . or steal one."

"Dad!" Alyson's eyes went wide. "No."

"No, no. You're right. We won't steal a car."

Even though he said he wouldn't, Alyson saw the look on his face. He would steal a car if he had to. If it meant getting his family to safety.

"Let's forget about taking a boat for a moment. The bottom line is we need our car. It's too far to walk to Wyoming. The borders are closed tight. Even if we could get past the checkpoints, there's the issue of fuel. We don't have enough to make it all the way to Wyoming, and who knows if we'll be able to find more along the way."

"What about Grandpa's connections?" Alyson asked, remembering their discussions of his trying to help.

Her dad shook his head. "I tried reaching out this morning, but . . . nothing. The phone wouldn't ring, and I couldn't get a text through. I sent them an email, but so far, they haven't responded."

They all sat quietly, each of them lost in their own thoughts about what lay ahead.

"We'll figure something out," Alyson said, surprising herself with the determination in her voice. "We have to." As much as she had wanted to stay and support the community, the intruders in their home had changed her mind. Now, all she wanted was to leave. The isolation of her grandparents' lodge seemed far safer than staying here.

Her dad gave her a smile. "That's the spirit, Alyson. We need to keep brainstorming and consider all our options."

As they sat around the kitchen table, picking at their breakfast of oatmeal and canned fruit, a wave of gratitude rushed over Alyson. She was not only grateful for the food they had, and especially thankful the men were stopped before they were able to clean out the pantry, but grateful for her family. Her mom's bruises were prominent this morning and her lip was swollen. A bandage covered the cut above her eyebrow, but she was alive, and they were together.

"Are you sure we can't try going on foot?" her brother asked. "We drive as far as we can before hiking through the wilderness or something?"

Their mom shook her head. "It's too far, Eddie. And too dangerous. We don't have the supplies or the skills for that kind of journey."

"Plus, where we were looking at to cross the state line from Oregon into Idaho, it's not wilderness like you're thinking," their dad added. "Not a forest, anyway. That area is the high desert. The temperature this time of year could be scorching. Dangerous, even. And we'd be back to needing to find a vehicle once we reached Idaho. It's too far to walk."

"How far?"

Alyson's parents exchanged a look, and her mom shrugged. "Six hundred miles?"

"Oh." Eddie's shoulders dropped. "That's a long way."

As they continued to debate various options between bites of oatmeal, each one seeming more far-fetched than the last, a knock at the door made them all freeze.

Her dad motioned for them to stay quiet as he approached the door, peering through the peephole. His shoulders relaxed slightly. "It's Mr. Verley and Mrs. Samms," he said, opening the door.

The two neighbors entered, looking around nervously as if afraid they might have been followed.

"Jim, Eva," her dad greeted them. "Is everything okay?"

Mr. Verley nodded, his eyes darting between her family members. "We need to talk," he said in a low voice. "About your plans."

Alyson's family exchanged worried glances. How much did their neighbors know?

"Why don't we all sit down?" Her mom gestured to the table. "We're finishing up breakfast. We have coffee, or tea if you prefer."

"I'd love a cup of tea," Mrs. Samms said as she took a place at the table. "Jim?"

"Sure. That's fine."

Once they were settled, with mugs of steaming tea in front of them, Mr. Verley leaned forward, his voice barely above a whisper. "I think I have a solution for you to get to Wyoming."

Alyson's pulse quickened. Could it be possible?

He continued, "I have a friend who knows someone transporting rations. With the right encouragement, he takes passengers."

"Passengers?" her dad asked, his brow furrowed. "You mean . . . smuggling people out?"

Mr. Verley shrugged. "It's risky, but it might be your best shot. And, well, if you'll take Eva and me, along with my dog Steve, of course, I'll make the arrangements. Eva and I want to get out of here, too, but at our age, we're not sure we can make the trip on our own."

The room fell silent as everyone absorbed that information. Alyson sifted through the risks and rewards, her thoughts spinning.

"What's the fee for transport?" her dad asked after a moment.

"Not cash money," Mr. Verley replied. "They want precious metals and gems. Gold, silver, jewelry . . . things with lasting value."

Her mom's hand went to her wedding ring. "How much are we talking about?"

He shook his head. "I'm not sure yet. But I imagine it won't be cheap. This guy is taking a big risk."

Her dad stood up and paced the room, as he often did when deep in thought. "It's dangerous. If we get caught . . ."

"If we stay, it's just as dangerous," her mom countered. "You heard what that police captain said last night. He's looking for any excuse to arrest you. To toss you in jail and keep you there. Not to mention the burglars . . . they're getting braver each day."

Alyson had told her parents what she'd overheard from the burglars, about being hired, but she didn't think they believed her. They'd waved the suggestion away, mentioning the same thing was happening all over Astoria.

She watched the conflict play out on her father's face. She understood his hesitation. The plan was fraught with risks. But as she looked around at her family, and at Mr. Verley and Mrs. Samms, she knew they had to take this chance.

"I think we should do it," she said, her tone steady, though her insides were anything but. "It's our best shot at getting to safety."

Eddie nodded enthusiastically. "Yeah, it'll be like a secret mission!"

Their dad shot him a warning look. "This isn't a game, Eddie. If we do this, we need to understand the gravity of the situation."

"We do understand, Dad," Alyson insisted. "But what choice do we have?"

"I think Alyson's right," her mom said. "It's a risk, but staying here might be even riskier."

After a long moment, her dad nodded. "All right, Jim. Can you get us more details? We need to know exactly what we're getting into before we commit."

Mr. Verley smiled, relief evident on his face. "I'll reach out to my contact right away. But we'll need to move fast. These opportunities don't come often, and they don't last long."

"How do they get us out?" Eddie asked.

"I'm not exactly sure of the details. I'll know more later. But you folks should start packing. Be ready to go. Things could happen fast."

As their neighbors prepared to leave, Mrs. Samms spoke up. "There's one more thing," she said, her voice trembling slightly. "We'll need to be prepared for . . . well, for anything. The roads aren't safe anymore. We might encounter difficulties."

The unspoken implication hung heavy in the air. They all knew what kind of "difficulties" she meant. Star Brights, desperate people, maybe even authorities looking to set an example of anyone trying to flee.

"We'll be ready," her dad assured her, though Alyson could see the worry in his eyes.

After their neighbors left, her family gathered in the living room, the reality of their situation sinking in.

"If we're actually doing this," her mom said, "we need to get things together. Mr. Verley said things could happen fast. We need to start packing."

"Will we take our car?" Eddie asked.

Alyson shook her head along with her parents. "Doubtful," their dad said. "The way Jim said he takes passengers tells me we'll be riding with him."

"All the way to Wyoming?"

"Hopefully so, son. Hopefully so."

"We need to be smart about what we take," Alyson's mom said. "I hope your folks will understand when we show up on their doorstep with little to nothing. Be sure to let them know, Rich. I don't want them to be upset. You know how your dad can be."

"I'll tell them. Let's start getting things together. Food, water, first aid supplies, clothes. And we need to start finding things of value to use for payment."

"What about weapons?" Eddie asked, his voice small.

The room fell silent. It was a question they'd all been thinking but had been afraid to voice.

Finally, her dad spoke. "We'll . . . we'll figure that out. Let's focus on the other things first."

As they began to make lists and gather supplies, Alyson experienced fear combined with determination. This was actually happening. They were leaving Astoria. Possibly forever.

Chapter 19

As they discussed the information Mr. Verley brought, they tidied up from breakfast. "How did he know we wanted to go to Wyoming?" Alyson's mom asked, her voice tense.

"I mentioned my family there," her dad said, a note of hesitation in his voice. "I didn't come out and say we wanted to leave but had said how I thought it may be safer. You know, since they're so isolated. He agreed it sounded like a great place to ride this out."

Eddie leaned against the counter. "Do you think it's smart that he told Mrs. Samms? You know, since she called the cops on us before for having a neighborhood meeting."

Alyson shook her head. "She apologized for that. She was being cautious. Since she used to be a nurse, she was worried it may spread."

"They haven't been talking much about that lately," Eddie said.

"Talking about what?" their mom asked as she closed the dishwasher.

"How it spreads. Remember? They were talking about it being a virus or spread by blood." He pointed at Alyson. "That's why we thought she might get it. Because of the blood."

Alyson rolled her eyes at her brother, but inwardly, a rush of grief hit her as the memory of that terrible day resurfaced. Megan thrown off the balcony, Jenna killed by Ryan, followed by Alyson fighting for her life and taking his. She could still remember the smell of the blood and the sticky feel of it.

"Eddie," their mom gasped, placing her hand on his arm. "Please."

Her brother looked down, regret in his voice. "Sorry."

"It's fine. You were right to worry," Alyson glanced at her family, meeting each of their gazes. "If I had it . . . but Eddie's right. There isn't a lot of chatter about finding a cure. Even the last presidential address didn't mention it. He didn't even have the CDC people there."

"The last few addresses have been like that," her dad agreed, moving to a chair at the breakfast bar.

"So, what does that mean?" Eddie asked. "Did they find a cure or not?"

Their parents shared a long look before both shook their heads. "My guess is not," their mom said. "That doesn't mean they aren't still looking. Perhaps they don't have any new information, so they're keeping quiet for now."

"Let's get started on our packing." Their dad stood and rubbed his hands together. "It's possible Jim will get the info, and we'll have only a short time to prepare."

"He didn't say how much we could take," Eddie said.

"No, but he did say the person hauls rations. My guess is he's in a semitruck. Chances are, we'll only be able to take what we can carry. Plan on a suitcase each." He looked at his wife of nearly twenty-five years. "A carry-on. Not that behemoth one that you like to take places."

Alyson's mom smiled sweetly. "I know how to pack light."

"Sure you do," he said with a laugh before dropping a kiss on her lips.

Alyson smiled. It was good to see her parents getting along again. The tension had lessened considerably after Mr. Verley and Mrs. Samms's visit. Even though the idea of sneaking out on a ration truck had risks, huge risks, at least it was a viable option.

"Let's do this," her mom said. "Put everything on your beds that you think you need to take. Your dad and I will do the same. We'll whittle it down from there. I think . . ." Her voice faded away as the room went silent. "Power's out again."

"At least it's daytime, so we don't need lights to pack," Eddie said.

~~~~~

Alyson stood in her bedroom, staring at the pile on her bed. One suitcase. Not even a real suitcase, a carry-on. How could she possibly fit her entire life into such a small space? As she pulled a drawer open, the light on her dresser came on, the power returning at least for the moment.

"Alyson?" her mother's voice called from downstairs. "How's it going in there?"

"I'm working on it," she replied, her voice wavering slightly.

Her mom's steps sounded on the stairs before she appeared in the doorway. "It's not easy, is it?" she said softly, understanding in her eyes.

Alyson shook her head, fighting back tears. "Mom, how do I choose? Every little thing feels important."

Her mom crossed the room and wrapped an arm around Alyson's shoulders. "I know, sweetheart. But we have to be practical. Think about what we'll actually need on the journey."

As they sorted through Alyson's belongings, making tough decisions about what to take and what to leave
~~~~~

behind, a knock at the front door echoed through the house.

"That'll be Jim and Eva," her dad called out. "Can someone get that?"

Eddie ran down the stairs. The door opened, followed by the click of dog nails on hardwood.

"Steve!" Eddie's excited voice carried up the stairs. "Great to see you, buddy!"

"Let's go find out the latest news."

In the living room, Mr. Verley and Mrs. Samms were settling onto the couch, while Steve sat obediently at Mr. Verley's feet.

Alyson's dad emerged from the kitchen, a tray of coffee mugs in hand. "So, Jim," he said, handing out the drinks, "what's the word from your contact?" Even though they'd been rationing their coffee, there was no longer a need to do so. Might as well enjoy it while they could.

Mr. Verley's face grew serious. "Well, I've got good news and bad news. The good news is, he's willing to take us all, including Steve here. We'll meet with him tomorrow morning, early. If all goes well, we'll be on the road before the end of the day."

"And the bad news?" her mom asked, her grip tightening on her mug.

Mr. Verley sighed. "The fee. It's . . . well, it's astronomical."

A heavy silence fell over the room. After all their planning, would it all fall apart because of money?

"How much?" her dad finally asked, his voice tight.

He named a figure that made Alyson's eyes widen. It was more than she'd ever imagined.

"That's impossible," her mom whispered. "We wouldn't even be able to come up with that in cash . . . certainly not in gold or jewelry."

"Now, hold on." Mr. Verley held up a hand. "The amount is flexible. It's based on whether the contact will accept what we offer. It's a judgment call on his part. And that is to get you all the way to Wyoming."

"You told them where we're going?" Her dad's eyes widened.

"Not exactly. But I gave them the general idea. Told them we needed to get to Cody. He said they'd be willing to get us to the Montana–Wyoming state line."

"And then what?" her mom asked.

"My folks will meet us there," Alyson's dad said.

"You knew about this?"

His gaze drifted to the floor. "We'll discuss it later, Beth."

She narrowed her eyes and shook her head. "We most certainly will."

"So, what you're saying is, we need to bring more than we think we'll need? To have room for negotiation?"

Mr. Verley nodded. "Exactly. Bring whatever you can. We can use it to barter if needed."

As the adults discussed the logistics of payment, doubt settled over Alyson. What did they have that was valuable enough? Her gaze fell on her mother's wedding ring, glinting in the morning light. Would they have to part with it?

"There's one more thing," Mrs. Samms spoke up, her voice soft but firm. "About Steve."

All eyes turned to the dog, who wagged his tail at the attention.

"They balked at first about taking him," Mr. Verley explained. "But they finally relented. The contact knows him, knows how well-behaved he is. Said he's more human than dog."

Eddie grinned, scratching behind the dog's ears. "He sure is. Aren't you, boy?"

"Even so, it's going to be stressful," Mr. Verley said. "Even as well-behaved as Steve is, he still could give us away. A growl or whine at the wrong time . . . we're taking a chance, as is the driver. In exchange, I offered my contact and his friend, the driver, my house once we're gone. He can have everything left behind. My car, furniture, food. That seemed to be the winning offer. You could do something similar. If he doesn't accept what you offer, tell him he can have what is left in your house."

"That's what I'm going to do too," Mrs. Samms said with a sad smile. "Not that my house has much of value. It's mainly memories of . . ." She shook her head as tears filled her eyes.

Alyson was in elementary school when Mrs. Samms lost her husband. The families weren't close, but she remembered that her mom made a casserole for her.

"Especially since we can only take a backpack each," Mr. Verley added.

"What?" Alyson and her mom said in unison. "A backpack?"

"Right," he nodded. "And not one of those big ones used for multiday backpacking adventures. A small one. Like a schoolbag."

"Oh no," her mom sighed. "That's— "

"It's not much," Mrs. Samms agreed.

As the conversation turned to the practicalities of traveling with a dog, Alyson found herself drifting back to the issue of packing. One backpack each. And not even a big hiking backpack, but something more reasonable in size.

"Alyson?" Her father's voice broke through her thoughts. "Why don't you and Eddie show Mr. Verley and Mrs. Samms what you've got laid out so far? They might have some good advice."

For the next hour, the living room became a hive of activity. Armloads of clothes were brought down. Her mom scoured closets and found old schoolbags and a medium-sized backpack. Bags were emptied and repacked, items debated and discarded. Mr. Verley, drawing on his experience as a former Boy Scout leader, offered advice on what was truly essential.

"Remember," he said, holding up a small bottle, "water purification tablets. They weigh almost nothing and could save your life. These should be enough for all of us, but if you have some or plain bleach, you should bring it."

"How about the tablets we use to clean the hot tub?" Alyson's mom asked. "Would those purify water?"

"Yes, bring some of those. We can also boil water, but those are quicker and won't require fuel."

Mrs. Samms, meanwhile, focused on first aid supplies. "We should each carry a basic kit. You never know when you might get separated."

"Add water purification to each kit, for exactly that reason," Mr. Verley added. "One person holding everything won't help us a bit if we do get separated."

As they worked, her dad pulled Mr. Verley aside. Alyson strained to hear their conversation.

"Jim," her father said in a low voice, "about tomorrow morning . . ."

Mr. Verley nodded gravely. "Yes, we'll meet the contact to make the final arrangements. Early, before the neighborhood starts stirring."

"And you're sure about this guy? We can trust him?"

"As much as we can trust anyone these days. He's our best shot, Rich. Maybe our only shot."

With those words hanging heavy in the air, Mr. Verley and Mrs. Samms exchanged a glance, signaling their departure. "We should get going," Mrs. Samms said softly. "There's still much to prepare."

As the day wore on, the reality of their situation began to sink in. This wasn't merely a theoretical plan anymore. Alyson was sad yet also hopeful.

Alyson moved through the house, her hands lingering on familiar items, trying to hold on to the sense of home. In her bedroom, she paused before her bookshelf, fingers tracing the spines of beloved novels she'd have to leave behind.

"You can bring one," her mother's voice came from the doorway. "For the journey."

Alyson turned, tears pricking her eyes. "How do I choose?"

Her mom crossed the room and pulled her into a tight hug. "I know it's hard, sweetheart. But remember, we're not letting go of things entirely. We're also moving toward something. Safety. A chance for a better life."

"A chance for a life," Alyson muttered, tears filling her eyes.

"Yes," her mom agreed with a sniff. "That is my hope. Or as your dad says, his *prayer* is that we will be safe there."

Alyson stepped back. "He has been saying stuff like that lately. Talking about praying and God. I thought he didn't believe in God."

"It's not that he doesn't believe in God. He doesn't have the zealousness of his parents."

"But you don't believe. We've never gone to church."

Her mom smiled. "It's complicated. Right now, we need all the help we can get. And if God is the one to help us . . . I don't know. Let's focus on what happens next."

Chapter 20

The Reynolds house was quiet in the predawn darkness. Alyson lay in bed, wide awake, her thoughts focused on the journey ahead. Had she even slept? She wasn't sure. The front door creaked open, breaking the silence and making her sit up quickly. Her father was leaving to meet Mr. Verley and his contact.

Soft footsteps from below told her that her mother was awake too. Alyson slipped out of bed, taking one last look at her room. Would this be the last morning she ever woke up here? The smell of coffee drifted up, familiar and comforting. She slid into her slippers before heading downstairs.

Her mom was in the kitchen, hands wrapped around a steaming mug. She looked up as Alyson entered, offering a hesitant smile. "Morning, sweetheart. Couldn't sleep either?"

She shook her head and settled onto a stool at the breakfast bar. They sat in silence for a moment, both acutely aware of her father's absence and what it meant.

"So," her mom said, her voice overly bright, "did you hear about that movie star's new haircut? The one everyone's talking about?"

Alyson blinked, struggling to process the abrupt shift. Then it clicked. Her mother was striving for a sense of normalcy. "Oh, um, yeah," she played along. "It's . . . different, isn't it? She did it herself. Thought it'd be safer than going to a beauty salon. I can't believe she shared the photos."

"I admire her bravery," her mom continued, setting down a mug of coffee in front of Alyson. "It must take a lot of confidence to do something like that and share it with the world."

Alyson took a sip of the steaming coffee, appreciating the warmth. "Yeah, it does. I guess she's trying to adapt, like everyone else."

Her mom nodded, her gaze drifting to the window. "We're all trying to adapt, aren't we?" She hesitated before continuing in a lower tone, "But some changes are harder than others."

For the next hour, they engaged in a strange dance of small talk, discussing trivial matters from a world that no longer existed. Celebrities, TV shows, fashion trends . . . all were inconsequential now, but it was a welcome distraction from the reality of their situation.

The sound of the front door opening again made them both freeze. Her dad entered the kitchen, his face etched with fatigue and worry.

"Well?" her mom asked, unable to keep the tension from her voice.

He sank into a chair and ran a hand through his hair. "It's done. All the plans are made."

Alyson leaned forward, her heart racing. "So, what happens now?"

"We leave after dark. Tonight."

"Tonight? That's so soon," Alyson whispered, her voice trembling slightly.

Her mom squeezed her hand. "It's for the best, sweetheart. The quicker we leave, the safer we'll be."

"We'll walk to the meeting spot. Someone will pick us up there and take us to the next location."

"And he's done this before?" her mom asked, her knuckles white around her mug.

"That's what he says. If we do what we're told, we'll be fine."

A heavy silence fell over the kitchen. Finally, Alyson voiced the question they were all thinking. "What about the cost?"

Her dad's face tightened. "It's astronomical, like Jim said. The deal I made . . . it's not great." He reached into his pocket and pulled out a familiar glint of gold. "But it could have been worse."

Her mom gasped as he handed her her wedding set. "Oh, Rich . . ."

"They'll clean out our houses after we leave," he continued, his voice hollow. "They seemed happy about it. Apparently, they've heard about our neighborhood, exactly like those robbers did."

Alyson and her mom exchanged shocked glances. "How does everyone know about our neighborhood?" Alyson asked, her brow furrowed with concern.

"Is there a leak somewhere?" her mom asked. "Are we being watched?"

He shook his head, looking troubled. "I'm not sure. Jim thinks word spreads fast these days. People are always looking for safe havens or easy targets. We might have become both without realizing it."

"The smugglers won't bother any of the other neighbors, right?" Alyson asked, concerned about all those she'd grown so fond of. They didn't need any more issues in their quest for survival.

"They said they wouldn't, only our houses. Jim believes them. I guess I do too. They seemed honest. Considering they run a human smuggling operation."

With the deal made and the agreement that anything left behind on the property, including both cars, would be property of the contact and the smuggler, her dad told them to double check they had everything they couldn't bear to part with. "I thought we could cache a few of our things we can't take. Things we'd hate to lose. I'd like to think we'll be back when everything settles down."

"Cache how? Like leave with a neighbor?" her mom asked.

"No, that's too risky. What if we bury it behind the retaining wall? We could cover it with bark and no one would notice. I didn't think of it yesterday, or we could have done it in the dark. I only thought of it because Jim told me that's what he did."

As he explained his plan to cache some of their belongings, Alyson experienced a surge of emotions. The idea of burying their treasured possessions was both hopeful and heartbreaking. "What if we can't come back?" she asked, her voice barely above a whisper. "What if someone finds it?"

Her dad placed a comforting hand on her shoulder. "We have to believe we'll return someday, Alyson. And if we don't . . . well, at least we tried to preserve a piece of our lives here."

Her mom nodded, her eyes glistening with unshed tears. "It's worth the risk. There are some things I can't bear to leave behind for someone else. Things my parents left me."

As they gathered items for the cache, Alyson found herself lingering over old photographs and childhood mementos. Each object seemed to hold a lifetime of memories, making the reality of their departure even more painful.

The rest of the day passed in a blur of activity. The packing continued. The bags were emptied, and every item was scrutinized, debated, and either packed or discarded before being repacked.

Her dad took care of making several caches for things they couldn't take but didn't want to lose, mainly memorabilia that had been passed down to her mom. Alyson added a few things to it, as did Eddie. Her dad said all that was important to him was going to Wyoming. The look he gave them brought tears to Alyson's eyes.

After lunch, she took a few minutes to check on the garden. Her dad didn't want her to walk to the end of the block alone, insisting on going with her. Eddie also went along for something different to do.

Looking over the neat rows of the freshly planted garden, Alyson noted the subtle signs of growth. Tiny green shoots pushed through the dark soil, some barely taller than blades of grass. The tomato plants were not yet large enough for cages, but she could imagine them growing tall and sturdy, their vines heavy with clusters of ripe, red fruit.

Soon, the cucumber vines would begin to stretch, searching for something to climb. Lettuce leaves formed small clusters, their edges bright and delicate. It wouldn't be long until they could begin harvesting for salads.

The soil was still damp from last night's watering, and a few weeds had already crept in, their stubborn stems poking up between the rows. A lone bee hovered over the scattered blossoms of marigolds planted at the edges, meant to ward off pests. The sight was humble but promising, a quiet reminder that life, fragile as it was, could still take root even now.

A pang of sadness washed through her. She wouldn't be there to see the end result of their hard work.

"You did good, Alyson. Real good," her dad said as he draped his arm around her shoulder. "You're the reason this looks like it does."

"Did I do enough?"

Her dad was quiet for a moment before he squeezed her shoulder. "You've done more than enough. It's okay to let others take care of the rest."

The words offered little comfort, but she nodded, determined not to reveal the ache in her chest. She understood they had to go. It was the sensible choice, though she resented being forced to leave.

As evening approached, a knock at the door signaled the arrival of Mr. Verley, Mrs. Samms, and Steve. Mr. Verley carried two small backpacks, which he set on the kitchen table with a somber expression. Even Steve was wearing something like a backpack or saddlebag.

When Mr. Verley caught Eddie and Alyson staring at Steve, he explained, "We used to do some hiking. If it was more than a few miles, I liked to bring along supplies in case something went wrong. You know that whole Boy Scout motto. Steve carried his own food and a water dish." He motioned to a bottle. "Even his own water." He kneeled to pet his dog. "Didn't you, boy?"

Steve wagged his tail and smiled, as much as a dog could smile. Alyson couldn't help but feel a pang of envy at the bond between the two of them. She'd always wanted a dog, but her parents had never agreed. Now, she wondered if having a loyal companion like Steve might make their dangerous journey a little less frightening.

"He seems so calm," Alyson observed.

Mr. Verley smiled sadly. "Dogs are intuitive creatures, Alyson. I think Steve knows something big is happening, but he trusts us. That's the beauty of dogs. They live in the moment and face whatever comes with unwavering loyalty."

"I wish I had a dog," Eddie whispered, low enough for only Alyson to hear. She nodded in agreement.

"I brought some . . . supplies," Mr. Verley said, unzipping the bag. He pulled out a handgun and handed it to Alyson's father. "For protection. Just in case."

Her mom shook her head but said nothing. While she had been vocal in the past about guns, even she knew things were different now.

Her dad took the weapon, his expression unreadable. "I hope we won't need these."

"So do I," Mr. Verley agreed. He turned to Mrs. Samms. "Eva has protection too. Something small and easy to conceal, but it'll do the job if needed."

"Do you know how to use one of those?" Alyson's mom asked.

Mrs. Samms gave a single nod. "I do. And I'm grateful to my late husband for making sure I did. At the time, I thought I'd never need the knowledge. But now, I wish I'd stayed in practice. Jim showed me how to work it, and we even shot it a few times without bullets."

"Dry fired," Mr. Verley clarified.

"Good," Alyson's dad agreed. "Dry firing gives a good feel for shooting." A cloud passed over his face. Was he remembering the other night when he'd used his pistol to shoot the intruder? Alyson thought maybe he was, but she wouldn't ask.

Her mom watched the exchange, her face pale. When Mr. Verley asked if she wanted to carry a gun, she shook her head firmly. "No, I . . . I can't."

He nodded in understanding. "At least take this knife. For peace of mind."

Her mom's face grew increasingly pale. When he demonstrated the automatic knife, she jumped back, her hand flying to her mouth.

"I don't— " she began, her voice shaky.

"Take it, Beth," Alyson's dad insisted, his tone gentle but firm. "I know it's scary, but we need to be prepared for anything."

After a brief hesitation, she accepted the knife with a nod, her fingers trembling slightly as she gripped the handle. Alyson had never seen her mother look so vulnerable, and it sent a chill down her spine. If her parents were this frightened, what horrors did they believe they'd encounter on their journey?

Then Mr. Verley turned to Alyson and Eddie, offering each a knife as well. "These are for emergencies only," he said sternly. "Understood?"

Much like her mom had, Alyson paused before taking the knife. Though smaller and without the blade extended, the memory of the kitchen knife she'd used to stop Ryan came rushing back. She shook her head. "I don't know if I should. If I can."

Her dad turned to her and placed his hands on her shoulders, meeting her gaze. "You did what you had to do before. To save your own life. This can be the same. A way to keep you alive. Keep you safe."

Mr. Verley handed her dad the knife, who held it in front of her. Its red metallic grip gleamed in the sunlight. Cautiously, she reached out a finger and ran it along the handle. She glanced at Eddie. His knife looked identical but brown. "How does it work?"

"There's a button right on the side," Mrs. Samms said, pulling her own pink-handled knife from her pocket. "Jim gave me this for Christmas. Not exactly the gift I'd expected, but now I'm glad for it." She demonstrated how the knife worked. "Mine has a stiletto blade. Yours may be different."

"Alyson's is a double edge too," Mr. Verley said. "Eddie's is a tanto edge, and Beth's is a serrated dagger. They're all automatic and ready to use. I'll bring along a couple of whetstones so we can keep them in good shape." He turned to Alyson's dad. "You have a cleaning kit for the pistol?"

"I do. I'll bring it." He gently pressed the knife into Alyson's hand. "You got it?"

"Okay. I'll take it."

"Eva?" Mr. Verley said. "Why don't you spend a few minutes with Beth and the children, showing them how to work these? They're all the same brand, one I know and trust, simply different models of automatic knives. I have a selection of folding pocketknives and fixed blade knives too. They have a multitude of uses."

"I already have a pocketknife," Eddie said, his voice full of enthusiasm. "It's not very big, but I put it in my backpack." He pointed at his backpack against the wall. "You must really like knives, huh?" He hesitated a moment before adding, "And guns."

"They're tools," he responded. "Tools that can be of use to us." He pulled another knife-looking item out, handing it to Alyson's dad. "This is a multi-tool. It has seventeen different items."

"I have one," he said. "Made in Portland. One of my clients gave it to me as a Christmas gift a few years ago. It was still in the box. I packed it."

"Good. That's good. Beth, would you like to carry this one? Eva has one already, and so do I."

She reached out her hand to take it, seeming to be less concerned about this item than the switchblade. "This is the thing with pliers and scissors and even a nail file?"

"I don't believe this one has a nail file, but it does have some useful gadgets." He looked at the children. "Sorry, I don't have any of these for you, but I do have Swiss Army knives." He glanced toward Alyson's mom, quirking an eyebrow. "These do have nail files."

Eddie's eyes lit up as he accepted the Swiss Army knife, turning it over in his hands with a mixture of excitement and trepidation. "This is so cool," he murmured, before catching his mother's worried gaze. "I mean, uh, thanks, Mr. Verley. I'll be careful with it."

Alyson received hers with a solemn nod. "Thank you," she said, meeting Mr. Verley's steady gaze. She already knew the power of such a tool. The kitchen knife in her apartment had saved her life when Ryan attacked. She slipped the Swiss Army knife into her backpack and adjusted the automatic knife in her pocket, feeling its pressure against her leg.

It wouldn't be long now until the sun set and it would be time to leave, time to meet the contact and leave Astoria possibly forever. She checked her watch again, counting down the minutes until darkness.

Chapter 21

Darkness brought a tense silence that settled over the group. Alyson's dad checked his watch and gave a small nod to the others. "It's time."

They shouldered their backpacks, each taking one last look around the house they were leaving behind. Alyson's throat tightened as she realized this might be the last time she ever saw these walls, these rooms that had been her entire world for so long. She'd lived there most of her life, leaving only to go away to college. Even when living in Portland, she'd always known her bedroom was waiting. She could come home whenever she wanted.

Stepping out into the night, she couldn't help but notice how different their neighborhood looked. The familiar houses loomed in the shadows, their dark windows almost accusing.

They'd discussed driving to the meeting spot since the contact would be taking their car as partial payment anyway, but the risk of being discovered was too high. Though the occasional vehicle still passed, walking had become far more common. Being out after dark, though, was against the rules. They were taking a chance.

The weight of her backpack, the unfamiliar presence of the knife in her pocket, the quiet of the deserted streets . . . it all created a surreal atmosphere, as if she was a character in some post-apocalyptic movie. She fell in line behind her brother, shaking her head as the VR set attached to a loop on his backpack bounced with each step.

She still couldn't believe her parents had allowed him to bring it. Her mom had insisted he needed the space in his backpack for important things that may be necessary on the trip, but she finally gave in when he showed how he could attach it to the outside. Alyson found it a bit ridiculous, though she understood. She'd managed to fit two books into her overloaded backpack.

The meeting location was a little over two miles from their home, near the Astoria Column, but the route was uphill. With the elevation change, combined with the care they were taking to remain unseen, they expected the trip to take about an hour.

"We're fine on time," her dad whispered as they stopped for a rest. "Everyone, drink some water."

Bright headlights sliced through the darkness, sweeping over the group and washing them in harsh white light. Alyson froze, her heart pounding as she squinted against the glare, unable to make out the vehicle or its occupants.

Her breath caught, and her muscles tensed as the urge to flee surged. Beside her, Eddie's hand found hers. She slipped her other hand into her pocket, her fingers curling around the handle of the knife Mr. Verley had given her.

"Stay where you are!" a harsh voice barked from behind the blinding lights. The sound of a car door opening and closing echoed in the still night air.

Alyson squinted, trying to make out the figure approaching them. As he stepped into view, the first thing she saw was the gun in his hand, its metal gleaming in the headlights.

"I told you I'd be watching you," the voice said, a smug satisfaction evident in its tone.

"Captain Davis." Her dad's voice was tight with barely controlled anger. "What's the meaning of this?"

Davis chuckled, a sound devoid of any real humor. "Oh, I think you know exactly what this is about, Reynolds. I've been waiting for this moment."

He circled the group slowly, like a predator toying with its prey. "I must admit, I'm a little disappointed. I thought those men would do what they were hired to do."

Alyson's mom drew in a sharp breath. "You . . . you sent those men to our house?"

"Bingo," Davis sneered. "Give the lady a prize. Too bad they were so incompetent. Forced me to take matters into my own hands."

Alyson's stomach churned. This man, this *police captain*, had sent men to their house to rob and kill them. "But why?" she managed to choke out.

Davis's face contorted with rage. "That officer who died because of your father's recklessness? He was the son of my best friend." His voice trembled with anger and sorrow. "I promised to look out for the kid when his old man passed. I watched him grow up, from a little boy who used to follow us around, to a young man who wanted nothing more than to make a difference in this world."

He paused and took a deep breath. "When I decided to transfer here from Southern Oregon, he followed. As soon as there was an opening, I made sure to get him on. Brought his wife, kids, and mom. Started a new life. And now he's dead, all because you people couldn't follow the rules. Do you have any idea what that does to a person? To know you failed someone you cared about? His mother . . . she trusted me to keep him safe. And I had to look her in the eye and tell her he was gone. Gone because of you."

He clenched his fists, his body shaking with rage. "I buried a friend. A son. How many more, huh? How many more lives are going to be ruined before you realize the consequences of your actions?"

Alyson tried to find a way out of this nightmare. She was sure they were all going to die here, on this dark street, at the hands of a man sworn to protect them. And why? Because of some Shakespearean version of honor?

"You won't get away with this," Mr. Verley said, his voice steady despite the fear Alyson could see in his eyes.

Davis laughed, the sound sharp and cruel in the night air. "Oh, but I will. You'll all simply . . . disappear. It happens all the time these days, doesn't it? People vanishing into thin air. I guess you all know the women won't simply vanish. They'll have a purpose." His eyes drifted toward Alyson. "Especially you. There's a fine price on young, attractive women."

Eddie spoke up, his voice small but determined. "How did you know where to find us?"

The captain's grin widened. "I have my ways, kid. You'd be surprised how many eyes and ears I have in this town."

As one, Alyson's family turned to look at Mrs. Samms. She had called the police on them before, after all. Could she have betrayed them again?

Mrs. Samms's eyes widened in shock. "No, no, it wasn't me," she insisted, her voice trembling. "Jim? Tell them. It wasn't me."

Davis's laughter cut through the tension. "You think there aren't plenty of people willing to snitch for a little extra food? I asked my sources to keep an eye out for anything suspicious happening at your house."

He leaned forward and lowered his voice conspiratorially. "If you're going to bury your family heirlooms, you should do it after dark, where prying eyes can't see."

Alyson's father stiffened beside her as Eddie released her hand. The realization hit hard. They'd been watched, every move fed back to this madman. Her fingers clenched tighter around the handle of the knife, the only thing grounding her in the moment.

Davis straightened, his grin taking on a sharper edge. "And those prying eyes? They're not only watching. They're ready to act. All it takes is one call from me, and they'll be here. You thought you could outsmart me with so many people in my pocket?"

Her dad's voice cut through the mounting tension. "You think all this loyalty is real? People follow you because they're scared or hungry, not because they believe in you. That's not strength. It's desperation. Same as you."

The smirk on Davis's face faltered, but only for a moment. "I'll admit, I'm surprised to find you walking," he continued, ignoring the jab. "Not sure where you think you're going to go. I mean, how far can a couple of old folks walk? Unless . . ." His eyes narrowed as a new thought seemed to occur to him. "There've been rumors of people being smuggled out."

He made a clucking noise with his tongue and shook his head in mock disappointment. "Guess I should've waited until you got where you were going. Catching the smugglers would be a huge feather in my cap." His eyes gleamed with a predatory light. "No worries. I'm sure this one will be happy to tell me."

Before anyone could react, Davis lunged forward, grabbed Alyson by the arm, and yanked her toward him. She cried out in pain and fear, struggling against his iron grip.

"Let her go!" her dad shouted, stepping forward.

Everything happened at once. Steve, sensing the threat, launched himself at Davis, teeth bared. The captain swung his gun around. A shot rang out, deafeningly loud in the quiet night. Alyson pulled the knife from her pocket and pressed the button to extend the blade before swinging it in Davis's direction. The knife met a sharp resistance before yielding and slipping from her grip.

Alyson lost her balance and tumbled to the ground; her arms instinctively covered her head as she fell. More shots followed, along with shouts and the sound of a scuffle.

When the commotion died down, she slowly raised her head, her heart hammering in her chest. Her lips were tingly and numb. She took a deep breath to ward off the panic attack she could sense coming on. She pressed her hand onto the ground, and the cool grass helped to ground her. She took in a breath before shifting her gaze to the others.

The scene before her was one of nightmarish confusion. Captain Davis lay on the ground, motionless. A pool of blood was spreading beneath him, and to Alyson's shock, she saw a red-handled switchblade protruding from his chest. The same knife she'd had in her pocket. She bit her lip as she forced back the storm of emotions threatening to overwhelm her.

Mrs. Samms stood nearby, her hands shaking as she holstered her gun. "I . . . I had to," she whispered, her voice barely audible. "He was going to kill us all."

Alyson glanced from the gun to the body. Had the blade or the bullet killed the man? She didn't know, but she understood it had to be done. Even though Mrs. Samms said he was going to kill them, Alyson knew the plans he had for her were worse than death.

"Alyson?" The voice was far away, muffled and distant. Her lips tingled again, the sensation creeping across her skin like a warning. Her fingers trembled as she caressed the ground, pressing against it to steady herself. Each breath came too fast, too shallow, and the world seemed to blur at the edges. She fought to stay focused, but the panic was creeping in, pulling everything further out of reach.

"Are you hurt?" the voice said again, closer this time. "Alyson? Answer me."

"Dad?"

He was kneeling next to her. "Are you okay?"

She shook her head. "Did I— "

"You did what you had to do. Just like Eva. Now, we need to go. Someone may have heard the shots. Can you get to your feet?" He helped her up. "You're not injured?" he asked, his voice hoarse with concern.

Alyson shrugged, unable to form words. She looked around at the others. Everyone seemed shaken but unharmed. Steve whined softly, pressing against Mr. Verley's leg.

"Is he hurt? Is Steve hurt?" Eddie asked, his voice trembling. A dark spot stood out against the dog's light fur.

Mrs. Samms kneeled and examined the wound. "He was hit. His shoulder. I can't tell how bad it is."

Mr. Verley's hands shook as he reached for his dog, fighting to keep his voice steady. "We need to move. We'll check on him as soon as we're safe."

"I'll carry him," Alyson's dad said, placing a hand on his shoulder. "You take Eva and my family. Get them to safety."

Mr. Verley hesitated for a moment, finally nodding. "Thank you, Rich."

Her dad turned to her. "Are you ready?"

"I'm okay. Let's go." It was a lie, of course. Alyson didn't know if she'd ever be okay again. First Ryan, then the hoodlum on the city street, and now a police officer. All dead because of her. Well, she wasn't certain the man on the street was dead, but she suspected he may be. Three murders by her hand.

She furrowed her brow. Three murders. Did that make her a serial killer? The thought was so absurd she almost laughed out loud. At least the absurdity of it helped to bring her back to the present.

"I'll carry your backpack," Eddie offered, reaching out his hand. Her dad passed it off to him with a quiet "thank you" before carefully lifting the large dog into his arms, trying not to jostle the injured shoulder. Steve whimpered softly but didn't struggle.

"Let's go," Alyson's mom urged, looking around nervously. "We can't stay here."

Mrs. Samms kneeled beside the captain's body, her face pale as she checked his vitals. With surprisingly steady hands, she retrieved the knife and wiped it clean on the grass before folding it and passing it to Alyson. "You may need this later."

Swallowing the lump that formed in her throat, she took the knife with a nod and cast one last glance at Captain Davis's body. The man who had threatened their lives, who had pursued them with such hate, now lay still and harmless. There was no joy in his death, only a profound sadness at the waste of it all. He should have been working alongside them, helping the town of Astoria through its darkest hour. Instead, he had chosen to create strife.

Mr. Verley took Mrs. Samms's hand, leading her away as the rest followed closely. Her dad brought up the rear, cradling Steve protectively.

They moved quickly, Alyson's heart pounding with fear and adrenaline. Every shadow seemed to hold danger, every sound a potential threat. After a couple of blocks, her dad said he needed to rest. He leaned against a tree and held Steve as Mr. Verley comforted the dog while checking the wound.

"It isn't bleeding too much," he said. "That's good, right?"

"Probably," Mrs. Samms agreed. "Put him on the ground and I can check him."

"We're almost there." Mr. Verley shook his head. "Once we reach the meeting spot, you can give him an exam."

"Let's go," Alyson's dad said, pulling the dog close as he pushed himself from the tree.

They walked in silence for a couple more blocks. "Only a little farther," Mr. Verley whispered. "How's Steve?"

"Doing okay," her dad said, his breath coming in ragged gasps.

She glanced at her dad. Something in his voice made her wonder if he was telling the truth.

Finally, they reached the pickup location. "Let's get behind the trees," her dad said as he was moving in that direction. "Out of the open."

"They should be here soon." Mr. Verley removed his pack and made his way to his dog. "Is he . . . alive?"

"He's alive and squirming. Not happy about being carried." He placed the dog on a carpet of wilting grass. Steve whined and stood up.

"Easy, boy," Mr. Verley said. "Let me take a look."

"Dad?" Eddie asked, concern in his voice.

"I don't think it's too bad. We'll get him patched up," her dad said firmly. "He'll be okay."

Mrs. Samms knelt beside Steve, her hands gently probing the injury. "I'll take a look," she said, her voice steadier now that she had a task to focus on. "I may not be a veterinarian, but I've patched up my fair share of people over the years. This can't be too different." She lowered her voice to a whisper before adding, "I hope."

As she examined the wound, Steve whimpered softly but remained still, seeming to sense the importance of the moment. After a few tense minutes, Mrs. Samms let out a relieved sigh.

"It looks like it's more of a graze than anything," she announced, the tension in her shoulders easing slightly. "The bullet skimmed his shoulder, tearing the skin but not penetrating deeply. He's a lucky boy."

Eddie, who had been hovering anxiously nearby, let out a choked sob of relief. "So, he'll be okay?"

Mrs. Samms nodded. "Yes, I think so. But we'll need to keep the wound clean and make sure he stays off it as much as possible. Jim, will you grab the first aid kit from my pack? I'd like to clean and bandage this before the, um . . . before your *friends* show up."

Mr. Verley quickly retrieved the kit. As Mrs. Samms worked, cleaning the wound with antiseptic wipes and carefully wrapping it with gauze, the others kept watch, acutely aware of how exposed they were.

"How are you doing, Steve?" Mr. Verley gently stroked his dog's head. He responded with a soft whine and a tentative wag of his tail.

"There," Mrs. Samms said as she secured the last of the bandage. "That should hold for now. We'll need to change it regularly and keep an eye out for any signs of infection. Hopefully, he won't get bumped around too much on our journey."

"Thank you, Eva. I hope so too." Alyson's dad checked his watch. "Our contact will be here soon, and we need to be ready to move quickly."

As if on cue, the distant rumble of an engine filled the air. The group froze, exchanging worried glances. Was it their ride to safety, or had Captain Davis's body been discovered?

"Get ready," Mr. Verley whispered. "If it's them, we'll need to move fast."

"Stay hidden. If it's not them . . ." Her dad's voice faded away as his hand gripped the butt of his pistol.

The sound grew closer, its low rumble cutting through the night. Alyson's hand found Eddie's as the vehicle slowly approached their hiding spot.

Chapter 22

The hum of the approaching engine swelled into a throaty growl, and a battered pickup truck materialized out of the darkness. It rolled to a stop twenty feet from their position behind the trees.

"That's him." Mr. Verley stepped out from the cover of the trees and raised his hand.

A gruff voice called out from the driver's seat, "Let's go."

There was no time for hesitation. After lifting Steve into the truck bed, Alyson's dad helped the others climb in. She sank beside Eddie, the cold metal digging into her, her breath coming fast and shallow.

"We're okay now, Aly," her brother said, sounding much more confident than he should.

"Are we?" she whispered.

The truck lurched forward before they were fully settled, tires spitting gravel as it sped up. Alyson clung to the side, her hair whipping in the wind as they drove away from Astoria and everything she'd ever known.

Grateful for the jacket tied around her waist, she pulled it on as her mom signaled for Eddie to do the same. Once her jacket was in place, Alyson pulled the collar up toward her ears. Not great, but better. She had a gaiter and gloves in her bag; she'd use those if it got any colder.

For over an hour, they rode in tense silence, the landscape a blur of shadows and fleeting glimpses of moonlit fields. Finally, the truck slowed and turned onto a bumpy side road.

"Where are we?" Eddie whispered, his voice barely audible over the engine.

Mr. Verley squinted into the darkness. "Jewell, I think. Small town off the Sunset Highway. Easy to miss if you're not looking for it."

"We've been here before, right, Dad? It's where the elk refuge is?"

"That's right. Not exactly an elk refuge. It's a wildlife area, but we did see elk here."

Alyson smiled at the memory of their last visit. They had come during the fall of her junior year in high school. The air was crisp, and the leaves were vibrant with autumn colors. She remembered the excitement in Eddie's eyes as they watched the elk graze, majestic and serene. He had been much younger. She glanced at her brother, noting how much he'd matured in the weeks since the trouble with the Star Brights had started.

The truck pulled up in front of a large shop. A man stepped out. "Let's go. Get inside." He motioned with his arm, beckoning them to come toward him.

"Go on, now," the driver called from the cab.

Alyson's dad jumped down first and extended a hand to Mrs. Samms, as Mr. Verley clambered out and helped Steve to the ground. Eddie didn't wait for assistance, and Alyson followed close behind. Her mom's feet had barely hit the dirt when the truck lurched forward, the driver clearly eager to be on his way.

"Thanks for the ride," her mom muttered as the vehicle disappeared down the road.

"Come inside," the man in the shop said again as they moved toward him. "It'll be a bit of a wait. The truck got held up."

Her mom frowned. "Held up?"

"Delayed," the man clarified, his tone impatient. "It's bringing a shipment out of Lincoln City. Taking longer than expected."

"Where will we go from here?" Her mom's voice was steady despite the tremor in her hands.

The man sighed heavily. "The less you know, the better."

"But maybe if we know, we can be better prepared to stay safe," Alyson chimed in, surprising herself with her boldness.

The man studied her for a moment before relenting. "Portland."

As he closed the door behind them, Alyson's mom pressed on. "Where do we go after Portland?"

"The check station at the state line."

"And then?"

"Boise," the man replied, his patience clearly wearing thin. "This load is a trade with the fine people of Idaho. You'll get out before then."

Her dad opened his mouth to say something, but the man held up his hand. "Don't worry. I know where you're heading. Wyoming. You'll switch vehicles. Idaho and Montana don't have the restrictions of getting in and out of the state, but there could still be difficulties. It'll be important for you to do everything exactly as you're told. No questions, got it?"

His gaze shifted to take each of them in before falling on Steve. The man's eyes widened. "Wait a minute. You didn't tell me the dog was injured."

"He wasn't," Mr. Verley explained quickly. "He is now. We had a little trouble. It's fine. He'll be fine."

The man ran a hand over his face and exhaled sharply. "This better not come back to bite me."

"It won't," Alyson's dad assured him. "But you may want to be careful when checking out my house. Seems there are spies in the neighborhood. Go at night. Get in, get out."

The man's mustache twitched as he smirked. "You think they're not already collecting payment? The moment you all climbed into that truck, the process started. By now, they're probably wrapping it up."

Mr. Verley's eyes narrowed. "We had a deal. No unnecessary damage. We all hope to return to our homes as soon as this is over."

"Relax," the man said, waving a dismissive hand. "They're professionals. They know the drill. They'll only take what's owed."

Alyson's dad glanced at Mr. Verley, and a silent understanding seemed to pass between them. They had no choice but to trust this man. "How long until the truck gets here?" her dad asked, his voice tight with suppressed tension.

He shrugged. "Couple of hours, I'd guess. Go ahead and relax." He indicated a sagging couch and a couple of shabby office chairs in the corner.

Mr. Verley tended to Steve while the others took turns sitting or pacing as time ticked slowly by. The man had disappeared into another room, doing who knows what. Once Mr. Verley was satisfied his dog was doing okay, he turned to Alyson. "Let's clean your knife, sharpen the blade, and make sure it's ready in case you need it again."

Alyson's heart started beating rapidly as she remembered the knife sticking out of Captain Davis. She'd done what she had to do, but that didn't make it any easier.

"Can I help?" Eddie asked.

The siblings followed Mr. Verley to a small kitchen, where they cleaned and sharpened the knife. As they worked, he explained how to achieve a sharp, well-maintained blade. Alyson understood the need to keep it in top condition, but she truly hoped she'd never need to use the knife again.

After about two hours, the man poked his head out the door of the small office. "Shouldn't be long now."

A heavy silence fell over the shop, broken only by the distant sound of an approaching semitruck. The man straightened, all business once more. "That's your ride. Anytime you feel the truck slow, be ready. When it stops, assume the door is going to open. Absolute silence or the gig is up." He glanced at the injured dog and shook his head. "Understand?"

They nodded solemnly, the gravity of the situation seeming to settle over them like a physical weight.

The contact opened the overhead door, allowing a massive semitruck to back up inside. With the driver still at the wheel, the man unlocked the back of the truck and guided them to a hidden compartment in the cargo area, cleverly concealed behind crates that looked like canned goods.

"In you go," he ordered. "There's a bucket if you need it. But remember, if the rig is stopped, not a sound."

They climbed in one by one, her dad again carrying Steve. The space was cramped and dark. Alyson found herself wedged between Eddie and her mother, the warmth of their bodies both comforting and claustrophobic. Steve lay at their feet, his breathing steady but shallow.

The compartment door closed, plunging them into total darkness. Her mom gasped as muffled sounds and voices calling out instructions filled the air. With a lurch that made her stomach flip, the truck began to move.

As the truck rumbled along, her mom leaned in close. "Try not to worry," she whispered, her voice barely audible over the engine noise. "We've made it this far. We'll be okay."

Mr. Verley shifted uncomfortably, his hand resting on Steve's back. "I hope the wound doesn't get infected. We're not exactly in the most sanitary conditions."

"We'll check it as soon as we get out of this truck," Mrs. Samms reassured him. "The bandage should protect it."

Alyson's dad cleared his throat. "Let's try to get some rest. It won't take long to get to Portland, but we need to be alert when we arrive."

The journey was eternal. Alyson drifted in and out of a restless sleep, plagued by nightmares of Captain Davis's lifeless eyes and the sound of gunshots, along with her knife sticking from his chest. The air grew stale and heavy, and her limbs ached from the cramped position.

She had lost track of time when she noticed it. The semitruck began to slow. Not slow like they were taking a corner, but slow like they were preparing to stop. Everyone froze, hardly daring to breathe. Even Steve, as if sensing the tension, remained perfectly still.

The semitruck came to a stop. Muffled voices drifted through the walls, followed by the sound of the cargo doors opening. Alyson's heart hammered as footsteps approached their hiding spot.

"Let's get it loaded up," someone ordered. There was considerable clanking and banging over the next twenty or thirty minutes. None of them dared to move or even take a deep breath during that time. Steve had his head on his paws, his eyes closed.

Finally, someone said that was all of it. The cargo doors slammed shut, and the engine rumbled to life once more. It wasn't until they'd been driving for several minutes that Alyson allowed herself to exhale fully.

As the miles rolled by, Alyson's mind raced with questions. She knew there was a checkpoint at the state line, about six hours from Portland, but would there be others? What awaited them in Idaho? And even if they made it to Wyoming, what kind of life could they hope to build in this new, dangerous world?

The truck continued its journey through the night, carrying its hidden cargo of desperate souls toward an uncertain future. Alyson clung to the warmth of her family around her, drawing strength from their presence as she napped off and on.

Her dad fumbled with his watch, squinting at the dim glow of its face. "It's been about two and a half hours since we left Portland," he whispered. "We must be about halfway to Ontario and the state line."

He reached for Alyson's hand in the darkness. "I think . . . I think we should pray," he said, his voice thick with emotion.

Alyson was taken by surprise. Her family had never been religious, yet she could hear the desperation in her father's tone. She listened as his prayer started off shaky but grew more confident.

Mr. Verley joined in next, his prayer focused on Steve's healing and their successful journey. Mrs. Samms followed, her voice soft but fervent.

Alyson remained quiet, unsure of what to say or how to pray. But to her surprise, Eddie piped up, his childlike faith evident in his simple words. "God, please keep us safe and help us get to Wyoming. And make Steve's shoulder better. Amen."

After a moment of silence, her dad spoke again. "Let's get some sleep while we can. We'll need our strength for whatever comes next."

Alyson dozed restlessly for several hours before sensing the semi slowing again before coming to a stop. She closed her eyes and found herself silently praying for safe passage.

After a few minutes, the door shuttered open.

"What's in these crates?" a gruff voice asked.

"Canned goods," a voice replied smoothly. "Heading to a distribution center in Boise."

There was a pause, and Alyson could almost feel the suspicion radiating from the unseen inspector. "Mind if we take a look?"

"Be my guest," a second voice said, his tone casual. Was that their driver? Alyson assumed it must be.

She held her breath as she heard crates being moved. Beside her, Eddie trembled slightly, and she reached out to squeeze his hand in the darkness.

"What's the holdup?" the driver asked, a note of tension creeping into his voice.

"New orders," came the curt reply. "We're doing full searches of all vehicles crossing the state line. Too many smugglers looking to exploit the disorder."

Full searches? Alyson exchanged panicked glances with her family, though in the darkness, she could barely make out their faces.

The sound of crates being moved grew closer. Any moment now, their hiding spot would be discovered.

Outside, voices rose in turmoil, accompanied by the sound of hurried footsteps. Their driver's voice cut through it all. "What's going on?"

"Security breach at the perimeter," someone yelled back. "All units, respond!"

The inspector cursed. "Fine. We're done. Get this truck out of my way!"

The cargo doors slammed shut, and the truck's engine roared to life. As they pulled away from the checkpoint, Alyson could hardly believe their luck. Whatever had happened at the perimeter had saved them from certain discovery.

The heartfelt prayers from earlier echoed in her mind. Was it actually luck that had saved them? Or had God been watching over them? For the first time in her life, she found herself considering the possibility that there might be more to faith than she had ever believed.

"Thank you," she whispered into the darkness, not sure who or what she was thanking, but feeling a sense of gratitude, nonetheless.

As the truck picked up speed, the tension slowly eased. Alyson allowed herself to hope. They had made it across the state line. They were one step closer to safety, to a new beginning.

Chapter 23

The semitruck lurched to a stop, the sudden silence deafening after hours of constant engine noise. Alyson held her breath, straining to hear any clues about their location. They hadn't been driving long. Only about half an hour since the inspection at the state line. The sound of the driver's door opening and closing echoed through the trailer, followed by muffled footsteps approaching the rear.

Bright light flooded their hiding spot as the compartment door swung open. She blinked, her eyes struggling to adjust after so long in darkness.

"Out," the driver grunted, his face impassive. "Quickly now."

They scrambled to comply, muscles protesting after hours of cramped inactivity. Steve, too, struggled to his feet. "Easy now," Mr. Verley said.

"Should I carry him?" Alyson's dad asked.

"Let's see how he does," Mrs. Samms replied as Steve walked with a slight limp, not much different from the rest of them after so many hours in their cramped hiding space. The dog whimpered softly as they emerged into the cool air.

The sudden brightness stabbed at Alyson's eyes, forcing her to squint and turn her head. Spots danced across her vision, and she blinked rapidly, her lashes wet from the sting of light after so long in the dark.

Wiping her eyes, she took in their surroundings. They were behind a nondescript building, its weathered brick facade offering no clues to their exact location. The driver didn't wait for questions. He climbed back into his cab and pulled away without another word.

"Well," Alyson's mom said, her voice trembling slightly, "that's that, I suppose."

Mr. Verley shook his head as his eyes scanned the empty lot. "Let's not jump to conclusions. We were told someone would meet us here. We should wait."

"Where are we?" Eddie asked.

"Idaho?" Mr. Verley didn't sound completely sure of his response.

Steve carefully laid in a spot of sun, the dry, brown grass crunching softly beneath him. Mrs. Samms knelt to examine the wound. "It doesn't look any worse. I think he's doing okay, all things considered."

The minutes ticked by, each one heightening Alyson's anxiety. Had they been abandoned?

"Well . . ." her mom said, glancing around. "If we're in Idaho, at least we're past the checkpoints, right? We can figure things out."

"Let's not worry yet." Mr. Verley sat on the grass next to Steve. "We were told they'd get us to the Montana-Wyoming state line. I still have faith that is what will happen."

"And then what?" her brother asked.

"Your grandparents will meet us there," her mom said. "That's the plan, anyway. Right, Rich?"

As her dad opened his mouth to say something, the low rumble of an approaching engine cut him off, drawing everyone's attention.

"Is that them?" Eddie asked, a hint of fear in his voice.

"Let's hope," Beth replied.

A cargo van, its white paint faded and dust-covered, rolled into view. A luggage rack on the roof was piled high with boxes and fuel cans, tightly secured with ropes. The front windows were down, and strands of gray hair streamed out in the breeze. The driver's door swung open, and a woman stepped out, her face creased in a wide, genuine smile.

She radiated the essence of an aging hippie, with loose salt-and-pepper locks accented by a few braided sections on the left, adorned with colorful beads. Her flowing, vibrant dress clashed with the sturdy hiking boots she wore. Despite the deep lines marking her face, her eyes gleamed with a youthful energy.

"Well, aren't you a sight for sore eyes," she called out, her voice warm and tinged with a slight Southern drawl. "I'm Maggie. Y'all ready to hit the road?"

They exchanged wary glances before Alyson's dad stepped forward. "We were told to expect a ride to— "

"That's me." Maggie nodded, her smile never faltering. "Now come on, let's get you loaded up before anyone takes much notice. We got you out of that commie state, but they ain't above coming to look for you. Heard of it happening before."

With a mixture of relief and apprehension, they piled into the van. The interior was sparse, with bench seats lining the walls to face each other in the cargo area. Steve settled at their feet, chuffing softly.

As Maggie pulled onto the road, Alyson's shoulders relaxed slightly, the tension easing. They were moving again, one step closer to their goal.

"I've got food in the cooler. Water in the jugs," Maggie shouted over the wind rushing through the open windows, her voice barely carrying back. "Help yourselves whenever you need it. We'll have a bathroom stop a bit down the road."

"You think they'll come looking for us?" Alyson's mom asked with a tremor in her voice.

"Who? The gestapo? Are you important?"

"Important? No . . ."

"Then you'll probably be fine. They don't have any jurisdiction in Idaho. We're still a free state. Well, as free as anyone with the Star Brights running around."

"You do this often? Help people— "

"Escape the commies? You betcha. We've got a whole network trying to get people out of Oregon, Washington, and California. There're others in other states, but we each operate independently.

"We had to pay," Eddie said. "They took everything left in our houses."

"Mm-hmm. That's how it works. And what our network can't use directly will be traded on the black market for what we do need. We appreciate your contribution." She cackled out a laugh that sounded like nails on a chalkboard, sending shivers down Alyson's spine.

"Where are we exactly?" her dad asked, glancing out the window. The landscape was a stark contrast to the towering evergreens and lush greenery of Astoria.

"I picked you up a little outside of Caldwell, Idaho. In about seven or eight hours, we'll be in Missoula. That's where my part of this little adventure ends, and you'll meet up with a new driver."

"It'll be around midnight before we get there," her dad said, checking his watch.

"That's right. Got a place for you to rest up before hitting the road tomorrow. You've got folks set to meet you, right?"

"Yes, on— "

Maggie lifted a hand. "I don't need to know the details. I'll get you to Missoula. The next person will worry about where to drop you off."

The area seemed like a combination of farmland and small towns. As they passed through the communities, Alyson noticed a difference in the atmosphere.

"People seem . . . friendlier here," she remarked, watching a group of neighbors chatting animatedly on a street corner.

Maggie nodded, glancing in the rearview mirror. "We haven't been hit as hard by all this craziness. Folks are wary, sure, but they're pulling together instead of tearing each other apart."

"We were doing that in our neighborhood," Alyson said, a bit of defensiveness in her tone. "We started a garden, checked on people, and did other things to work together."

"Sounds right nice," Maggie replied, looking in the rearview mirror to meet Alyson's gaze. "And yet, here you are."

Her dad leaned forward, closer to Maggie's seat. "Not everyone had the same sense of camaraderie. Things were becoming dangerous."

They'd only been driving about an hour when Alyson saw a sign announcing they were in Horseshoe Bend. Maggie pulled into a small gas station.

"All right," she said, turning to face them. "Bathroom breaks and leg stretches. Keep it quick, and try not to draw attention. We don't want anyone to know you're escaped commies. They might think you're infected just 'cause of where you came from." She cackled again as she opened her door.

As they took turns using the restroom and walking Steve, Alyson marveled at the relative normalcy of the scene. People walked by, nodding at the newcomers. A young couple laughed as they shared a snack by their motorcycle. Other than the restroom, there wasn't anything available at the gas station. No snacks and no gas, but people seemed to accept that was how it was.

"It's like stepping back in time," her mom murmured, voicing Alyson's thoughts.

"Ready to go, folks?" Maggie motioned them back to the van. "Someone want to ride up front? Keep me from lookin' like the hired help."

"I'll sit up front with you," Alyson's dad offered.

As Maggie pulled back onto the quiet highway, she said, "We'll stop in the forest and put some fuel in. I've found it's best not to advertise that we have it. I make sure to fill up away from prying eyes."

"Do we have enough to get to Missoula?"

"Well, sure. What kind of professional driver would I be if I couldn't get you where you need to go." She let loose her loud laugh again. This time, it didn't bother Alyson as much, instead she smiled along with the woman.

As they left Horseshoe Bend, the landscape began to change. The road wound through the small town of Garden Valley before entering the vast expanse of the Boise National Forest. Towering pines replaced the open farmland, and the air grew cooler as they climbed in elevation.

"We'll be on this highway for a while," Maggie explained, her eyes fixed on the winding road ahead. "It's beautiful country, but it can be treacherous. And it looks like it's going to rain." She pointed at the darkening sky as she shook her head. "Hate to roll up the windows. This old van has an odor problem."

Alyson crinkled her nose as she sniffed the air, but she didn't smell anything too terrible. It was a little musty, but it could be worse.

Maggie kept up a steady stream of cheerful chatter, telling stories of her life in Idaho and the changes she'd seen since the troubles began. When Mrs. Samms asked where Maggie lived, she was evasive and answered with, "Oh, here and there. I've been traveling a lot, helping folks like you."

The van rounded a sharp bend, and Maggie slammed on the brakes, skidding to a halt. A fallen tree blocked the road ahead, its massive trunk spanning the narrow mountain path.

"Oh no," Maggie muttered. "This ain't good. Not good at all."

Those in the back leaned forward to peer out the windshield. "What's wrong?" Mr. Verley asked.

Maggie's eyes darted nervously between the road and the rearview mirror. "That tree didn't fall on its own. We're in trouble, folks. Big trouble."

Alyson's stomach tightened as the implications settled over her.

"What do we do?" her dad asked, drawing his pistol.

Maggie's voice was tight with fear. "We can't stop. They'll be waiting for us to get out. I'm going to try to get around it."

As she spoke, a shot rang out. Maggie flinched but kept her hands steady on the wheel.

"Get down!" her dad roared, scrunching into the front seat.

Alyson dropped to the floor, her heart pounding so hard it thudded in her throat. Her mom crouched beside her in an instant, pulling her close with one arm and reaching out to draw Eddie into the protective circle of her embrace. The van rocked as bullets peppered its sides.

"Hold on tight!" Maggie shouted as she pressed the accelerator.

The van lurched forward, tires spinning on loose gravel. Maggie angled toward the narrowest part of the fallen tree, aiming for a gap barely wider than the van itself.

Metal screeched against wood as they scraped past the trunk. Alyson felt a jolt as they bounced over smaller limbs.

They were through, but the danger wasn't over. Bullets continued to whiz past as Maggie swerved wildly, trying to put distance between them and their attackers.

A deafening crash filled the van as the rear window exploded, showering glass over the huddled passengers. Her mom screamed, tightening her hold on Eddie and Alyson, her body protecting them.

"Everyone okay?" her dad called out, his voice strained.

Before anyone could answer, another shot rang out and Maggie cried out in pain. Her body jerked, and the van swerved dangerously close to the edge of the road.

"I'm hit," Maggie gasped, her hand leaving the wheel to clutch her shoulder. Blood seeped between her fingers, staining her colorful dress a dark crimson.

Alyson watched in horror as Maggie's face paled, her grip on the wheel weakening. The van began to veer off course, tires skidding on loose gravel.

"Maggie!" Alyson's dad lunged forward to grab the wheel. "Hold on! Alyson! You need to drive."

Alyson nodded, her heart racing. "How— "

"No time to talk," her dad cut her off. "Eddie, Beth, help me get Maggie out of the seat. Jim, watch our backs!"

In a flurry of movement, they managed to pull Maggie from the driver's seat, allowing Alyson to slide in. Her hands shook as she gripped the wheel, acutely aware of the firefight and the ongoing danger.

"Floor it!" Mr. Verley yelled from the back. "They've got ATVs, and they're still coming!"

Alyson's heart raced as she glanced in the rearview mirror. Sure enough, two ATVs were roaring up behind them, their drivers hunched low over the handlebars and each with a passenger, firing their gun at every opportunity. The four-wheelers were gaining ground quickly.

"Hang on!" Alyson shouted, pressing the accelerator to the floor. The van's engine whined in protest as they hurtled up the mountain road.

A sharp turn loomed ahead. She gritted her teeth, fighting to keep control as the van's tires skidded on loose gravel along the edge of the pavement. The nimble ATVs drew closer.

"They're trying to force us off the road!" her dad yelled, bracing himself against the dashboard, as he leaned out the window, pistol in hand.

One of the ATVs pulled alongside the van, its rider reaching out to grab the driver's side window. Alyson swerved hard, clipping him and forcing him into the oncoming lane.

"Eddie, stay down!" her mom screamed as a bullet punched through the side panel.

"Looks like a sharp bend is coming up," Mr. Verley called out. "If you can make it, they might overshoot!"

Alyson saw the hairpin turn approaching fast. It was risky, but they were out of options. She held her breath, keeping the accelerator down as they barreled toward the bend.

At the last possible second, Alyson wrenched the wheel to the side. The van tilted precariously, tires squealing in protest. For a heart-stopping moment, Alyson thought they would flip.

Then, mercifully, the van righted itself. Behind them, one of the ATVs failed to make the turn, sailing off the road and down the mountainside. The other, caught off guard by the sudden maneuver, skidded to a stop, buying them precious seconds.

"You did it!" Eddie cheered, his face a mix of terror and exhilaration.

But their reprieve was short-lived. The remaining ATV was already in pursuit again, its engine roaring with renewed determination.

As they sped down the winding mountain road, the ATV gaining ground, Alyson's knuckles were white on the steering wheel. The van, heavier and less maneuverable, was at a clear disadvantage on the treacherous terrain.

"We can't outrun them," her dad said, his voice tense. "We need another plan. If we let them get close enough, I might be able to get off a shot. Hit the driver or . . . maybe a tire." He sounded less than confident.

A flash of lightning lit up the sky, followed by a crack of thunder that rattled her chest. The wind whipped through the open window as rain exploded from the clouds, pelting the windshield and soaking her arm. She didn't dare take her hand off the steering wheel to roll up the window, not on this winding road.

"This could work in our favor," Mr. Verley said. "The ATV may have a harder time in this weather."

Alyson nodded, squinting through the rain-streaked windshield. "But so will we. I can barely see the road."

"Keep going," her dad encouraged. "Be smart. Let them take the risks." He still had his window down, but now he was watching the side mirror.

Through the rearview mirror, Alyson could see the ATV's headlight bobbing behind them, drawing closer despite the rain. The rider was either skilled or desperate, possibly both.

"They're making their move!" Mr. Verley called. "Coming up fast. I'll try to stop them. Be ready, Rich." He had his pistol out and aimed toward the quad.

She glanced in the mirror to see the four-wheeler rapidly approaching.

"Go to the other side of the highway," her dad said. "Drive toward oncoming traffic."

"But . . . but what if . . ."

"Just do it."

Alyson switched to the other lane, and the four-wheeler shot forward, vanishing from her mirror in seconds. Mr. Verley must have had them in his sights because he started firing his gun.

"Come on, come on," her dad muttered, his eyes glued to his mirror. "There!" He moved faster than she could believe possible, firing off several rounds.

The sound of gunshots echoed through the van, followed by a screech of tires and a loud crash. Alyson's heart raced as she gripped the steering wheel, fighting to keep the van steady on the rain-slicked road.

"Did you get them?" Eddie asked, his voice trembling with both fear and excitement.

Their dad lowered his gun, his face sad yet relieved. "Either me or Jim. We hit their tire. They went off the road."

"Reload," Mr. Verley said. "Be ready in case that didn't do it."

"I'll be out of bullets," her dad said.

"Yep," Mr. Verley agreed. "Me too. We'll do what we can."

Alyson risked a glance in the rearview mirror. Through the curtain of rain, she could make out the overturned ATV, its wheels spinning uselessly in the air. There was no sign of the rider.

"Is it over?" her mom asked, her arms still protectively wrapped around Eddie.

Mr. Verley peered out the back window, scanning the road behind them. "I don't see anyone following. I think we lost them."

A collective sigh of relief filled the van. They had escaped, against all odds. Alyson's heart was pounding as she eased off the accelerator, her hands shaking with residual adrenaline. "Is everyone okay?"

A chorus of shaky affirmatives answered her, along with a weak groan from Maggie, sprawled on the floor with Mrs. Samms by her side, tending to her wound.

"We're not out of danger yet," her dad reminded everyone, glancing back at their injured driver. "Eva? How's Maggie?"

"She's alive, but we need to stop the bleeding. I don't . . ." Her voice faded away as she continued to work on Maggie.

The silence in the van was thick, broken only by Maggie's shallow breaths and the occasional hiss of the tires on the road. Alyson's grip tightened on the wheel, her eyes scanning the rearview mirror as if expecting someone to appear from the shadows.

The road ahead disappeared into the heavy rain, its twists and turns swallowed by the darkness. They had escaped, yes, but for how long? And at what cost?

Chapter 24

The van rumbled along the winding mountain road, its engine a constant reminder of their precarious situation. Alyson's hands gripped the steering wheel tightly, her eyes scanning the road ahead for any sign of danger. In the passenger seat, her father sat vigilantly, his now reloaded pistol at the ready.

In the back, Mrs. Samms worked tirelessly on Maggie, her hands moving with years of practice despite the van's constant jostling. The rest of the group watched in tense silence, the gravity of their situation weighing heavily on them all.

"Cold?" her dad asked, working to adjust the heater. Alyson tried to roll up her window, but it wouldn't budge. Her dad said a bullet might have hit the door and broken the glass and they would check it when they stopped. He rolled his up, cutting some of the wind, but with the back window blown out, the vehicle was far from warm. At least the rain had stopped.

"How's she doing?" her mom asked softly, her eyes fixed on Maggie's pale face.

Mrs. Samms shook her head. "Not good. The bullet went deep, and she lost a lot of blood. I'm doing what I can, but . . ." She trailed off, focusing once again on her patient.

Mr. Verley cradled Steve, the dog whimpering softly as if sensing the somber mood. Eddie sat silently, his young face a mask of worry and fear.

After about thirty minutes of driving, Mrs. Samms's voice cut through the quiet. "I'm sorry," she said, her tone heavy with regret. "She's gone. Maggie's dead."

A sharp intake of breath swept through the van, followed by an oppressive silence. Alyson's throat tightened, her eyes stinging as she blinked back tears. Maggie, who had risked everything to help them, was gone.

"What do we do now?" Eddie asked, his voice small and frightened.

Her dad turned in his seat to address those in the back. "We need to decide what to do with her body. And quickly."

Her mom spoke up, her voice trembling. "We need to get her home. It's the least we can do after everything she did for us."

"Do we even know where her home is?" Mr. Verley asked. "Or who to contact?"

"She wouldn't say," Mrs. Samms reminded them.

Alyson glanced at the glove compartment. "Is there any registration for the van? Or did Maggie have a purse with ID?"

Her dad shook his head as he opened the glove box. "A couple of maps, but not much else. I didn't see a purse, did anyone?"

"I found a bag of clothes," her mom said, moving around the back. "Let me check."

"She wouldn't have carried anything that could identify her, not with the work she was doing," Mr. Verley said.

After a couple of minutes, her mom agreed. "There's a couple of days' worth of clothes, plus a few toiletries. Nothing else."

A heavy silence fell over the group as the reality of their situation sank in. They were in the middle of nowhere, with a dead body and no way to contact Maggie's loved ones and friends.

"We can't leave her on the side of the road," Mrs. Samms said firmly. "She deserves better than that."

Mr. Verley cleared his throat. "I saw a shovel handle sticking out from the luggage rack earlier. Maybe . . . maybe we should bury her."

"Bury her?" Eddie echoed, his eyes wide. "Like, here in the forest?"

Their dad nodded slowly. "It might be our only option. We're still in the national forest. There are logging roads all over. We could find a quiet spot . . ."

"Is it safe?" their mom asked, worry evident in her voice. "What if someone sees us?"

"It's pretty dark," Alyson observed, glancing at the sky through the windshield. The rain had stopped, but heavy clouds still hung low, hastening the arrival of night. "It'll be fully dark soon."

Mr. Verley leaned forward. "It's the right thing to do. Maggie risked everything to help us. We owe her this much."

After a moment of contemplation, Alyson's dad nodded. "All right. Let's find a logging road and give Maggie the best burial we can."

It was another five miles down the road before her dad pointed. "Look. Up ahead. Let's try that."

Alyson steered the van onto a narrow, unpaved road that branched off from the main highway. The forest pressed in close on both sides, branches scraping against the vehicle's sides. The headlights cut through the growing darkness, illuminating a path that seemed to lead deeper into the wilderness.

After about five minutes of slow, careful driving, they came upon a small clearing with a pile of brush along one side. Alyson's dad touched her arm. "This looks good. Let's stop here."

As they piled out of the van, the enormity of what they were about to do settled over them. Mr. Verley and her dad retrieved the shovel from the luggage rack and also found an axe, while her mom and Mrs. Samms carefully wrapped Maggie's body in a patchwork quilt they found in the back of the van.

The ground was hard and unyielding under their tools. Her dad and Mr. Verley took turns with the shovel, each strike making them pause briefly before going again. Eddie, eager to help, used a small hand trowel they'd found in the van to clear away loose soil.

"This is going to take forever," her mom murmured, wringing her hands anxiously.

Mrs. Samms stepped forward, taking the axe. "Let me try." She began to chip away at the rocky earth, creating cracks that made the digging easier.

"While we work on the grave, Beth, why don't you see if you can find something to cover the broken windows? Maybe clean up the glass?" her dad suggested.

"Okay. Alyson? Eddie? You can help."

Alyson started at the driver's door, hoping to get the window up. A hole in the door suggested her dad was right about the issue. On the inside, there was a bulge, but the bullet hadn't punctured through. "Going to need to cover this one too," she said, shaking her head.

After finding a roll of heavy-duty garbage bags and duct tape in a plastic crate in the back, Alyson and Eddie taped up the windows while their mom cleaned the glass and blood out of the van. Alyson and her mom discussed the trouble with the driver's side window. Black plastic wasn't suitable, especially since they'd had to use that on the destroyed back window, making the rearview mirror unusable.

"Do we have any clear plastic?" Alyson asked, rummaging in the van again.

"There're a few white grocery sacks, but those won't be see-through either. I guess the driver will just have to bundle up."

"Bundle up?" Alyson shook her head. "It's not like we brought winter clothes, Mom."

"Yes, Alyson. I'm aware. But everyone brought jackets and light gloves, right? A stocking cap? Even though it's summer, we prepared for chilly evenings. It'll be fine."

"If you say so."

"Do you have a better idea?" her mom snapped. "Because if you do, tell me what it is. We're out here in the middle of a forest, with a dead woman's van, and limited supplies." Her eyes welled with tears.

Alyson understood her mom's response was born out of the stress of Maggie's death along with them being shot at. "Sorry. You're right. It'll be fine."

Her mom reached out to touch her shoulder, her hand resting there for a moment. "Let's help Eddie finish up."

When they finished, they returned to the burial site, taking turns with the digging. The physical labor gave them something to focus on, a brief reprieve from their grief and fear. As the sky darkened completely, the van's headlights threw long shadows over their work. Dampness clung to their faces, their movements slow, each breath labored under the enormity of what they were doing.

Her dad stepped back from the hole. "I think . . . I think this will have to do," he said, his voice rough with exhaustion. The grave was shallow, but it was the best they could manage under the circumstances.

They moved Maggie with care, ensuring the quilt stayed wrapped around her as they settled her into her final resting place. Alyson fought back tears the entire time, but Mrs. Samms let hers fall freely, streaking down her face and soaking into the quilt or dropping on the ground below.

"We should say something," Eddie suggested as they gathered around the hole in the ground. "Like a funeral."

Their dad nodded, clearing his throat. "Maggie, we didn't know you long, but you risked everything to help us. Your courage and kindness in the face of danger showed us the best of humanity in these dark times. We promise to carry on your spirit of helping others."

"Thank you, Maggie," Mrs. Samms whispered.

A lump rose in Alyson's throat as tears pricked her eyes. This woman, a stranger a few hours ago, had given her life to help them reach safety. The truth of that sacrifice settled around her, sharp and undeniable, as she glanced at the others. Would Maggie's loss be the only one they'd face?

Once the grave was filled, they moved some of the heavier logs from the brush pile to cover it. "I wish we had stones, but this will have to do," her dad said. "Hopefully, it'll keep it from being disturbed by wildlife. Plus, we'll be able to find her again. When this is over, maybe we can get her home."

"Wherever that may be," Mrs. Samms added.

As they stood in silence, paying their final respects, a twig snapped in the forest behind them. Alyson whirled around, her heart racing. Had they been followed?

Her dad raised his gun and scanned the tree line. "Everyone back to the van," he whispered urgently. "Now! Alyson, you're driving."

They scrambled back into the vehicle. Alyson's hands shook as she turned the key in the ignition. The engine roared to life, seeming impossibly loud in the quiet forest.

"Go," her dad commanded, his eyes still fixed on the surrounding woods. "Back to the main road. Quickly."

Alyson maneuvered the van back down the logging road, her knuckles white on the steering wheel. Every shadow seemed to hide a potential threat, every movement of leaves a sign of pursuit.

As they turned back onto the highway, a collective sigh of relief went through the group. They had given Maggie a proper burial, and for now, at least, they seemed to have avoided detection.

"Keep heading east?" Alyson asked, pointing in front of her.

Her dad consulted a map he'd found in the glove compartment. "Yep. We need to keep heading east. Stay on this road. It'll take us to Missoula. That's where Maggie was supposed to hand us off to the next contact."

"But how will we know who to meet?" her mom asked. "Maggie was our only link."

They were silent for many minutes before Mrs. Samms spoke up. "We keep going. Use the fuel we have. Get more if we need it . . . somehow. We go to where we're supposed to meet Rich's family."

"Steal the van?" Eddie asked.

"We don't have any other option."

"She's right," Mr. Verley agreed. "The secretiveness of the network is important, and they knew the risks. They'll suspect what happened when we don't show up at the meeting place."

"Can we leave them a note?" Eddie asked. "So they know where to find Maggie?"

"Where would we leave that note?"

There was silence in the van as it rumbled on. Alyson rolled her shoulders, trying to push down the memories. Captain Davis, the ambush, Maggie's death, the impromptu burial . . . so much had happened in such a short time.

"I think the forest is ending," Alyson said, then pointed to the fuel gauge. "We need to put gas in. Maggie had planned to do it in the forest."

"You're right," her dad agreed. "And we should check the map to see what towns, if any, are between here and Missoula."

Alyson found another side road and drove up a short distance. Her dad and Mr. Verley took care of adding fuel from one of the cans while the others stretched their legs.

"Might as well put the second one in," Mr. Verley suggested. "The tank'll hold it. That will leave us a final five gallons."

"It won't be enough to get us where we're going." Her dad shook his head.

"We'll figure it out."

As they finished refueling, a rustling in the nearby bushes made everyone freeze. Steve's ears perked up, and a low growl rumbled in his throat.

"What was that?" Eddie whispered, his eyes wide with fear.

Their dad motioned for silence, his hand moving to his gun, as did Mr. Verley's. For a tense moment, they all held their breath, straining to hear any further noise.

A deer burst from the undergrowth, bounding across the road and disappearing into the forest on the other side. The group collectively exhaled, nervous laughter breaking the tension.

"We're all on edge," their mom said, placing a comforting hand on Eddie's shoulder. "But we need to stay focused. We've got a long way to go."

As they piled back into the van, Alyson couldn't shake the feeling that their troubles were far from over, and the next time it may not be a deer.

The van pulled back onto the highway, its headlights cutting through the darkness. Ahead lay Missoula, and hopefully, the next step in their journey to safety. But as the miles rolled by, Alyson knew that reaching their destination was only half the battle. The real challenge would be surviving long enough to get there.

Chapter 25

The van rolled down the road, the night's darkness pierced only by the occasional headlights of passing cars and the distant glow of nearby towns. Alyson's mom took the wheel, giving her a much-needed break. In the passenger seat, Mr. Verley kept a vigilant watch, his eyes sweeping their surroundings.

Alyson leaned back on the bench seat, her brain refusing to settle even as her body begged for sleep. The events of the past few days played on repeat in her head, a constant reminder of how fragile their safety was.

"I don't think it's much farther to Missoula," Mr. Verley said. "From there, we get on I-90 and head east. We'll be early to the meet-up spot with your family, but that'll hopefully be fine."

Alyson's dad leaned forward. "We'll try to call my family as soon as it's daylight. They're usually up early. If the phones are working, we can let them know about the change."

"We can go straight to their lodge, right?" her mom asked. "We have the van— "

"We'll see. I'm concerned about the fuel. It was smart of Jim to notice the stalled car on the road. Punching out the gas tank gave us enough to almost fill one of the empty fuel containers, but that's still not going to get us there."

"We'll do the same thing with each car we see," Mr. Verley said. "I mean, if it's obvious they've been abandoned and it seems safe to do so."

"I hate that we're destroying private property," her mom huffed. She lifted her gaze to the rearview mirror. "Uh-oh. We might have trouble."

Alyson raised her head to look out the back window but couldn't see anything with the black trash bags covering it.

"We've got company!" Mr. Verley called out, his voice tense.

The vehicle behind them rammed into their rear bumper. The van lurched forward, tires screeching as her mom fought to maintain control.

"Hold on!" she yelled as the mysterious attacker struck again.

Her dad was instantly alert, reaching for his gun. "Eddie, Alyson, stay down!"

The van swerved as her mom tried to evade their pursuer. Mrs. Samms clung to Steve, trying to keep the dog calm amid the unprovoked attack.

"Can you see who it is?" Alyson asked, her heart pounding.

Mr. Verley shifted to the rear of the van and peeled back a corner of the garbage bag to get a better view. "Could be a Star Bright, could be someone desperate. Doesn't matter. Either way, they're not giving up!"

Her mom's voice was shrill. "There's an exit coming up. Should I take it?"

"No," her dad decided. "Too risky. We don't know what's waiting for us off the highway. Keep going, try to outrun them."

"Outrun them? In this big lug?"

The chase continued for several tense minutes, the attacker relentlessly pursuing them. Somehow, her mom managed to keep them on the road, but their options were running out.

"Wish I could have brought a rifle," Mr. Verley said, his handgun at the ready. "Something long range to reach out and touch them. As it is, we don't have enough bullets to send any warning shots."

"If they get close enough, use the pistol," her dad said. "I'll do the same."

"Make every shot count," Mr. Verley added.

"There's another vehicle up ahead." Her mom's voice was surprisingly calm. "Might be working with the car behind us."

Alyson lifted her head to see what she was talking about. A large truck took up the right lane.

"Beth," Mr. Verley said urgently. "Speed up and cut in front of the truck. Use it as a barrier."

"What if they're together? If he rams us— "

"I don't think they are. We need to risk it."

"I'll try." As she drew level with the truck, she made her move, swerving sharply in front of it. The truck driver blared his horn and swerved into the lane she'd vacated. The maneuver worked. Their pursuer was cut off, forced to slam on their brakes to avoid hitting the truck.

"It worked!" Eddie exclaimed, peering out the side window.

"Turn off your headlights," Mr. Verley said. "Try not to press the brakes. We didn't lose them. All we did was slow them down. They could be back."

"I don't think so . . ." Eddie said. "The truck stopped. So did the car. I think . . . Oh no. The truck driver got out, and so did the guy in the car. They're fighting."

Alyson was watching the fight unfold as they took a bend, and the men left her view.

"What's happening?" Eddie asked.

"Don't worry about it," their dad said. "Beth, take the next exit. We need to assess the damage and make sure we aren't being followed."

Her mom nodded and guided the battered van off the interstate at the next opportunity. She drove for a few more minutes before pulling off onto a secluded side road.

As they came to a stop, the group let out a collective sigh of relief. The immediate danger had passed, but the encounter had left them all shaken.

"Is everyone okay?" her dad asked, looking around at his family and friends.

"Let's see how bad it is," Mr. Verley said as everyone piled out. They spent a few minutes walking around the van, shining flashlights on various areas.

"The bumper is bent, but other than that, everything looks fine," her dad said. "Notice any issues with the steering?"

"It was driving okay."

A sound drifted through the night air. A voice, singing softly.

"Not again," Eddie whispered, his eyes wide with fear. "Is it a Star Bright?"

They all fell silent, listening intently. The singing continued, the melody hauntingly familiar.

"Shh," Mrs. Samms said. "Listen carefully. That's not a star song. Don't the Star Brights only sing songs about stars?"

"Are you sure it's not 'Twinkle, Twinkle, Little Star'?" Eddie asked, his voice trembling.

Their dad shook his head, a look of surprise on his face. "No, it's 'Jesus Loves Me.' I recognize the tune."

The group exchanged confused glances. If it wasn't a Star Bright, who was singing out here in the middle of nowhere?

"We need to check it out," he decided. "Jim, you stay here and watch the van. Alyson, Eva, you're with me."

Alyson nodded, her hand instinctively going to the automatic knife in her pocket. Her dad checked his sidearm, ensuring it was ready if needed.

"Be careful," her mom called softly as they prepared to investigate.

The trio moved cautiously through the darkness, following the sound of the singing. The voice grew louder as they approached, clearly belonging to a child.

As they rounded a large boulder, they saw her. A little girl, no more than four or five years old, sat huddled on the other side. Her clothes were dirty, her face streaked with grime and tears. Despite her obvious distress, she continued to sing softly to herself.

"Dad?" Alyson whispered.

He shook his head as they exchanged looks of concern. What was a child doing out here alone?

"Hello there," Mrs. Samms called gently, not wanting to startle the girl, as Alyson's dad scanned the area, looking for anyone who might be with her.

The singing stopped abruptly as the child's head snapped up, her eyes wide with fear.

"It's okay," Alyson said, crouching down to appear less threatening. "We're not going to hurt you. Are you lost?"

The little girl shook her head, fresh tears welling up in her eyes.

"What's your name?" Mrs. Samms asked, her voice soft and reassuring.

"Zoe," the girl whispered.

"Hi, Zoe. I'm Alyson, and this is Eva. That's my dad. His name is Rich. Can you tell us how you got out here?"

Zoe's lower lip trembled as she spoke. "We were driving. Mommy and Daddy and me. Daddy started acting funny. He . . . he tried to hurt Mommy. She told me to run and hide. I heard screaming, and then it got quiet. No one came and got me."

Alyson's throat constricted as she looked at the little girl. She glanced at her father, seeing her own concern mirrored in his eyes. They couldn't leave Zoe here, but bringing her along could put them all at risk. They still didn't know how the disease spread. Even though Alyson hadn't turned into a Star Bright after having Ryan's blood on her, that didn't mean Zoe wasn't infected.

"How long have you been out here, Zoe?" Mrs. Samms asked gently as she touched the girl on the wrist. Alyson could tell she was not only offering comfort but also checking her pulse and watching the girl as she breathed.

She shrugged. "I'm hungry."

"Do you hurt anywhere? Your stomach or head or . . . anywhere?"

"I'm a little tired."

Alyson's dad nodded, clearly making a decision. "Let's take her back to the van. We'll figure this out."

"Can you walk?" Mrs. Samms asked, offering Zoe her hand. Alyson also reached out her hand, and they helped the girl to her feet. As they approached the van, Zoe clung tightly to Alyson, her eyes wide with fear and uncertainty.

When they returned, Alyson's mom looked from Alyson to the girl and back again. "A child? Out here?"

Zoe shrunk to Alyson's side. "It's okay. That's my mom. My little brother is next to her and our friend Mr. Verley. See the dog? His name is Steve."

Her mom immediately took charge, her maternal instincts kicking in. She wrapped a blanket around Zoe's shoulders and offered her some water and a breakfast bar from their supplies.

"Sip the water slowly," Mrs. Samms said. "And only the one bar for now. Let's see how your stomach does with that."

Alyson watched as her father pulled Mr. Verley aside, speaking in hushed tones. She couldn't hear what they were saying, but their expressions told her it wasn't good news.

"Alyson, can you stay with Zoe and Eddie in the van?" her dad asked. "Your mom and Eva will keep watch. Jim and I need to check something out."

Alyson wanted to protest, to demand answers, but she knew now wasn't the time. She nodded and climbed into the van with Zoe and Eddie.

Through the windows, Alyson watched as her father and Mr. Verley disappeared into the darkness. Zoe stretched out on the bench seat and rested her head on Alyson's lap, while Eddie fidgeted nervously beside them.

Finally, after about twenty minutes, they returned. Alyson strained to hear the conversation they were having with her mother and Mrs. Samms but caught only fragments.

". . . both deceased . . ."

". . . Washington State . . ."

". . . can't take her back there . . ."

Alyson's heart sank as she pieced together the tragic reality. Zoe was an orphan now, alone in a world that had become increasingly dangerous.

Alyson's dad approached the van, his face etched with worry. "Alyson, can you come out for a minute? Eddie, stay with Zoe, okay?"

Gently moving out from under Zoe so as not to wake her, she made sure to slip the blanket back over the young girl. Outside, her dad explained the situation in hushed tones. They had found Zoe's parents, both dead. The father had likely turned into a Star Bright. They couldn't leave Zoe behind, but taking her with them added another layer of risk to their already perilous journey.

"What do you think, Alyson?" her dad asked, surprising her with the question.

Alyson glanced back at the van, where Zoe slept peacefully, unaware of the tragedy that had befallen her. "We have to take her with us, Dad. We can't leave her here."

"Could be dangerous," Mr. Verley said, shaking his head. "Haven't heard much about kids her age turning into Star Brights, but that's not to say it won't happen."

Remembering the research Alyson had done, she agreed with him. In fact, she'd seen zero reports of anyone as young as Zoe becoming a Star Bright. She did recall several around her brother's age, but the bulk of the infected were between the ages of seventeen and thirty-five. This age range had been something the scientists had mentioned as odd.

Her dad nodded, his eyes showing both pride and concern. "That's what we decided too. It's the right thing to do."

"Rich, we should probably . . ." Mr. Verley trailed off, glancing at Alyson.

"Agreed. Alyson, we need to return to Zoe's parents' car. Can you stay here with your mom and keep an eye on things?"

She nodded, understanding the unspoken message. They needed to siphon fuel and gather whatever supplies they could find. It seemed wrong, but she knew it was necessary for their survival.

With their newly acquired supplies and the van refueled, they prepared to move on. Alyson settled into her seat and glanced at Zoe, who remained asleep beside her. She couldn't stop wondering what other challenges waited for them on the road ahead. They had saved a little girl, but at what cost to their own safety?

If Zoe began to turn, they would have to subdue her. Somehow. Staying vigilant and ready to act at the first sign of danger was their only option. The thought of what might be required if Zoe became a Star Bright made Alyson's stomach twist.

With her mom behind the wheel, the van pulled back onto the highway, headlights cutting through the predawn darkness. As they drove, Alyson sent up another silent prayer—for Zoe, for their journey, and for the strength to face whatever came next. This praying thing was becoming a habit.

Chapter 26

Alyson drifted in and out of a restless sleep, her body swaying gently with the motion of the van. The events of the past couple of days had left her exhausted, but true rest remained elusive.

How long had they been traveling? Time seemed to blend together. They'd left their home in Astoria after dark on July 1st. What was today? She was too tired to try and figure it out. Closing her eyes, she drifted off into a light sleep. She was vaguely aware of the soft breathing of those around her, Eddie and Zoe curled up nearby, her parents in the front seats while Mr. Verley and Mrs. Samms used the other bench seat in the back. Steve was sleeping on the floor.

The sudden deceleration of the van roused her fully. Alyson blinked, disoriented, as sunshine streamed in the windshield.

"Rich," her mom said, her voice tight with fatigue, "I need to swap out. I'm getting too sleepy to drive safely."

Her dad nodded. "Remember last summer when we drove through here? There's a truck stop ahead in Columbus where we can pull off. From there, we'll take the back roads. It's shorter and, hopefully, quiet through the small towns."

As the van exited the interstate, Alyson took in their surroundings. They had stopped here last year on their much-too-long drive from Astoria to her grandparents' lodge. The truck stop had been busy, completely unlike today.

There were a few cars parked off to the side and several semitrucks in a lot behind the gas station. One of the doors of the building was busted out. A sign hung on the other stating the place was closed, for all the good that did.

"It's been looted," Alyson said.

"Stay alert," her dad warned as they exited the van. "It may seem empty, but that doesn't mean it is."

Alyson nodded, her hand instinctively going to the knife in her pocket. She scanned the area, feeling the hair rise on the back of her neck. Were they being watched? They'd seen people walking along the interstate earlier, but this area was clear and quiet.

"I'll check the store," Mr. Verley offered, his hand resting on his holstered gun. "There might be some supplies left."

Her dad nodded. "Take Eva with you. Beth and I will keep watch out here with the kids."

"Will you keep Steve? Let him relieve himself?"

"Sure, no problem."

As Mr. Verley and Mrs. Samms cautiously approached the store, Alyson turned her attention to Zoe. The little girl stood close to her, wide eyes taking in their surroundings.

"Are you okay, Zoe?" Alyson asked softly.

Zoe nodded and pointed to the golden arches sign across the street. "I'm hungry," she whispered.

Eddie, overhearing, chimed in. "Man, I wish that was open. I'd give anything for a burger and fries right now."

"I want a Happy Meal," Zoe murmured, her voice barely audible.

Alyson's chest ached at the small, innocent wish. It was such a simple, ordinary request, children craving fast food, but in their harsh new reality, it didn't exist. She knelt next to Zoe and met the little girl's eyes. "I'm sorry we can't go to the restaurant, but we have some granola bars and dried fruit. Would you like some of that?"

Zoe nodded and Alyson rummaged through their supplies to find the food. As she handed it to Zoe, the little girl began to hum softly. Alyson tensed for a moment before recognizing the familiar tune of "Jesus Loves Me." The song that had led them to Zoe in the first place now served as a poignant reminder of the child's innocence in the face of unimaginable loss.

Steve took care of his business while standing near her parents. He tensed before wagging his tail; his ears flopped slightly as he watched Mr. Verley and Mrs. Samms return from the store.

"Not much left," Mr. Verley reported. "Looks like it's been picked clean. But we did find some maps, a can of baked beans, and a can of spaghetti." He gave an exaggerated shudder, which caused Eddie and Zoe to laugh.

Alyson's dad nodded, accepting the meager finds. "Every little bit helps. Were the restrooms functional?"

"Close enough," Mr. Verley said, while Mrs. Samms made a face and added, "They're disgusting."

"Let's use them anyway. Jim, can you and Eva watch over the van, and I'll take my family and Zoe inside? We'll spend a few minutes here before getting back on the road."

"I'll take a turn driving," Mrs. Samms offered.

While the family walked toward the truck stop, Alyson held Zoe's hand, keeping a watchful eye on their surroundings. As Mrs. Samms said, the restrooms were disgusting. One of the toilets had overflowed. Her dad insisted they all use the women's, much to Eddie's dismay, while he stood guard outside. "What about you?" her mom asked.

"It's easy for me. I'll take care of things before we start driving again."

Her mom gave him a smile and shook her head when a voice drifted in from the hallway. "Oh! I'm so happy to see you!" A woman stepped into view, blocking the bathroom doorway. "There hasn't been anyone around. It's crazy what's happening."

Alyson's father instantly tensed, his hand moving to his sidearm. Alyson pulled Zoe behind her, pressing back against the bathroom wall.

Movement in the mirror caught her attention—a man appeared behind the woman, his reflection showing that terrible, twisted smile she'd seen on Ryan's face before everything went wrong. The sound of his humming raised the hair on her neck.

"Twinkle, twinkle, little star . . ." The woman's friendly expression contorted as she joined the melody, her body swaying slightly, as her eyes glazed over. In the confined space of the bathroom, the sound seemed to bounce off the tiles, surrounding them.

The woman lunged at Alyson's mom, slamming her against the paper towel dispenser. Her dad fumbled to draw his weapon in the tight space, the shot going wide and splintering tile as the man rushed forward, still humming that horrible tune.

"Eddie, get Zoe out!" Alyson shouted. "Go, go!"

"But what about Mom?"

"I'll help her. Just go!"

As Eddie pulled Zoe toward the exit, Alyson charged forward. The woman had her mom pinned, fingers clawing at her throat. Alyson grabbed a fistful of the attacker's greasy hair and yanked hard, forcing her head back. The woman's singing turned to a snarl as she released her mom and spun toward Alyson, her movements surprisingly quick.

Behind them, her father grappled with the man, their bodies slamming against the bathroom stalls. The man's fingers wrapped around her dad's wrist, trying to wrench the gun away. The horrible melody never stopped, even as her dad drove his knee up into the man's stomach.

Alyson ducked under a wild swing from the woman and slammed her shoulder into her midsection, pushing her back. Her mom recovered and grabbed the woman's arm, twisting it behind her back. The woman threw her head back and caught her mom in the face, opening the cut further.

"The gun!" her dad shouted as he lost his grip on the weapon. It skittered across the wet floor, spinning under the sink. The man's humming grew louder as he slammed her dad against the mirror, cracking the glass. He jabbed his elbow back, catching the man in the throat, but he couldn't break free from his grip.

Alyson felt the woman's nails rake across her arm as her mom struggled to maintain her hold. The three of them stumbled, slipping on the wet floor. Alyson's back hit the edge of a sink and knocked the wind from her lungs. The woman's face was inches from hers, eyes wild and empty as she sang about twinkling stars.

The crack of the bathroom door being kicked open made everyone jump. Mr. Verley burst in with Mrs. Samms right behind him. "Star Brights!" Mr. Verley shouted, immediately grabbing the humming man and slamming him into the wall.

Mrs. Samms wielded a flashlight like a club, striking the woman who had Alyson pinned. The impact gave her enough space to break free. Her mom, having recovered slightly from the initial attack, hit the woman hard with a fist to the face.

In the cramped confines of the bathroom, the fight was brutal and desperate. Stall doors banged, mirrors cracked, and the singing grew more frenzied until Mr. Verley managed to knock the man unconscious with the butt of his gun. The woman, seeing her companion fall, broke away and fled through the hallway, her haunting melody fading into silence.

"Everyone okay?" her dad asked, helping her mom steady herself against the sink. She touched the cut on her face and nodded, though her hands were shaking.

Mr. Verley picked up her dad's sidearm and handed it to him.

"This bathroom, everyone in here— " Her dad looked at the door. "Where's Eddie?"

"The kids are okay, locked in the van with Steve," Mr. Verley said.

"We need to go," Mrs. Samms urged, checking the hallway. "That singing could draw more of them."

"And she could come back," Mr. Verley added.

The group hurried out of the building, watching over their shoulders for more Star Brights. Eddie was waiting for them and slid the side door open. "I locked everything," he said. "Steve's watching Zoe."

Alyson glanced at the bench seat where Zoe sat with her knees pulled up, the dog on the floor next to her, his gaze fixed on the girl. Her hands were still shaking from the fight, and the spot on her back where she'd hit the sink was starting to throb.

It took only a minute to get everyone in the van and pull out on the road, with Mrs. Samms behind the wheel.

"How are we doing on fuel?" Mr. Verley asked, his voice surprisingly calm, like they hadn't just fought for their lives.

"We're down to our last five gallons," her dad replied, his voice still unsteady, whether from the fight, fear, or both, Alyson didn't know.

"I would've siphoned from the cars, but it's too exposed. We'll have to hope we come across a stalled vehicle soon," Mr. Verley said. "What's our next move, boss?"

"Head on into town."

Mrs. Samm looked in the rearview mirror. "Get the first aid kit out. You need to clean those wounds."

"Did you get her blood on you?" Eddie asked, looking at his mom and then shifting his gaze toward Alyson.

"No," their mom replied. "It's just a scratch from the . . . the . . ."

"Brawl?" Allyson suggested, wincing as she shifted in her seat, her back protesting the movement.

Her mom laughed. An actual laugh. "I guess so. Never much thought of myself as a brawler, but I guess that's what it was." She touched the cut on her face gingerly. "Although I have to say, I prefer my spreadsheets and Zoom meetings to hand-to-hand combat."

"Are you okay?" her dad asked, taking the first aid kit. "Hold still and I'll clean that cut on your face." His hands were steady now as he opened the first aid kit, but Alyson could see the worry in his eyes as he examined her mom's wound.

Zoe hadn't said a word since they got back to the van, but she'd uncurled slightly from her tight ball, one hand resting on Steve's head. The dog hadn't moved from his protective position beside her, but his tail thumped softly against the floor when he caught Alyson looking at him.

Chapter 27

The part of Columbus they drove through was as quiet as the truck stop had been when they first arrived. Even so, Alyson couldn't shake the feeling of being watched. Were there Star Brights just waiting to pounce? Just like the woman and man, waiting until their guard was down?

There weren't houses on their route but rather businesses. Were people holed up inside, looking out the windows while waiting for the strange van to pass through? They made a right near a bar and grill, followed by a left about a block later.

"Okay, now we cross the river," her dad said, glancing up after putting a small bandage on her mom's face.

"What river is this, Dad?" Eddie asked. "The one by Grandpa and Grandma's place?"

"This is the Yellowstone River. They live off the Shoshone."

"Did you call them?"

"I couldn't get through. I'll try again shortly. The road is easy to miss . . . there it is. Take a left here, Eva. Stay on this road until it ends."

After asking Alyson if she needed anything, her dad pulled out his cell phone once again, trying in vain to reach their family in Wyoming. The lack of connection was a stark reminder of how isolated they truly were.

"Will it be a problem if you can't reach them?"

A shadow crossed over her dad's face before he gave a slight shrug. "Hopefully not."

"We'll need to wait, right?" her mom asked. "You told them what time to meet us based on the information you had? The time the contact gave you, which included spending a few hours in Missoula?"

"Mm-hmm," her dad replied while moving his finger across the phone screen. "I'm trying to send a text. To my mom's phone and my brother's."

The van wound its way along the country roads between Columbus and Joliet, the landscape a patchwork of rolling hills and open fields. Despite the beauty of the Montana countryside, Alyson found herself constantly scanning for threats. Every building, every curve in the road could hide danger.

After having several snacks and some water, Zoe had fallen asleep, her head resting on Alyson's lap. Eddie was engrossed in a tattered magazine they'd found. The adults spoke in hushed tones, discussing their route and the dwindling supplies.

Alyson's mind wandered to the future. *What will happen when we reach their place? Will it truly be the safe haven we hoped for?*

She knew there were others there, living with them, along with Uncle Brian. Had her cousins arrived? Her dad hadn't said anything about them when he told her the plans they had for meeting up. And what about Zoe? The little girl had latched onto Alyson, seeming to view her as a protector. She didn't seem sick, but would the people at the lodge assume she was?

Mr. Verley's voice cut through her thoughts. "Eva, slow down. There's a car up ahead, pulled off to the side."

Alyson's heart rate quickened as Mrs. Samms eased off the gas. The car in question was a sedan, its blue paint dulled by a layer of dust. It showed no signs of life.

"I'm going to check it out," Mr. Verley said, his hand already on the door handle. "We need that fuel."

Alyson's dad nodded, his expression tight. "Be careful. I'll cover you." He opened the side door and stepped out with Mr. Verley.

Alyson watched, her breath caught in her throat, as he approached the abandoned vehicle. Every second seemed to stretch into eternity as he lay on the pavement and worked to remove the precious fuel.

As he was finishing up, a sharp crack split the air. Alyson instinctively ducked as she realized what was happening. Someone was shooting at them.

"Jim!" her dad yelled, moving toward the front of the van and returning fire. "Get back to the van!"

Chaos erupted as bullets pinged off the van's metal frame. Alyson threw herself over Zoe and Eddie, shielding them with her body. The sound of shattering glass told her another window had been shot out.

"Go, go, go!" her dad shouted as both he and Mr. Verley dove back into the van, the fuel can clutched tightly in his hands.

Mrs. Samms slammed her foot on the accelerator, and the van lurched forward. Alyson's heart pounded in her ears as they sped away, the sound of gunfire gradually fading behind them.

As the immediate danger passed, Alyson sat up and checked on Zoe and Eddie. Both were pale and shaken but unharmed. She looked around the van, taking stock. Everyone seemed to be okay, but the new bullet holes and shattered window were stark reminders of how close they'd come to disaster.

"Is everyone all right?" her mom asked, her voice trembling as she glanced around, checking on them all.

A chorus of shaky affirmatives answered her. Jim lifted the fuel can high, his face hard with resolve. "At least we got what we came for."

Her dad was on high alert, his eyes constantly scanning their surroundings as Mrs. Samms navigated the winding road. "Keep going. We're not far from Joliet."

Alyson held Zoe close as the little girl whimpered softly. "It's okay," she whispered, stroking Zoe's hair. "We're safe now."

But even as she said the words, she knew they weren't true. Safety was a luxury they could no longer afford. Every moment, every mile was a risk.

The men got into their seats, and the van fell into an uneasy silence as they continued down the road. The stink of gas filled the air and Mr. Verley murmured how it wasn't safe to have it inside with them, but they needed to keep going. They shouldn't stop.

Alyson replayed the attack over and over. Who had shot at them? Were they Star Brights or desperate people trying to survive? And how many more threats would they face before reaching her grandparents' lodge?

"Um, Rich?" Mrs. Samms said from behind the wheel, her voice hesitant.

"Yes?"

"How far did you say it is to Joliet?"

"I'm not sure. Maybe ten miles. Why?"

"Something isn't feeling right. I think maybe they hit one of the tires."

Mr. Verley muttered something unsavory. "There's a road up there. I can't tell if it's a driveway or a side road. Better pull off so we can check it."

As she pulled off the road, Alyson surveyed the area. There was a dilapidated barn up ahead but no house.

"What do you think?" her dad asked.

"I think it's abandoned," Mr. Verley responded. "Hope so, anyway. Keep going, Eva. Pull behind it. Get out of sight, at least."

She guided the van behind the weathered structure, the tires crunching on gravel and kicking up dust. As the engine died, the silence seemed to press in on them.

Her dad turned to face the group. "Let's check the tire and figure out our fuel. How much did you get, Jim?"

"About three gallons. It's not much, but it'll help."

"All right. Alyson, can you check our food and water? Beth, see what you can do about patching that broken window. Use the garbage bags again."

"Pretty soon, we're going to have more bags than windows."

"Jim, let's take a quick walk around. Make sure we're alone. Everyone stay alert and be ready to move if we have to."

Alyson rummaged through their supplies, checking for any leaks or damage. Her mom opened a garbage bag and started taping it where the window had been, muttering under her breath about the makeshift repairs. Eddie used the little broom to sweep up the glass.

Her dad and Mr. Verley walked the perimeter of the barn, scanning for any signs of recent activity. They returned with tight smiles, her dad giving them all a thumbs up.

"Looks clear," Mr. Verley said, squatting down to inspect the tire. "We've got a slow leak here. Better put the spare on."

"Yep," her dad replied, glancing around. "We'll need to get moving."

"I'll change it," Mr. Verley said. "You keep watch. Everyone out, but don't go far. Even though the place seems empty, we've been fooled before. Eddie, can you give me a hand?"

With Eddie's assistance, Mr. Verley worked quickly, setting up the jack before taking off the old tire and putting on the spare.

"How's everything look?" her dad asked as he scanned the area.

"Food and water are good for now," Alyson reported.

"Window's patched, for what it's worth," her mom added.

"That about does it." Mr. Verley wiped his hands on his pants. "Thanks for your help, Eddie. You made it easier."

Eddie beamed as he gave a dip of his chin.

"All right," Alyson's dad said. "Everyone in. Let's get moving."

As Mrs. Samms started the engine and pulled back onto the road, the group settled into a tense silence.

"Alyson?" Zoe's small voice drew her attention. "Are the bad people going to keep finding us?"

Her heart clenched at the fear in the little girl's eyes. She pulled her close and lifted Zoe's chin with her finger so she could meet her gaze. "We're doing everything we can to stay safe. And we have a lot of brave, smart people looking out for us."

Zoe nodded solemnly. She surprised Alyson by wrapping her arms around her in a tight hug. "I'm glad you found me," she whispered.

Tears pricked at Alyson's eyes as she returned the embrace. "Me too, Zoe. Me too."

Chapter 28

The van rolled through Joliet. Highway 212 cut through the tiny town with a small park on one side and businesses on the other. The town's only gas station stood open, a few people milling about outside, but a large hand-painted sign proclaimed, "No gas." As they passed, a little girl on the sidewalk waved enthusiastically at the van.

"Look," Eddie said, pointing. "People!"

Zoe jumped up from the bench seat, her eyes wide.

But their moment of normalcy was short-lived. The girl's mother quickly appeared, grabbing her daughter's arm and pulling her behind the building, out of sight.

"So much for a warm welcome," Mr. Verley muttered from the passenger seat.

A pang of sadness struck Alyson as she watched the mother's reaction. It was a stark reminder of how much the world had changed. Trust, once given freely, was now a rare commodity.

"I wonder what it's like here," she mused aloud. "Do you think they've had trouble with Star Brights?"

Her dad shook his head. "Hard to say. But that kind of caution . . . it's not a good sign."

"Isn't there trouble everywhere?" Eddie asked. "You were doing research on the internet to find out where there were reports on Star Brights."

Shrugging, Alyson said, "I didn't check each and every town in the United States. I went state by state, and yes, every state had reports, even Alaska and Hawaii. After that, I went country by country. I didn't finish before . . . well, before it became overwhelming. Pretty much, there were reports from everywhere. Fewer, though, in low-income countries."

"Is that so?" Mr. Verley turned in his seat to look at Alyson. "The third-world countries aren't affected?"

Alyson gave him a prim smile. "They are, but not to the same degree as high-income countries. And, Mr. Verley, you should know that's considered an antiquated term and many find it to be offensive."

He crinkled his brow. "What is?"

"Third world," Mrs. Samms whispered.

"Really? Huh. So . . . I'm supposed to classify countries by how much money they make? Okay, fine. Do poorer countries have fewer Star Brights? Is that what you're saying?"

As they left the town of Joliet behind, Alyson gave a nod. "Much less. At first, I thought it was because of their location. Many of the lowest incidents are in Africa."

"Are you sure?" Mrs. Samms glanced in the mirror to meet Alyson's gaze. "That's interesting since many epidemics originate in Africa."

"I thought they started in Asia," Mr. Verley said.

"There too," Mrs. Samms replied with a nod while her eyes stayed on the road as she navigated a sharp bend. "Zoonotic diseases, which are infections that spread between animals and people, are especially prevalent in Africa. Large animals are killed and eaten, and small animals and rodents run rampant, so disease spreads."

Alyson's mom leaned forward in her seat. "But the most recent pandemic didn't originate in Africa, it started— "

"Asia is another hot spot for epidemics and pandemics," Mrs. Samms continued. "I was already retired but kept up on the research. There were some interesting studies during the pandemic on not only zoonotic diseases but urbanization and the continued use of live markets."

"That's how it started, right?" Eddie asked. "From someone eating bat soup?"

"Eddie!" their mom said, shaking her head. "That is not true. That's only a rumor."

"Right," Mr. Verley said. "It was started in a lab and was released on purpose."

Alyson's dad laughed. "Good one, Jim."

Mr. Verley turned to look at those in the back of the van. His face was serious. "I'm not joking. It was— "

"Jim." Mrs. Samms used the same voice with him that Alyson's mom used, the voice mothers use when their child says something embarrassing or inappropriate.

Turning back to face forward, Mr. Verley shook his head and muttered something Alyson couldn't quite catch. She pursed her lips. She had no idea he was one of those conspiracy theorists like Grandpa Dick. From the look her parents shared, they didn't know either. At least Mrs. Samms seemed normal, even slightly embarrassed that he could think such a thing.

"Looks like another town is coming up." Mrs. Samms lifted her chin to point.

"Yes, sorry," Alyson's dad said. "This is where we turn. Stay in the right lane, and you'll take a right here."

As she slowed for the turn, Alyson's eyes drifted toward the building on the left.

"What're they doing?" Eddie asked, his nose pressed against the only remaining back window on the driver's side.

Their mom stood and leaned on the bench seat the children were sharing so she could also look out. "Looks like a farmers' market or something."

"What town is this?" Eddie asked.

"Rockvale," their mom replied, pointing to a sign.

"Should we stop?" Mrs. Samms was already slowing the van.

"No, no." Mr. Verley shook his head. "Too risky."

"Agreed," her dad said. "Let's keep going. There're a few more little towns we need to pass through. Maybe we'll see something there that we will want to stop and check out."

Though he said the words, Alyson knew he had no intention of stopping. With her mom settled back in her seat, they crossed over a bridge with a fast-moving creek below them. When they visited the summer before, they'd gone on an all-day drive to visit some of the areas outside of Yellowstone and Cody.

Her grandparents owned an old school bus. Not the large kind, but the smaller, short-bus version. They used it for picking people up at the airport in Cody or taking them on tours. They even had a loudspeaker system set up so Grandma Ruth could play tour guide while Grandpa Dick or Uncle Brian drove. She'd tell passengers about the places they were passing, which felt so different from Oregon's lush, green landscape.

While there were a few green patches among the Wyoming countryside, most of the landscape was an unappealing brown. Grandma Ruth had said that if they had visited earlier in the spring, things might have been greener, but it was essentially high desert.

The streams, creeks, and rivers supported vegetation that thrived near the water, but farther out, the land was barren. Grasses and wildflowers grew in narrow ribbons of green, contrasting sharply with the surrounding dry earth. Trees like cottonwoods and willows clustered along the banks, their roots reaching into the cool water. The water's edge was a refuge for wildlife, with birds flitting about and small animals coming to drink.

Now, in early July, it looked much the same as it had last August. Maybe a little greener but not enough to make much of a difference.

Alyson's grandparents lived near the North Fork of the Shoshone. The fifty-two-mile stretch of the North Fork of Shoshone River between Cody and the east entrance to Yellowstone was referred to locally as the North Fork. Grandma Ruth had told them it was considered the most scenic fifty-two miles in America. Alyson agreed it had a unique beauty to it, but she didn't find it to be nearly as pretty as Astoria and the Pacific Northwest. Would she ever get used to the arid land?

"So, if Africa is usually a place where diseases start because of the rodents," Eddie asked, bringing up their previous conversation, "why aren't there more Star Brights there?"

"Because it's not a— " their mom started, but paused. "I'm sorry, Eva, what was the term you used?"

"Zoonotic or zoonoses."

"But if it's not caused by animals, what caused it?"

"Some diseases begin as a zoonosis but later mutate into human-only strains. Other zoonoses can cause recurring disease outbreaks, such as Ebola virus disease and salmonellosis. There're also bacteria to consider. That was something they looked at with these Star Brights."

"Why'd they stop talking about the cause? Are they still trying to make a vaccine?"

Mrs. Samms looked in the rearview mirror and met Alyson's gaze before shifting slightly to take in Eddie's. "I don't know. Things did become suspiciously quiet as far as what it is and how to stop it. It's . . . concerning."

The van grew silent as they approached the next small town, Fromberg. As with the previous two towns, Alyson noticed signs of a community trying to maintain some semblance of normalcy. In what looked like a park, a similar market to the one in Rockvale was set up. A man held up a string of fish.

"Think he got those out of the river?" Eddie motioned behind them. The road they were on skirted the edge of a river about half a mile back.

"Probably so," their dad agreed. "That's the Clark's Fork of the Yellowstone. I noticed it when I was looking at the map. It joins up with the Yellowstone River, which we crossed back in Columbus, somewhere around Billings, Montana."

"Did they name that after Lewis and Clark?" Mr. Verley asked.

"I think so. That sounds right, anyway."

"At least they're organizing," Alyson's mom observed. "That's something."

Her dad checked his phone again, frustration evident on his face. "My phone shows I should have service here, but I still can't get through to my parents. No response to emails or messages either."

"Don't worry," her mom said, reaching over to squeeze his shoulder. "We're on the home stretch now. It's only about thirty miles to the state line from here, right?"

"A little less probably. Maybe twenty-five?"

Alyson caught a flash of unease in his eyes. She pushed the thought aside, focusing instead on the landscape. They'd made it through Fromberg, and Mrs. Samms was picking up speed. They were so close now. She could almost taste the relief of reaching safety.

Soon, the van reached the town of Bridger, where there was once again evidence of the people working together. Why were these towns so different from the town of Columbus? Did it have to do with Columbus being on Interstate 90 and these towns being more isolated? She wasn't sure but suspected that it had something to do with it.

Each mile brought them closer to their goal, and Alyson's excitement grew. Zoe, who had been asleep for most of the journey, pulled on her sleeve. "Is this where your grandma and grandpa live?"

Alyson smiled down at her. "Not quite yet, but we're getting close. They live in a beautiful place with mountains and near a river. They have horses, cows, and even chickens. Lots of chickens. You'll love it there."

"Will we be safe?"

The question tugged at Alyson's heart as she pulled the little girl closer.

As they exited Bridger and turned onto Highway 72, Alyson couldn't contain herself any longer. "How far is it from here, Dad?"

He forced a smile. "Oh, I don't know for sure. Less than twenty miles, maybe? We'll pick up the river again."

"We'll be at the state line soon," her mom said, her voice filled with relief. "At the very least, we can wait until they show up at the appointed time."

Mr. Verley turned to look at the passengers in the back. Alyson noticed that he and her father exchanged a look before Mr. Verley quickly faced forward. His gaze was fixed on the window, while her dad appeared to be absorbed in his shoes. The knot of unease in her stomach, which had loosened as they neared their destination, tightened again.

"What?" Alyson asked, her voice sharper than she intended. "Dad? What is it?"

He sighed heavily and ran a hand through his hair. "Well, you see, I wasn't actually able to confirm the pickup with my parents."

The van fell silent as the implications of his words sank in.

"What do you mean?" her mom asked, her voice dangerously calm.

"I mean, I messaged and emailed. I've tried calling. I'm not certain they got the info."

Her mom spoke slowly, each word deliberate. "You mean you don't know if they know they're supposed to pick us up? And you're telling us this just now?"

"You lied— " Alyson began, but her dad cut her off.

"Not exactly lied. I just . . . I thought it would work out. I didn't want to worry everyone more than necessary."

Her mom's face was a mask of anger and disbelief. "I can't believe this, Rich. After everything we've been through, you kept this from us? We've risked our lives. We've . . ." She trailed off, glancing at Zoe, clearly not wanting to upset the child.

Mr. Verley tried to intervene. "It seemed smart at the time. We couldn't risk staying in Astoria, and we needed a destination. Something to work toward."

"A destination?" her mom's voice rose. "We've risked our lives for a destination that might not even be waiting for us?"

Eddie, who had been uncharacteristically quiet, spoke up, "But Grandma and Grandpa are still there, right?

They're at their lodge? Even if they don't know we're coming?"

"Yes, as far as I know. But remember, communication has been spotty everywhere. We don't know exactly what the situation is there."

Mrs. Samms, who had been focused on driving, joined the conversation. "Well, I guess we drive the rest of the way. Find more fuel and make it work. We've come this far. We can't turn back now."

Alyson stared out the window as the next twenty miles passed in uncomfortable silence. After they passed through the small town of Belfry—that one not showing the hustle and bustle of the other towns, but Alyson suspected that may be because the highway skirted the town instead of going smack dab down the middle of it—they crested a hill and were once again following the river.

It was a pretty area with a mixture of dry plains and stunning scenery. To the west, majestic mountains rose up, their snowy peaks and forested slopes creating a dramatic backdrop. If she wasn't so angry and disappointed with her dad, she'd ask him the name of the mountains. She knew her grandparents had mentioned them last year, but she couldn't recall the name.

Why did he lie? Did he think things would magically work out? Maybe they would and her grandparents would be there waiting for them. If not, they did have the van, and they could keep driving, but that would mean finding more fuel. They'd been watching since the last time they got gas, and almost got themselves killed, but there hadn't been any cars on this stretch of quiet highway.

"We're almost to the state line," her dad said. "I can make out the sign in the distance."

Alyson squinted, her heart beating hard. She could see the sign too. Even though she couldn't read it, she knew it was welcoming them to Wyoming. Was that . . . yes! There was a car parked in the pullout. They'd gotten the messages. Her grandparents were waiting for them!

Chapter 29

"They're here!" Eddie practically squealed. Even Zoe was bouncing in her seat with a wide smile. Alyson glanced at her parents. Her mom was also smiling, while her dad was leaning forward to look out the front window.

"Dad?" Alyson asked.

"Give me a minute. Eva, pull into the parking area on the Montana side."

Mrs. Samms pulled over near the "Welcome to Wyoming" sign. All eyes were on the double-cab truck across the highway. Alyson expected the door to open and her Grandpa Dick to step out, but nothing happened. The truck didn't appear to be running. Was it even occupied?

"Is it them?" Mr. Verley asked, staring intently at the truck. "Is that your family?"

"I don't think so." Alyson's dad sighed. "I'm going to check it out. Eva, keep the engine running. Get out of here if things go bad."

Her mom reached for his hand. "Be careful."

He gave a stoic nod as he slid open the door of the van. Her mom moved to the bench with the children, all of them staring out the window, watching as he crossed the road. He carefully approached the truck, keeping his distance. Alyson heard him call out, asking if anyone was inside.

After a moment, he walked around the vehicle, finally stopping on the passenger side. She couldn't tell for sure what he was doing, but seconds later, the front passenger door opened. After a few minutes, the door closed, and her dad popped back into view. He jogged across the road.

When he opened the van door, Eddie said, "It's not them, is it?"

"No. Not my parents. The truck is abandoned. It's been cleaned out, but the registration was still inside. Showed they were from Meeteetse, a town in Park County but farther south."

"So, your folks didn't get the message." Her mom's voice was hollow.

"I guess not. I'll try again." He pulled out his phone as Mrs. Samms shut off the engine.

After several minutes of her dad messing with the phone, he shook his head. "Sorry."

Zoe spoke up. "What happens now?"

It was the question on everyone's mind, but no one seemed to have an answer.

Alyson looked at her father, a mixture of anger and fear churning in her gut. "Dad, what are we going to do?"

He ran a hand through his hair, the weight of their situation evident in every line on his face. "We'll keep going."

Alyson couldn't help but wonder if they'd made a terrible mistake. They'd left behind everything they knew and faced countless dangers, all for the promise of safety that now seemed out of reach.

"Well," Mr. Verley said, breaking the tense silence. "Sitting here is leaving us exposed. Think that truck has any fuel in it?"

Alyson's mom turned to her dad, her anger now tempered with worry. "How far is it to your parents' place from here?"

He looked at the sky, his face filled with thought. "Around a hundred miles, give or take."

"I don't think we can make it, not on the fuel we have." Mrs. Samms motioned to the truck across the road. "You'd best check it. Even if we can get a gallon, it'll get us closer. I don't fancy the idea of walking, but . . ." She tapped her hands on the steering wheel.

Mr. Verley nodded and gathered up the items he'd previously used to punch a hole in the fuel tanks and drip out every bit of gas he could. Her dad went with him, standing guard while Mr. Verley did the deed.

The group in the van fell silent again, each lost in their own thoughts. The safety they'd been chasing for days seemed further away than ever.

Zoe tugged on Alyson's sleeve. "Are we going to be okay?" she whispered, her eyes wide with fear.

Alyson pulled the little girl close, wishing she had a better answer. "We're going to figure this out," she said, trying to inject confidence into her voice. "We've come this far. We're not giving up now. As Mrs. Samms said, we don't want to walk, but we can if we need to."

"I'm a good walker." Zoe smiled.

"I'm sure you are, but a hundred miles?" Alyson's mom said skeptically. "With an injured dog? Plus, your feet are going to get sore pretty quickly. I'm not sure it's realistic."

"Let's see how much fuel they can get," Mrs. Samms said, her voice steady and reassuring.

As her mom, Mrs. Samms, and Eddie continued the discussion, Alyson found her gaze drawn to the "Welcome to Wyoming" sign. She remembered how excited she'd been last summer when they'd stopped here for photos. That had been the beginning of an adventure.

Originally, she hadn't wanted to visit her grandparents, knowing the trouble that was likely to occur between her grandpa and her mom, but her dad had played up the visit and spoke of all the fun things they'd do. And, overall, it was fun.

Things were definitely different now. Now, it was as if they were standing on the edge of a cliff, with no clear path forward.

"So . . ." she began, hesitating as all eyes turned to her. "We drive as far as we can with the fuel we have. We've got nothing to lose, right? Maybe we'll find more abandoned cars to siphon from along the way."

Mrs. Samms nodded slowly. "It's about all we can do. We're better off moving than sitting still. Maybe we'll be surprised, and they'll get a decent amount of fuel from this truck. It looks like it probably has a big tank."

"And who knows," Eddie added, "maybe we'll run into someone who can help us."

Their mom let out a humorless laugh. "Because we've had such great luck with strangers so far?"

"We can't think like that," Mrs. Samms said firmly. "We have to believe there are still good people out there. Otherwise, we lose hope."

A few seconds later, Mrs. Samms sighed. "That didn't take long enough for them to have gotten much." She pointed at the men, who were now walking back.

"We didn't get more than a gallon," Mr. Verley said into the open window. "We'll put it in, plus what we have in the other gas can. That'll be it. We'll . . ." He shrugged before moving to the back of the van where the gas cap was.

The van swayed as Alyson's dad retrieved the gas can from the luggage rack. After a few minutes, both men returned to the van. The smell of gas on their hands was strong. Her mom handed them each a wet wipe without comment.

"How much gas did you put in?" Alyson asked.

"Maybe four gallons?" Mr. Verley replied, looking to Alyson's dad, who gave a nod and added, "Sounds about right."

"That'll help," Mrs. Samms said. "This thing probably gets, what? Fifteen miles per gallon or so? I'm sure there was at least a gallon remaining."

"Maybe somewhere around there," Mr. Verley agreed.

"Okay. Good. We keep our eyes open for other cars and maybe we'll get another gallon or two. What's the next town?"

"I don't think there's anything to speak of between here and Cody," Alyson's dad said.

Her mom shook her head. "There's a place up ahead, remember? We stopped for sodas. It was a little restaurant."

"It was a bar," Eddie corrected. "They served food, and it smelled good, but people were drinking too."

Alyson remembered the sign outside had advertised ornery bartenders and camping available. "It wasn't a town, though. A bar and campground along the river . . . in the middle of nowhere."

"Right." Her dad nodded. "Cody is the next real town. Maybe we'll find fuel there." He glanced around the van. "All right, then," he said, a hint of his old determination creeping back into his voice. "Let's go."

As Mrs. Samms started the engine, Alyson experienced a mix of emotions swirling inside her. Fear, anger, hope, and determination, all battled for dominance. Zoe's tight grip on her hand sparked a fresh sense of purpose in her. They had to make it, not only for themselves but for this little girl who had already lost so much. And for Eddie, still just a child himself.

They pulled back onto the road. They had reached their goal, crossed the state line they'd been racing toward for days. But now, as they drove into the unknown, Alyson realized that their journey was far from over.

In fact, it appeared to be only the beginning.

The road stretched out before them, a ribbon of uncertainty leading into the heart of Wyoming. As she glanced around at the barren landscape, Alyson sent up a silent prayer—for safety, for guidance, and for the strength to face whatever challenges lay ahead.

They were in Wyoming now. They had made it this far, against all odds. And somehow, someway, they would make it the rest of the way. Even if it had to be on foot.

They only traveled for about ten minutes when they started down a hill. Mr. Verley pointed and said, "Is that your bar in the middle of nowhere?"

"That's it," her dad agreed. "Looks busy."

Even from a distance, it was easy to see the parking lot was filled with cars. "Another farmers' market?" Alyson asked.

"Might be," Mr. Verley agreed.

Alyson's mom surprised everyone when she said, "I want to stop."

"No, Beth. It's too— "

"I want to stop." Her words were clipped. "When we stopped for sodas last year, the lady was very nice and told us how much she loved working there. How she'd moved to the area a few years before and everyone was like a big family."

"Things are different now."

"Maybe they are, but people are the same, right? Down deep, the good are still good."

"Not if they start singing about stars." Zoe's voice was small as she shook her head. "My daddy stopped being my daddy when he started singing."

Alyson wrapped her arm around the little girl as Zoe buried her face in her side. "Shh. Shh," she crooned while Zoe cried.

Her mom looked crestfallen. "I'm sorry, Zoe. I should have thought . . ." With a sigh, she dropped her shoulders. "I'd still like to stop. Maybe they can tell us what's happening or they'll know where we can get more gas and can give us news about the area. We haven't spoken to anyone about anything since Maggie. And without the internet working, we're essentially blind."

"I agree with Beth," Mrs. Samms said, slowing the van as they reached the bridge crossing over the river. "Jim?"

He flung his hands in surrender. "Fine. I'm not sure it's smart, but I guess if we're careful."

"I still don't like it," Alyson's dad muttered.

"I don't like that you brought us here under false pretenses," her mom snapped.

As they approached the parking lot, Mrs. Samms turned on her blinker and took the left into the space. Alyson could feel people turning in their direction as Mrs. Samms maneuvered to a spot at the edge of the lot, close to the highway.

There must have been at least fifty cars in the parking lot, along with ATVs, motorcycles, bicycles, and even horses tied close to the lawn. The lawn, where people were camping last summer, was filled with tables and blankets. From the edge of the lot, Alyson couldn't make out anything being offered, but it was definitely some form of a farmers' market.

They got out of the van, with Zoe holding Alyson's hand. As the group approached the lawn, a hush fell over the crowd. Alyson's eyes widened as she noticed dozens of hands moving to the sidearms on their hips.

Chapter 30

The tension at the campground-turned-farmers-market was intense. While no one had drawn their weapons, it was clear they wouldn't hesitate to do so if threatened. Hands hovered near sidearms, ready to act at a moment's notice.

"Mom?" Eddie's voice was small and young, betraying his fear.

Their mom, sensing the delicate nature of the situation, took the lead. Her voice was warm yet respectful as she addressed the crowd. "Hello, everyone. We don't mean any harm. We actually passed through here last summer and stopped for sodas. The waitress was so friendly, and we remembered how well we were treated and how she said that everyone here was like family." She glanced around, smiling.

People scowled in response.

"Mom," Alyson whispered, "this isn't working."

She swallowed loud enough for Alyson to hear it. "Um, yes, anyway. We won't take up your time. We hoped we might be able to get some information."

She paused, gauging the reaction of the onlookers before continuing. "We've managed to get out of Oregon and we're on our way up the North Fork to my husband's family's property."

"Oregon?" someone spat. "That's just what we need."

"Get back in your van," another voice barked.

"Shh. Don't be rude," a woman hissed, her voice sharp.

From the back of the crowd, a gravelly voice called out, "Who are your people?"

Alyson's dad stepped forward, placing a supportive hand on his wife's shoulder. "My parents own a lodge a few miles outside of Yellowstone. Richard and Ruth Reynolds. They bought it a few years ago."

There was a moment of tense silence before an older man in a worn baseball cap pushed his way to the front. He squinted at Alyson's dad, recognition dawning on his weathered face. "I know Dick Reynolds," he said, adjusting his cap. "Did some work at their place." He glanced around at the gathered group, a hint of amusement in his eyes. "He did mention he had a son that lived on the Left Coast."

A ripple of laughter spread through the crowd, and the atmosphere noticeably lightened. The ice had been broken.

Her mom seized the moment to press on. "We were hoping to get some information on how things are going. We had expected our family to meet us at the state line, but . . ." She trailed off, giving Alyson's dad a pointed look.

No one answered, but they did have questions of their own about what was happening in other areas. The group answered as best they could before the bulk of the crowd moved away, returning to the market and visiting among themselves. The man in the cap was among those who apparently had better things to do.

Another man, this one wearing a weathered straw cowboy hat, moved near them. He nodded solemnly. "Things aren't good in Park County, but they could be worse. At least here in Clark, we're not being bothered much. We've had a few Star Bright incidents, but we dealt with them. Sad situation." He pointed at the cut on her mom's face covered with the bandage. "You run into some trouble?"

"Some, yes," she agreed with a nod. "But we're okay."

"Seems we never know when there's going to be trouble. Almost weren't sure we should get together. But with it being Independence Day, it seemed right to acknowledge it. Won't have any fireworks or anything, but this swap meet made sense."

He went on to explain the situation in Cody and how the National Guard had locked down the town. "They only let people through at set times, 7:00 a.m., noon, and 5:00 p.m. Best time is seven o'clock, when things are a little less crazy. They only take a certain number, so if there's already too many, you wait until the next time."

Mr. Verley, who had been quietly observing, spoke up. "Will we be able to keep the van?"

"Far as I know," the man replied, his gaze shifting to their battered vehicle. "Looks like you've found some trouble along the way."

"It found us," Alyson's dad replied.

He whistled low. "I'll say. You folks have fuel?"

"Not much. We don't know if we have enough to get to my folks' place." He gestured toward the market area. "Anyone bartering for fuel?"

"A few," the man confirmed. "Some farmers with fuel tanks think it'll go bad before they can use it. But the trade prices are steep. The gas stations in the neighboring towns are either shut down or open for official use only." He eyed the weary group. "You folks might want to camp here tonight. People will start closing up shop in a couple of hours. The owner lets people use the lawn for camping. You have tents?"

"We don't," her dad admitted. "We could stay in the van if he'd let us park in the lot."

The man shrugged. "Probably be fine. Go see if you can make your deal for fuel. I'll be around until the end if you want to talk more."

Her dad reached out his hand. "I'm Rich Reynolds."

"Martin Feller."

They shook before her dad introduced the rest of the group.

"Come see me when you've finished your trading," Martin said before walking away.

The group stayed together as they made their way around the market, which was a combination farmers' market, offering a very modest amount of produce and baked goods, along with a swap meet.

The fuel trader was easy to find. After some negotiation, they managed to secure three gallons of fuel, though the price had been steep. Even though they'd left most of their goods to the smugglers, they'd kept small things for this purpose. They had some jewelry and old coins. Plus, Mr. Verley had a nice watch. They would have tried for more fuel, but the farmer capped it at three gallons.

Using a necklace given to her for their tenth wedding anniversary, Alyson's mom was able to make a deal for some much-needed food. While they certainly hoped they'd be at the lodge by tomorrow night, they were beginning to realize nothing was guaranteed in this new world.

Alyson noticed her mom wasn't wearing her wedding set. She hadn't traded it but had likely slipped it into her pocket to prevent it from being considered as part of the negotiations.

As the market wound down, Martin approached them again. "Instead of staying in the lot, you might prefer to come to my place, right up the road. I used to do that rent-a-room online thing. Got a couple of small cabins you can stay in."

He pointed to a woman engaged in conversation nearby. "That's my wife over there. She said to invite you to dinner. Old Hank, he's the one who did work for your folks, he's her brother. Told her your folks seemed like good people."

The offer was unexpected but welcome. As the group considered their options, Alyson took in their surroundings. The Clarks Fork of the Yellowstone River rushed nearby, its constant flow providing a soothing backdrop. In the distance, the majestic silhouette of the mountain loomed, its distinctive shape unmistakable against the vast Wyoming sky.

The beauty of the landscape stood in sharp contrast to the tension and uncertainty they'd lived with for days. Alyson gingerly stretched her back, wincing at the tenderness where she'd hit the sink during the truck stop fight. The muscles had stiffened during the drive, and standing still made her all too aware of every ache from the confrontation.

As her parents exchanged glances of agreement, Alyson caught a glimpse of hope. Despite the obstacles still ahead—and the constant reminder of how dangerous their journey had become—she believed they would succeed.

Her mom spoke first. "It would be nice to sleep in a real bed."

Mr. Verley and Mrs. Samms agreed, and even Zoe seemed excited at the prospect.

"Thanks for your kind offer," her dad said, again reaching for Martin's hand. "We appreciate it."

As they followed Martin's truck up the paved road heading toward the mountain range, Alyson couldn't help but feel a mixture of emotions. They were still far from safe, still far from their ultimate destination. But for tonight, at least, they had found a moment of respite.

It wasn't long before Martin turned on his blinker and they pulled into a driveway. The ranch-style house was surrounded by fields full of cattle. With the flat treeless land, you could almost see forever. The surrounding views of the mountain range were amazing. To the east, other mountains were visible in the distance.

Martin introduced his wife, Jan, before sweeping his arm to encompass the landscape Alyson had been admiring. "God's country. We've lived here for over thirty years and never grow tired of the views."

"The wind does get to be a bit much," Jan added. "But days like this make it worth it."

Eddie pointed toward the mountain. "My grandma told us about that mountain last year."

"Yes, Heart Mountain. It's like a beacon of home." Jan smiled. "The Crow named it, believing the mountain resembled a buffalo heart."

Eddie nodded. "And it ended up there because it moved right? The mountain was somewhere else first?"

"Kind of," Jan agreed with a nod. "It's generally agreed that the mountain formed after a massive landslide, but how exactly that happened is unknown. Maybe an earthquake. Maybe . . ." She paused as she smiled at the group. "Maybe God just made it that way."

A few days ago, Alyson would have rolled her eyes at the statement. Today, things were different. They'd had some tough times, especially with the death of Maggie, but they were here, in Wyoming. Maggie's van was battered, but they may have enough fuel to make it to the lodge. If everything went as it should tomorrow with getting through Cody, they'd be there tomorrow night.

If everything went as it should . . .

Chapter 31

The aroma of sizzling beef filled the air as the group gathered on Martin and Jan's back patio. The sun was beginning to dip toward the horizon, casting a warm golden light across the vast Wyoming landscape. Heart Mountain stood sentinel in the distance, its unique shape a constant reminder of the wild beauty that surrounded them.

"These steaks are from our own herd," Martin explained as he expertly flipped the meat on the grill. "Nothing beats home-raised beef."

Jan emerged from the house, carrying a large bowl of salad. "And these greens and radishes are straight from our garden," she added with pride. "It's still early in the season, but we're starting to see some results."

As they settled around the table, Alyson couldn't help but marvel at the spread before them. After rationed supplies and constant uncertainty, the meal seemed like a feast fit for royalty. She almost imagined she was a princess herself, having showered and changed clothes.

When they first arrived, Jan showed them to two cabins. Mrs. Samms had quickly asked Alyson's mom if the men could be put in one cabin and the women in the other. While Mrs. Samms and Mr. Verley were friends, maybe even more than that, she wasn't comfortable sharing a cabin. "It wouldn't look right," she'd whispered, gesturing toward Zoe and Eddie.

The Fellers had even come up with a solution for the broken driver's side window, producing a couple of rolls of clear packing tape and using it to cover the window in horizontal and then vertical strips, both inside and out. It wasn't pretty, but it would cut down on the wind and still allow the driver to use the side mirror.

"This is incredible," Alyson's mom said, her voice filled with gratitude. "We can't thank you enough for your hospitality."

Martin waved off the thanks. "It's nothing. Out here, we take care of each other. It's how we've always done things, and it's how we'll get through these tough times."

As they ate, the conversation flowed easily. Jan spoke about her garden, explaining the challenges and joys of growing food in their climate. "Soon, we'll have more vegetables ready. The tomatoes are coming along nicely, and the peas are starting to climb."

Martin chimed in about their cattle operation. "We've been ranchers for over three decades now. It's not always easy, but it's a good life."

"What about the winters?" Mr. Verley asked. "I imagine it gets pretty harsh out here."

Martin nodded. "It can be tough, no doubt. The cattle do fine. They need food and water, of course, but it's not so taxing that I can't help Jan's brother out with construction projects during the colder months. Indoor projects, mind you. Keeps us busy and brings in some extra income."

As the meal progressed, they learned more about the area. Other farms in the region grew corn, wheat, barley, and alfalfa. "We'll be fine as long as the electricity stays on and the fuel holds up," Jan said. "We need those to keep the water going, especially for irrigation."

Alyson's dad furrowed his brow. "You need fuel for irrigation? Why were people trading?"

"Gasoline doesn't have a very long shelf life. Most of the irrigation uses electricity, or the pumps might use diesel or propane. Some of the propane pumps, of which there aren't many, can run on gas. Those trading figure they can use other things rather than letting their gas sour. Most of the trade is for food. We all know that's a hot commodity."

"We didn't have food to trade," Eddie said, shaking his head.

"Figured not. I'm sure Jerry was happy with what you offered. He wouldn't have made the trade otherwise."

After dinner, as the sun dipped below the horizon, painting the sky in brilliant hues of orange and pink, Martin suggested a game of horseshoes. "It's a bit of a tradition around here," he explained.

As they gathered near the horseshoe pit, Jan turned to the children. "If you'd prefer, there's a path that leads down to the riverbank. It's completely safe, just stay out of the water. The river's still high from snowmelt and is running fast."

Eddie's eyes lit up at the suggestion. "Can we, Mom? Please?"

Their mom hesitated for a moment before nodding. "All right, but be careful. Alyson, you're in charge."

Alyson swallowed her irritation at being lumped in with the kids. At eighteen, she was an adult and would much have preferred to stay with the others. Forcing a tight smile, she said, "Sure, Mom."

"Take Steve with you?" Mr. Verley asked. "He needs the walk, but keep it slow. He's still a little stiff."

With Jan's assistance, Mrs. Samms had changed Steve's bandage earlier. As a ranch wife, Jan said she'd doctored dogs, cows, horses, and more over the years. "Even chickens," she'd added when gesturing to a coop beyond the garden space. Jan had said she thought the wound looked pretty good and commented how blessed they were that the dog wasn't injured more severely.

As the adults began their game, Alyson led Eddie and Zoe down the path toward the river. Steve stuck by their side while sniffing everything. The sound of rushing water grew louder as they approached, and soon they could see the Clarks Fork of the Yellowstone River, its waters swollen and swift.

"Wow," Eddie breathed, taking in the sight. "It's crazy fast!"

Alyson nodded, keeping a watchful eye on Zoe. The little girl seemed entranced by the rushing water, her eyes wide with wonder.

As they walked along the riverbank, Eddie began to pester Alyson with questions about their grandparents' lodge. "Do you think they'll have horses?"

"They had them last year, didn't they?"

"Will we get to ride them?"

"I don't know, Eddie," Alyson replied, her patience wearing thin after days of stress and uncertainty. "We don't even know if they're still there, remember?"

Eddie's face fell. "But Dad said—"

"Dad doesn't know for sure," Alyson snapped, immediately regretting her harsh tone. "I'm sorry. I'm just . . . worried."

"Well, you don't need to be so mean about it."

"Look. I said I was sorry, didn't I?"

"Yeah, but still, you could be nicer."

As the argument carried on, their voices rising slightly, Zoe covered her ears for a moment before breaking into a run.

"Zoe, wait!" Alyson called out, fear rising as she saw how close the little girl was to the water's edge.

What happened next seemed to unfold in slow motion. Zoe's foot slipped on the muddy bank, and before either Alyson or Eddie could react, she tumbled into the rushing river.

"Zoe!" she screamed, breaking into a run. Eddie was right behind her, Steve on his heels barking out an alert.

The current yanked Zoe downstream, its force dragging her with terrifying speed. Just as she seemed on the verge of being lost to it, a thick branch caught her arm, halting her for a brief moment.

Alyson's breath caught, but the relief was short-lived. The branch snapped, and Zoe was swept away again. Her mind raced, scrambling for any water rescue techniques she'd ever learned. "Eddie, get help!" she yelled, her focus never leaving Zoe's struggling form in the water.

As Eddie sprinted back toward the house, Alyson raced along the riverbank, frantically scanning for a way to reach Zoe. Steve continued to voice his concern, barking and running with Alyson.

The little girl fought to keep her head above water, her terrified cries barely audible over the roar of the river. Zoe slowed, possibly snagged on something, her head disappearing under the water before she surfaced and continued struggling against the current.

Alyson spotted a fallen tree jutting out over the water a short distance ahead. She sprinted toward it. "God, if you're really there, I could use your help now," she pleaded as she ran, with Steve right behind her.

Scrambling onto the trunk, Alyson inched her way out over the rushing water. Steve continued to bark as shouts rang out in the distance. Help was on the way, but would it come in time?

As Zoe drew closer, Alyson braced herself. "Zoe!" she called. "Reach for my hand!"

The little girl's eyes locked onto hers, filled with terror but also a spark of hope. As the current carried her nearer, Zoe stretched out her arm.

Alyson leaned out as far as she dared, fingers straining, her breath catching as she feared she'd miss. Miraculously, their hands connected.

The current's force nearly dragged Alyson in as she clung to Zoe's arm. With every ounce of strength, she pulled the child toward her, but Zoe's weight and waterlogged clothes made it nearly impossible.

As Alyson's muscles screamed in protest, she felt a firm grip on her legs. Glancing back, she saw her dad, anchoring her to the tree trunk.

With his help, she managed to pull Zoe from the water's grasp. As soon as they were safely on the riverbank, Mrs. Samms scooped Zoe into her arms, sobbing with relief. Steve also went to the girl, checking her over and licking her on the cheek. She was coughing and shivering while she cried.

Alyson collapsed onto the ground, her heart pounding and her muscles aching. The reality of what happened began to sink in. They'd come so close to losing Zoe. Her mom was at her side, wrapping her in a blanket and murmuring words of comfort.

As the adrenaline faded, guilt washed over her. If she hadn't been arguing with Eddie, if she'd been paying closer attention . . .

Her dad knelt beside her and placed a comforting hand on her shoulder. "You did good, Alyson. You saved her."

Alyson shrugged, unable to speak past the lump in her throat. She watched as Jan wrapped Zoe in a warm blanket, the little girl's sobs subsiding into hiccups.

Eddie approached, his face streaked with tears. "I'm sorry," he whispered. "It's my fault. If I hadn't—"

Alyson pulled her brother into a tight hug. "It's not your fault. We're all okay. How fast did you run? I can't believe how quickly everyone got here."

"Fast. Too fast." Eddie's face was red, and his breathing was labored.

As they made their way back to the house, the group subdued and shaken, Alyson couldn't help but reflect on how quickly things had changed. Only moments ago, they'd been enjoying a peaceful evening, almost able to forget the dangers that lurked in this new world.

The incident served as a stark reminder of how precarious their situation truly was. Safety wasn't guaranteed, not even when they reached the lodge.

Back at the house, Jan found clothes for Zoe to change into before busying herself making hot cocoa for everyone, while Martin asked if he should light a fire in the woodstove. "Probably not, dear," Jan replied. "It'll be just as warm to sit outside. Maybe light the firepit instead?"

Dressed in warm clothes that fit fairly well, thanks to Jan's grandchildren, Zoe sat close to Mrs. Samms on a bench near the firepit, unwilling to leave her side.

As they all gathered around the outdoor space, the tension from the riverside rescue slowly began to dissipate. Mr. Verley cleared his throat. "I think we all owe Alyson a debt of gratitude. Quick thinking and brave action. You should be proud."

Alyson's cheeks grew warm at the praise. "I just did what anyone would do."

"Not everyone would have been so quick to act," Mrs. Samms pointed out. "You showed real courage out there." She turned to Eddie. "And you. The way you ran . . . why, you could be in the Olympics."

That brought a ripple of laughter. As the conversation continued, touching on the rescue before drifting to other topics, Alyson found her gaze drawn to the mountains. The stars were beginning to appear in the darkening sky, countless pinpricks of light in the vast Wyoming night.

Tomorrow, they would face new challenges. The checkpoint, Cody, and the final stretch to the lodge all lay ahead of them. But tonight, at that moment, they were safe. And for now, that was enough.

Chapter 32

Alyson stirred from sleep as a light snapped on in the cabin, cutting through the predawn darkness. The events of the previous evening had haunted her dreams, while the bar from the sleeper sofa threatened to break her in half. Her entire body ached from the trouble with Zoe at the river and the confrontation with the Star Brights back in Columbus. Glancing at her phone, she saw it was barely four in the morning.

On the other side of the studio-style cabin, her mom and Mrs. Samms were already up, quietly packing their few belongings. Beside her, Zoe whimpered softly in her sleep. Alyson gently stroked the little girl's hair, soothing her back into a peaceful slumber.

"How did she sleep?" her mom whispered, nodding toward Zoe.

Alyson shrugged. "Some bad dreams, I think. But she seems okay now."

"Time to get her up so we can get going. At least she'll be able to sleep in the van."

Mrs. Samms shook her head in wonder. "It's truly a miracle she came through unharmed. She could have swallowed water or been injured. We're so blessed. We'll still want to monitor her closely. I didn't see any cuts, but she does have a nasty bruise on her thigh."

Sliding out of bed, Alyson visited the restroom and changed her clothes. The same clothes she'd worn since they left their home in Astoria. *How long ago was that? Three days? Four?* She closed her eyes. They left the night of July 1, after dark. The fourth was yesterday.

Independence Day. No wonder her clothes were starting to stink.

She'd showered and put on her clean clothes last night, but figured she might as well wear the dirty ones today. If all went well, they'd be at her grandparents' lodge by nightfall, and she could wash them there. With only what was in her backpack, she needed everything to last.

Her mom was already worried about what they'd wear if they couldn't get back to their home before winter. Even if they could, they had no idea what the smugglers had left behind. Had they emptied the house completely, or only taken what they thought had value?

Her dad and Mr. Verley both said they were sure the food would be gone, probably the electronics too. But what else would the smugglers have considered necessary? There had even been talk that, if the smugglers left anything behind, looters might break in and clean out the rest, leaving the house in ruins. They all knew they were gambling with the possibility of losing everything by leaving, but at least they'd be alive. That was the hope, anyway.

More than once, Alyson had thought they should have stayed. With Davis dead, he couldn't bother them any longer. Of course, Davis was dead because of them. Between Mrs. Samms's gun and Alyson's knife, they were killers. *Which impact had caused the fatality?* she wondered. She didn't know. They hadn't stuck around long enough to examine him beyond confirming his death.

No, they couldn't have stayed. She couldn't even be sure they wouldn't be captured and returned to Oregon to stand trial for the death of a police captain. Even if he was out for vengeance and acting outside of the law, they'd still be accused. They'd have to prove it was self-defense.

She could only hope that with the current situation with the Star Brights, his death wouldn't get more than a cursory investigation and the authorities would chalk it up to a casualty of the chaos sweeping through the region. But that was a fragile hope, one she couldn't afford to count on. Her current worry was they'd reach her grandparents' lodge and, at any moment, there could be a knock on the door, a sound that would shatter the fragile illusion of safety they'd managed to cling to.

That worry hinged on actually making it to the lodge and on her grandparents still being there. Her dad spent several pockets of time last night frantically trying to reach them, calling and texting repeatedly. He'd tried using everyone's cell phone and even asked the Fellers if he could use their landline, but the phone wasn't working, and none of the cell phone attempts went through.

The Fellers said the internet had been out for days in their area, or they'd offer the computer to try. Her dad had already been emailing, using the phone data when it would come up, sending numerous emails to their personal accounts and the lodge's email.

Alyson could see the mounting concern in both her parents. They hoped the silence was only because the internet was down. But the bigger fear remained that her grandparents had left the lodge or that something worse had happened. With the Star Brights out there and people growing more unpredictable, anything was possible.

As they finished packing, a soft knock on the cabin door announced the arrival of Jan. "Breakfast is cooking in the main house," she called softly. "The coffee is ready."

The women, with her mom carrying Zoe, made their way to the main house, where the aroma of freshly brewed coffee and sizzling bacon greeted them. In the kitchen,

Martin was flipping pancakes, while her dad, Mr. Verley, and Eddie were already seated at the table, looking slightly worse for wear but alert. Steve was stretched out on the floor in the nearby family room.

"Good morning, ladies," Martin said cheerfully. Maybe a little too cheerfully at the early hour. "Hope you all slept well, considering everything."

As they settled around the table, Jan began serving up plates piled high with pancakes, eggs, and bacon. "Eat up," she urged. "You may have a long day ahead of you."

Her dad nodded, his expression serious. "We need to be on the road by five fifteen at the latest. It's about a half-hour drive to Cody, and we want to be at the checkpoint well before it opens at seven."

As they ate, Martin filled them in on the latest news he'd heard. "Word is, they're being pretty strict at the checkpoints. Make sure you have your story straight and any documentation you might need."

"Story?" Mrs. Samms shook her head. "We don't have a story. Only the truth."

"Do you think they'll give us trouble?" Alyson's mom asked, worry creasing her brow.

Martin shrugged. "Hard to say." He glanced at Mrs. Samms and smiled. "But stick to the truth. You're heading to family, passing through Cody and not staying. That should be enough."

"Any luck reaching your folks?" Mrs. Samms asked as she took a bite of her eggs.

"Not yet."

"I tried getting onto my game," Eddie said. "I thought maybe if I could reach Jackson he could try getting ahold of our grandparents."

"Who's Jackson?" Jan asked.

"Our cousin." Eddie pointed at Alyson. "He and his sister live in Casper with their mom. We play VR games a lot, but I haven't been on since we left Oregon. I didn't even get to tell him we were leaving. We were so busy getting ready, and when I remembered, the internet was out. Again."

"Those games sure are popular," Martin said, shaking his head. "Our grandson wanted a virtual reality headset thing, probably like the one hanging off your backpack, but his folks put their foot down. Between school and ranch work, there's no time for that nonsense."

Eddie wrinkled his brow. "It's not only games on the VR set. I use it for exercise too."

"We get plenty of that moving cattle and working in the fields."

Nodding, Eddie said, "I guess they would. We only have a small yard. There's this sword fighting game that's a full-body workout. It's pretty fun. If the internet was up, I could show you how it works—"

"Eddie," their mom said softly, "finish your breakfast so we can go."

"Okay, I only meant—"

"Oh, I understand what you meant," Martin said with a smile. "There're people around here who love their video games too."

"We lost one of them," Jan said, her voice quiet. "Both him and his mom. She was a friend, and the boys went to school with our grandsons. He was what they called a gamer."

"What happened?" Eddie asked, eyes wide.

"Not sure. It's been a few months now. Before all this craziness started. He was driving home from Powell and lost control of his vehicle. He only had his permit and was getting in some driving time. Both of them died before they could get to the hospital."

"It was hard on our little community," Martin added. "Then, when all of this happened . . ." He motioned his arm in a circle. "We didn't even have time for proper mourning before everything fell apart. There've been a few more deaths, and each one takes a toll on us. Even people who haven't lived here long are family. We do what we can to help."

The room grew quiet, the Fellers's words hanging in the air. Eddie shifted uncomfortably, glancing at their mom as if searching for the right thing to say.

She gave his shoulder a gentle squeeze, her expression a mixture of gratitude and sorrow.

Martin cleared his throat, breaking the silence. "We keep going," he said, his tone steady. "That's what small towns like ours do. We lean on each other, even when it feels like there's nothing left to give."

Soon, it was time to leave. As they loaded up the van, Jan pressed a basket of food into Beth's hands. "Some sandwiches and snacks for the road," she said with a warm smile. "I know it shouldn't take you more than a couple of hours . . . at least that's what it used to take to get to the East Gate of Yellowstone. But these days, it's best to be prepared for anything."

Martin clasped Alyson's dad's hand firmly. "Good luck to you all. If something goes wrong and you can't make it to your folks' place, you're welcome back here. There's plenty of work to go around." He chuckled.

With final waves and heartfelt thanks, they climbed into the van and set off down the dark road. A swell of gratitude rose in Alyson as the lights of Martin and Jan's house faded into the distance. Their brief stay had been a welcome respite from the dangers and uncertainties of their journey.

As they drove, the sky slowly brightened. The barren land appeared to stir to life as they crossed a vast, flat expanse. Before long, the scenery shifted, and they descended into a small valley, with farmland to the right and hills rising to the left.

"Look there," Alyson's dad said from his position in the passenger seat. "That's the Chief Joseph Highway. Remember, kids? It was one of the drives we took last year. The large canyon was there where we stopped to use the facilities and walked around. We continued on to Cooke City, where we found another entrance to Yellowstone."

"That's right," her mom picked up the narrative as she turned on the blinker to switch lanes. Even though they were the only vehicle on the road, old habits were hard to break. "We had lunch in Cooke City, and they drove us down that winding road—"

"The Beartooth Highway," her dad added. "What'd my dad say they called it? The Road to the Sky?"

"Highway to the Sky," her mom corrected. "And it was. The views were incredible. That was an amazing drive."

"We stopped for pizza, right?" Eddie added. "We ended up in a little town where there were shops to walk around in and pizza before the drive home."

"Red Lodge." Alyson smiled, enjoying the conversation that was completely normal in an abnormal world. The little town had some great shops, including a specialty clothing store where they designed and sewed some of the pieces. She'd eyed a cute skirt, but it was out of her price range.

Would they be able to have such a day now? While she wished they could, she knew it was impossible. If the National Guard was monitoring travel in and out of Cody, she couldn't imagine they could simply drive up and say, "We're going on tour today. Be back later." Besides, with the gas stations closed, driving for fun couldn't happen.

A quiet fell over the van as they climbed a hill, the engine making a low growl and the vehicle slowing. "I guess this thing doesn't like the ups," her mom said.

Alyson kept quiet. They'd gone through the mountains in Idaho without the van protesting. As the incline steepened, the van bogged down further, its struggle evident in every shuddering motion.

"Rich?" her mom said quietly, worry evident in her voice. "What should I do?"

"I'm not sure. Just . . . just keep going, I guess."

"I agree," Mr. Verley said from his spot on the bench. "The old girl has had a hard trip. We need her to give us a little more."

Soon, they crested the top of the pass and started down, the van growling a little less and picking up speed. Her mom let out a loud sigh. "Okay for now."

As they emerged from the rugged mountain pass and onto the flat expanse below, the sun began to rise, showing off another mountain range in the distance. Alyson watched in awe as the first light peeked over the horizon, painting the landscape in hues of gold and pink.

"It's beautiful," she murmured, almost to herself.

"Sure is," Mr. Verley agreed, leaning slightly so he could see through the remaining window. "The sunrises here are amazing."

"Sunsets too," Mrs. Samms added. "Last night, the colors . . . I could get used to this."

"I hope so," Mr. Verley replied, reaching for her hand. Steve, maybe thinking he needed to get in on the action, lifted his head up and nudged their clasped hands with his nose.

Alyson found herself wondering if she, too, could get used to these wide-open spaces. The vastness was so different from the close, green world of Astoria. Yet there was undeniable beauty to it, a rugged grandeur that spoke to something deep within her.

Where her grandparents lived was forested, more like her home in the Pacific Northwest than this open area. She loved the trees and the smell of the pines when she visited last summer. The beauty of the area had begged her to stay.

But the difficulties between the adults had cast a shadow over the trip, with her mom and her grandpa constantly bickering and making snide comments toward each other. It was hard to fully enjoy the surroundings when tension filled the air. She certainly hoped they could figure out how to behave themselves this time. Now they couldn't easily pick up and leave if things were rough between them.

As they neared Cody, the unease in the van began to build. Eddie, who had been fidgeting in his seat for the last several miles, spoke up. "What if they don't let us through?"

Their dad's fingers drummed on the dash. "They will. We stay calm and tell the truth."

They reached the roadblock shortly after passing a sign advertising the Cody Shooting Complex. With the barricade in place on Highway 120, they were directed toward a pull-off.

It was a few minutes before six thirty in the morning, and they were the only vehicle in sight, though a small group of people on foot had already gathered. In the field off to the right, there were several large tents set up.

"Looks like they got quite the arrangement here," Mr. Verley whispered.

A stern-faced man in a military uniform approached the van. "State your business," he demanded, eyeing the battered vehicle suspiciously.

Alyson's dad cleared his throat, leaning forward to address the man who was on the driver's side. "We're heading to my parents' lodge up the North Fork. Richard and Ruth Reynolds. They own the East Gate Lodge and Cabins."

The man's eyes narrowed. "Up the North Fork? You're not planning to stay in Cody?"

"No, sir," her mom chimed in, her voice light and airy. "We're passing through on our way to the lodge."

"Are any of you carrying weapons?"

Her dad cleared his throat. "Y-yes."

He made a motion, and the van was surrounded by his colleagues. Rifles pointed at them. Her mom whimpered. Zoe, who was asleep next to Alyson, stirred only slightly.

"I need you all out of the van, one at a time. Leave your weapons in the van. Let's start with you." He motioned toward her dad.

Alyson watched as her dad slowly and methodically took the gun from the holster on his hip. He verbalized everything he was doing as he did it. When he was out of the vehicle and standing off to the side, her mom was ordered to exit next.

"I don't have a gun," she said, her voice trembling. "I-I have a knife in my pocket."

"Leave it on the seat."

When her mom was standing next to her dad, both with their hands in the air, the side door of the van opened.

"You first, Pops," the young soldier said, waving his gun at Mr. Verley. The man shifted his gaze to Steve, who was standing and looking alert. "Is that dog going to be a problem?"

"He will not be a problem, young man," Mrs. Samms said, her voice sharp. "Stop waving that gun in here. We have children, as you can well see."

The man glanced at Alyson, catching her eye and raising an eyebrow. He lowered the rifle slightly as he muttered, "Sorry. Please exit the van, one at a time. Leave your weapons inside."

Alyson gently nudged Zoe, who'd yet to stir even with the commotion. "Zoe, wake up, sweetie. We're at the checkpoint and need to get out."

After the others exited the van, leaving only Alyson and a sleepy Zoe, Alyson asked, "Can I carry her? She fell in the river yesterday. She's still pretty tired."

"You have any weapons on you?"

"I've already put them on the floor." She pointed at the switchblade and Swiss Army knife at her feet.

"You folks sure like your knives, don't you?"

Alyson shrugged. "May I carry Zoe?"

"Go ahead." He stepped back and gave them room to exit.

With all of them lined up, two of the soldiers searched the van while a man who was older than the rest walked over to them.

"You have family that owns a lodge up the North Fork? What'd you say their names are?"

Her dad repeated the information as the man scribbled on a piece of paper.

"And where'd you come from?" he glanced at the van with Montana plates.

"Oregon," her dad answered.

The man let out a low whistle. "That right? How'd you manage that? I thought they had that state locked up tight."

"We had a little help."

The military man snorted out a laugh. "I bet you did."

"Sir?" The young man who'd "helped" them out of the van came scurrying over. He caught Alyson's eye and gave her a wink.

"Yes?"

"There's nothing of consequence in the vehicle. Backpacks with clothes, a few photos, books, and a VR set. And a suitcase that looks like it belongs to the little girl." He motioned to Zoe, who was now standing next to Alyson, holding her hand. "A small amount of food and basic supplies. On the roof are three empty gas cans, five gallons each, a shovel, an axe, and a few other necessities."

The older man looked back at the group. "I guess when you escaped Oregon, you needed to travel light."

Alyson's dad gave a nod.

The man turned back to the other soldier. "Did you find identification?"

"Something for each of the adults." He pointed at Alyson. "Her too. She's eighteen."

Her cheeks burned under the weight of his gaze as he announced her age. The way he said it, he might as well have added, "She's of marrying age."

"Very well. Go ahead and put their van back together for them."

The younger man rendered a salute and again caught Alyson's eye before turning to go.

The older man—an officer, Alyson suspected, but she didn't know the difference based on his uniform—turned back to them. "And you're certain about your destination? The North Fork road is closed at the entrance to Yellowstone. It's a dead end."

"We understand," her dad replied. "My parents' lodge is only a few miles from the East Gate. We'll be staying there."

The guardsman studied them for a long moment. "All right," he finally said. "We'll escort you through town to the checkpoint near the rodeo grounds. From there, you're on your own. We leave at seven. You'll follow the red car." He pointed to a small red commuter car parked at the end of the pullout, already positioned to head toward Cody, a mile or two beyond the barricade.

"If you follow the silver car, you'll end up heading toward Meeteetse. Don't follow the silver car." He gave something resembling a smile. "We leave at 0700, sharp. You can get back in your van or mingle with the group over there." He pointed to those on foot. "There are latrines if you need them."

Alyson let out a sigh of relief as the man walked away. She glanced at Zoe, whose eyes were half-closed with exhaustion. "Everything's fine," Alyson whispered, a mixture of weariness and triumph in her voice. "We'll be at my grandparents' lodge soon."

Chapter 33

As they followed the red car through the streets of Cody, Alyson, who was taking her turn driving, was struck by how empty the town appeared. Shops were boarded up, and the few people visible hurried along with their heads down, avoiding eye contact.

"It's like a ghost town," Eddie whispered, his face pressed against the window. "Think they have a farmers' market somewhere?"

In the passenger seat, Alyson's dad rolled down the window. He took a deep breath. "It's still early. A little chilly. Maybe the day hasn't started."

"I don't know," Mr. Verley said. "The entire feel of it is different from some of the other towns we went through. This is more like Columbus and how it seemed deserted."

Her mom nodded solemnly. "This was a bustling little town last summer. Lots of tourists. My guess is it was exactly the same . . . until it wasn't. So much has changed in such a short time."

"What happened there?" Mr. Verley asked, pointing to the Irma Hotel, now with part of the building missing.

"Nothing good," her dad replied. "Brian told me about it. There was an explosion, the same day things went bad in Portland."

"Star Brights?" he asked.

"Not sure. They think so, but things went so crazy so fast, I'm not sure how much investigating was done to determine the cause."

"That's too bad," her mom said. "That hotel's been there for years. Since Buffalo Bill built it in the early 1900s.

Remember how we went there for brunch last year? It was a beautiful building."

As they drove, Alyson's mind wandered to the challenges that still lay ahead. Once they reached the east end of town and the pilot car left them, what would happen? It was almost an hour's drive to her grandparents' lodge. Would they be there? Would it be the safe haven they so desperately needed?

At the rodeo grounds checkpoint, they were stopped one final time. The young guardsman who had helped them out of the van earlier was the driver of the red escort car. Alyson wondered if that was his usual assignment or if he'd coerced someone to get it.

The way he smiled at her gave her little doubt of his interest. She wanted to smile back, to let him know she welcomed the attention, but to what end? In minutes, she'd be on her way to the lodge and was unlikely to return until this whole mess was over. The guard would no longer be needed, and he'd go back home, wherever that may be.

"This is as far as we go," he said, leaning in the window. "It's unlikely you'll meet many cars. Maybe some of the locals that live in Wapiti, a small town up the road about twenty miles. With Yellowstone locked up tight, it's a dead end. There may be some walkers. I'm stationed here sometimes, and we'll have people walk up, but it's not a lot. Definitely not like what we see on Highway 120, either coming from Montana or Meeteetse. That road is still busy." He looked at Alyson and smiled. "By the way, I'm Dustin. Dustin Buchanan. Maybe . . ."

"Thank you for your help," she said quickly. "I think we're ready to go now."

He took a step back. "Be careful of rocks. The road ahead is clear for now, but be warned, conditions can change quickly. There have been a few rockslides. Nothing too big, but still." He gave a nod.

"We'll watch for them," Alyson's dad said solemnly. "Thank you for your assistance."

As the guardsman stepped back, Alyson put the van in gear. She held her breath as they slowly pulled away from the checkpoint. She couldn't help but glance in the rearview mirror. Dustin was still standing there, watching them go.

They had made it through Cody. The final leg of their journey lay ahead.

"How much farther?" Eddie asked, peering out the window at the rugged landscape as they left the town behind.

"About an hour to the lodge," their dad replied. "Assuming the road is clear."

As they drove out of Cody, following the road that would lead them toward Yellowstone National Park, Alyson experienced both excitement and apprehension. They were so close now, but would they encounter more troubles?

The beauty of the area was undeniable. Towering cliffs rose on either side of the road, their rocky faces streaked with vibrant colors. The Shoshone River rushed beside them, the water moving fast.

As they approached Buffalo Bill Reservoir, the landscape opened up, revealing a vast expanse of water surrounded by rugged hills. The morning sun glinted off the reservoir's surface, creating a dazzling display.

"I remember this," Eddie said, his face brightening. "We stopped here last year to take pictures."

Their mom nodded, a wistful smile on her face. "It feels like a lifetime ago now."

About fifteen minutes later, they passed through the small town of Wapiti. A few locals were out, tending to gardens or animals, but they quickly ducked out of sight as the van approached.

"Look!" Zoe pointed excitedly. "Those are big deer."

"Elk," Alyson's dad said, sounding almost proud. "They're one of the reasons we came here. Elk, deer, bighorn sheep . . . all are common up the North Fork."

"Nature's thriving," Mr. Verley observed, as the group watched the small elk herd seemingly unconcerned by their presence.

Mrs. Samms nodded. "It's beautiful, but also a bit unsettling. Like we're intruding on their world now."

As they continued past Wapiti, the road began to climb, winding its way through increasingly rugged terrain. The van's engine strained against the incline, a reminder of the vehicle's weariness after their long journey.

"Uh, Dad?" Alyson said, worry in her voice.

"Keep going."

"I will, but the gas gauge is also low. I hope we have enough to make it there."

"If nothing else," her mom piped up from her seat in the back, "we walk the rest of the way. We're almost there now. We'll figure it out."

Alyson lifted her gaze to the rearview mirror. Her mom sounded more positive than she'd been during this entire journey. Was it simply the excitement of being so near the lodge and ending this interminable trip? Or had she accepted this was the best choice for their current circumstances? Sure, she'd said the right words when agreeing that Wyoming would be safer. But Alyson hadn't missed the sadness in her eyes, coupled with the subtle blame she directed toward her husband.

"Look!" Zoe pointed out the window. A group of bighorn sheep were perched on a nearby cliff, watching the van pass with mild curiosity.

"See!" Alyson's dad exclaimed. "I told you there were wild sheep."

"Is that little one a baby?"

"I think it is. Looks like there are quite a few lambs. I'm glad to see that."

For a moment, the tension in the vehicle lifted as everyone marveled at the sight. It was a reminder of the wild, untamed nature of this place. A nature that seemed, at least for now, unconcerned with the troubles of the human world.

As they continued up the canyon, Alyson found herself lost in thought, driving as if by remote. The journey from Astoria had been fraught with danger and uncertainty. They had faced Star Brights, hostile strangers, and natural perils. Yet somehow, against all odds, they had made it this far. Maybe that's exactly why her mom was so happy.

She thought of the people they had met along the way. Maggie, who had given her life to help them escape. Martin and Jan, whose kindness had provided a brief respite from their struggles. She smiled as she thought of Dustin, the guardsman. Could she see him again?

Ryan's face flashed in her mind, his vacant eyes staring back at her, the handle of the kitchen knife protruding from his body. Alyson blinked rapidly, but not before she saw the man on the street in Portland, after she had pummeled him with the piece of concrete. The image of Captain Davis's body, with her red-handled knife sticking out of his chest, lingered in her mind. She shifted in her seat, feeling the weight of the same knife in her pocket, its handle pressing against her hip.

"We're getting close," her dad announced, a note of excitement creeping into his voice and snapping Alyson back to the present. She took a breath, willing her body to relax.

"I forgot how beautiful it is up here," her mom murmured, echoing Alyson's thoughts.

Mr. Verley nodded in agreement. "It's something else, all right. Makes you feel small in the grand scheme of things."

As they continued up the canyon, the conversation in the van turned to speculation about what they might find at the lodge. Would Alyson's grandparents be there? How had they fared during the crisis? Had any of their other relatives made it?

"I hope Maddie and Jackson are there," Eddie said, referring to their cousins. "It'd be nice to have some other kids around."

Alyson nodded in agreement as her dad reminded them there were a few extra people living at the lodge, friends of his parents. There was at least one girl, maybe around her age.

As they rounded a sharp bend in the road, Alyson slammed on the brakes. A scattering of rocks blocked their path. None of the rocks were overly large, but it wouldn't be safe for the van to simply drive over them. They'd end up walking for sure.

Her dad groaned. "We'll have to clear it."

Mr. Verley nodded and reached for the door handle. "Let's make it quick. I don't like being exposed like this."

Alyson glanced around. They weren't completely exposed. With the North Fork of the Shoshone on their left and a rock cliff on their right, they were pretty much in the middle of nowhere. They hadn't even seen people since Wapiti. It was only them and the wildlife, combined with the sounds of the rushing river.

"I'll help, Dad," Eddie offered, already following Mr. Verley out of the van.

"Me too," her mom said. "The soldier said we may encounter this. At least it's only small stuff."

"Zoe, you stay in the van with Alyson," Mrs. Samms said. "You too, Steve." She ruffled the dog's head before joining the others.

As they exited the van, Alyson glanced around. While they did seem isolated, she was beginning to agree with Mr. Verley that they were exposed. With the way the road curved, she couldn't see but twenty feet in front of them and about double that behind.

She glanced at Zoe, who was clutching her stuffed animal tightly as she began to hum. Alyson stilled, not even daring to breathe. When the tune finally came in clear, she let out a sigh. "Jesus Loves Me."

While the song was harmless, it was still nerve-racking to hear humming in this crazy world. She should talk to Zoe about it. Maybe tell her that there was a time and place for humming, but she should only do it when she was around family. Alyson shuddered to think what may happen. Singing or humming in today's world was a risk to one's health.

"Zoe? Sweetie? Why are you humming?"

Instead of looking at Alyson, she pointed to a car-sized boulder along the edge of the highway. Alyson could only catch a glimpse of it due to the angle of the still-intact window. "I don't—"

"People," Zoe said.

Alyson's gaze snapped to where Zoe was pointing. From behind the large boulder at the road's edge, figures emerged like specters materializing from the rock itself. Their appearance was sudden and jarring in the previously serene landscape.

"Don't move!" bellowed a man brandishing a makeshift weapon, a thick tree limb bristling with menacing metal spikes. His voice echoed off the canyon walls, shattering the tranquil atmosphere.

Another attacker, his face obscured by a bandanna, leveled what appeared to be a hunting rifle at the group. "Out of the van!" he demanded, his tone leaving no room for negotiation. "Now!"

The world beyond the van burst into motion as at least half a dozen attackers surrounded them, some with medieval-looking weapons but others with firearms. Her dad's and Mr. Verley's hands moved to their weapons. In a heartbeat, they had drawn their sidearms and taken defensive stances.

"Back off!" Her dad's voice boomed, steady and authoritative despite the chaos. "We don't want trouble, but we will defend ourselves!"

Mr. Verley stood shoulder to shoulder with her dad, his pistol unwavering as he scanned the group of assailants. "Think carefully about your next move," he warned, his voice low and dangerous.

Alyson's mom was in front of her brother, while Mrs. Samms was still bent over, retrieving one of the cereal-bowl-sized boulders.

The standoff crackled with tension, the air electric. Neither side seemed willing to back down, each group assessing the other, calculating risks and potential outcomes.

The distinctive sound of multiple weapons being cocked pierced the air. From around the bend to the west, a new group emerged on the road. They moved with military precision, their weapons far more sophisticated than those of the initial attackers.

"Everyone on the ground!" a commanding voice rang out. "Weapons down, hands where we can see them! Now!"

The unexpected arrival threw the scene into further disarray. The original attackers, caught off guard, hesitated. Alyson's dad and Mr. Verley exchanged a quick glance, their expressions a mixture of confusion and wariness.

"Do it," her dad said, nodding at Mr. Verley. Her mom had yanked Eddie to the ground, and they were kneeling, with Mrs. Samms doing the same. Steve, standing up in the van, let out a low whine.

As Alyson hushed Steve, the original attackers made their choice. Instead of complying, they whirled to face the new threat, raising their weapons.

"No way," the man with the spiked club snarled. "We ain't going down without a fight!"

In an instant, the air erupted with gunfire.

Chapter 34

Alyson instinctively threw herself over Zoe, shielding the little girl with her body. The van's windshield exploded inward, showering them with glass. Steve let out a low growl, his ears flattening against his head as he crouched protectively near Zoe's feet.

The sound of gunfire erupted outside the van, deafening in its intensity. Alyson could only imagine the mayhem unfolding beyond her limited view. The air filled with shouts and screams she couldn't quite make out.

Through the shattered windshield, Alyson caught brief, fragmented glimpses of the chaos outside. Blurred figures darted in and out of view, their movements quick and erratic. The sharp crack of gunfire filled the air, punctuated by the occasional ping of stray bullets striking the van's exterior. But from her position, huddled protectively over Zoe, she couldn't discern the details of the battle raging around them.

The firefight was intense but mercifully brief. In less than a minute, the gunfire ceased, leaving silence in its wake. Zoe was crying. Alyson's eyes burned with tears as she fought to steady her breath, the panic creeping closer. She pressed her hands onto the van's floor, trying to anchor herself. What about her family? Were they okay?

A sharp command sliced through the tense silence. "No one move!"

From the van's floor, Alyson heard her father's voice, half disbelief, half hope. "Dad? Is that you? Don't shoot! It's Rich and Beth. The kids are here, too, with some friends."

There was a pause, then a gruff voice answered, "Rich? Is that really you, son?"

Alyson's heart leaped at the sound of her grandfather's voice. She cautiously lifted her head and peered through the shattered windshield to catch a glimpse of the scene unfolding outside.

Her grandpa embraced her dad, both men visibly relieved. Alyson let out a sigh of relief when her mom helped Eddie out of the ditch along the river side, both appearing uninjured. Mr. Verley and Mrs. Samms were also okay.

"Alyson?" her father's voice called, as Grandpa Dick turned to hug Eddie. "It's okay. You can come out now. Bring Zoe and Steve with you."

Hesitantly, Alyson shifted her position, careful to avoid the shards of glass scattered across the van's interior. She glanced at Zoe, who was still clinging tightly to her stuffed animal, eyes wide with fear and uncertainty.

"It's all right," Alyson whispered, giving the little girl's hand a reassuring squeeze. "That's my grandpa out there. We're safe now."

As the situation de-escalated, she cautiously helped Zoe out of the van, Steve padding quietly behind them.

"Alyson? Why, look at you. You've become even more beautiful in the last year." Grandpa Dick moved toward her. "You look almost exactly like your mom."

As the family reunited and her dad introduced everyone, someone from Grandpa Dick's group approached, his expression tight. "There are no survivors among the attackers. It might be them . . . I'm not sure."

Her grandpa's face hardened. "Is the girl with them?"

The group exchanged glances, shaking their heads as her grandpa explained, "One of our people's been kidnapped. We're out here to find her, get her back."

"We'll keep looking," the man assured him. "Why don't you take your family and get them situated?"

Eddie piped up. "Where's Uncle Brian?"

Grandpa Dick's expression softened slightly. "He went to Casper. Went to get his kids and his ex-wife. We're hoping he'll be back soon." He gestured toward the battered van. "Let's see if that thing still runs. Looks like it's been through the wringer, even before today's shooting."

Alyson's dad rested his hand on her grandpa's shoulder. "I can help you look for your missing person."

"Me too," Mr. Verley offered, his voice determined.

Grandpa Dick nodded, a hint of pride in his eyes. "Maybe. We have certain protocols we follow. We'll have to check with our medical adviser."

"Protocols?" Mr. Verley asked, a snap to his tone.

The other man from her grandpa's group spoke up. "We're going to keep looking. Use the radio when you're on your way back."

Grandpa Dick turned to Mr. Verley. "We've had a few issues. Had to put some plans in place for everyone's safety."

Mr. Verley opened his mouth to speak, but Alyson's dad said, "We understand. Don't we, Jim?"

"I guess there's no choice in the matter."

Grandpa Dick met his gaze. "You're right about that. We'll do what's necessary to keep everyone safe around here."

Her dad and Mr. Verley brushed the glass off the van's seats while the rest of them piled in the back, except Eddie, who grabbed his backpack before asking to ride with their grandpa in the pickup.

Grandpa Dick seemed to hesitate a moment before agreeing with a nod.

The engine sputtered to life, protesting but functional. Her dad took the wheel, and the van followed behind the old farm truck. As they drove, he pointed out landmarks. "That's the guest ranch where the group my dad's people have joined up with is from. The owner lives there year-round, the same as my folks.

"Last time I spoke with my folks, they said he'd brought up some people to live there, too, and help with security. A little further up is Pahaska Tepee, closer to Yellowstone. Those folks are with us too. I'm sure we'll meet them all soon. This is one of the reasons I wanted to come here. Because of the way they're working together."

"But they said a girl has been kidnapped," Alyson's mom said. "How'd that happen?"

Her dad shook his head. "I'm not sure. It's happened since I last spoke with him. I guess we'll get the details soon enough."

The landscape unfolded before them, a testament to nature's enduring beauty despite the trouble of the human world. The North Fork of the Shoshone River rushed alongside them, its clear waters a stark contrast to the turmoil they'd left behind.

Finally, they crested a hill, and the East Gate Lodge came into view. The main building, a grand log structure, stood proudly amid a cluster of smaller cabins.

On the wide porch of the main lodge, a figure stood waiting. As they drew closer, Alyson recognized her grandmother, Ruth. The older woman's posture was tense, her arm in a sling and her eyes wary as she watched the unfamiliar van following her husband's pickup.

The moment Eddie leaped from the truck, his backpack slung over one shoulder, Grandma Ruth's demeanor changed instantly. "Eddie! Oh, my boy. You're here. You're safe!" she cried, rushing down the steps to envelop him in a fierce one-armed hug.

The reunion that followed was a whirlwind of tears, laughter, and hurried explanations. Alyson found herself wrapped in her grandmother's embrace. The normally stoic woman, showing a rare vulnerability, clung to her as if afraid to let go, her voice thick with emotion. "Alyson, I'm so glad you're here. You have no idea how worried we've been."

"What happened to your arm?" Alyson asked, trying to avoid jostling her grandmother too much.

"Don't worry about that now. I'm fine and so happy you are here and safe."

As the initial excitement settled, Grandpa Dick turned to her dad and Mr. Verley. "I need to head back out and join the search." He glanced toward a woman on the porch. "Think my son and his friend can join the search before we put them in quarantine? We could use the help."

She hesitated, her eyes scanning the newcomers while taking in the battered van they'd arrived in. "Sorry, no. We need to follow protocols."

Mr. Verley scoffed, but her dad gave a nod. "We understand."

"We'll get everyone settled and comfortable," Grandma Ruth said. "We've had an, uh, incident. We make sure everyone is free of the sickness when they arrive."

"Sorry, son," Grandpa Dick said with a sigh. "I'll stop by when we're finished. When we've found her and have her back home."

"We're not sick," Alyson's mom argued. "None of us have any of the symptoms of those Star Brights."

"I'm sure you're fine." Grandma Ruth gave her an uncomfortable smile. "From the looks of your vehicle, you had a rough trip."

"You have no idea." Her mom's eyes filled with tears.

"I'll get you all settled in. You can rest, and we'll talk about how things have been here. We've made sure it's comfortable. I've even stayed in the quarantine cabin myself. Trust me, it's fine. We'll take good care of you. Our group is growing. Right now, we have several people out on the search party."

"Do you have room for us?" Eddie asked, glancing around. There was a woman with two young children around Zoe's age. Another group of women huddled inside the open door of the lodge, seeming to listen intently.

"Of course we do. We always have room for family. Now, let's get you settled. We can drive to the cabin if you'd like. Or walk if you prefer to stretch your legs. It's the one your cousins stayed in last year. It just emptied out. Another group was using it to quarantine, but their time ended."

"Were they okay?" Eddie's eyes were wide.

"They were fine."

"You said someone was kidnapped?" Alyson's mom asked. "Are we safe here?"

Grandma Ruth pursed her lips. "I believe so. We've increased security and . . . and we will find her. Bring her back."

Alyson's mom didn't look convinced.

"I'd rather walk," Eddie said.

Their mom agreed with a nod. "I don't want to ever get back in that van."

"That's fine then," Grandma Ruth said. "Perhaps Rich can drive the van?"

"Sure, Mom." He gave his mother a smile. "But I'm with Beth. It's served its purpose, but I don't know how much the old thing has in it."

"What about Steve?" Eddie motioned to the dog, who wagged his tail in response.

"Well, I don't suppose he needs to quarantine, but I'm sure he'd be happier staying with you all."

"Let's go, Steve." Mr. Verley tapped his leg. Even though Steve's wound was healing nicely, he moved stiffly, as they all did after several days stuck in the van.

"Maybe I'll be able to get my phone to work as a hotspot in the cabin," Eddie suggested. "Then I can play my game." He motioned to his VR headset still secured to his backpack.

"Doubtful," Grandma Ruth said. "There wasn't much of a cell signal up here before, and now the towers don't seem to be working at all."

"Oh." Eddie sighed, his shoulders drooping. "Jackson and I really like playing together. I was hoping he'd bring his VR set so we could have some fun."

"There's going to be plenty of things to do," their mom said. "You're not going to have much time for video games, especially after we're finished with quarantine."

Zoe's small hand slipped into Alyson's. "Are we home now?" the little girl asked, her voice tinged with both hope and uncertainty.

Alyson squeezed her hand gently. "Yes, Zoe. We're home. And we're safe."

As they walked toward the cabin, Alyson couldn't shake the feeling that while one chapter of their journey was over, another was quietly beginning. The world beyond their refuge was still dangerous and uncertain, but here, surrounded by family and the rugged beauty of Wyoming, they had arrived at the place they'd been heading toward all along. A place to call home.

The adventure continues in *Tally the Stars: Lights of the Collapse Book 3*.

Tally the Stars: Lights of the Collapse Book 3

What was supposed to be a relaxing summer turns into a fight for survival…

Kaelyn Fisher is spending her summer break before senior year with her grandparents in Cody, Wyoming. But a shooting at her doctor's office, followed by an explosion at the historic Irma Hotel, changes everything.

As the Star Brights begin taking over their once-peaceful town, Kaelyn and everyone she cares about find themselves in unimaginable danger.

With no safe place left, they make the difficult choice to leave their home and seek refuge with friends near Yellowstone Park.

But the sanctuary they're hoping for may be anything but safe.

Can Kaelyn and her grandparents escape the growing violence, or will leaving home be their fatal mistake?

Thank you for spending your time on our new Star Bright adventure.

If you have five minutes, you'd make this writer very happy if you could write a short review on Amazon, Goodreads, Bookbub, or your favorite review site.

I appreciate you!

Join my reader's club!
As part of my reader's club, you'll be the first to know about new releases and specials. I also share info on books I'm reading, preparedness tips, and more.

Please sign up on my website:
MillieCopper.com/Freebie

Also by Millie Copper

The Havoc in Wyoming Series

When a series of coordinated attacks devastate the United States, the people of Bakerville, Wyoming, must come together to survive. Unfortunately, not everyone has the town's best interest at heart. Some are striving for personal gain during the apocalypse.

The Montana Mayhem Series

A group from Bakerville, Wyoming strikes out on their own while searching for the desires of their heart. Unfortunately, the road will not be easy, and sometimes the heart is hardened and deceitful. When things don't work out as they hoped, will they become stranded in the wilderness? Or will each be able to find their way home?

The Dakota Destruction Series

After a series of coordinated attacks devastate the United States, Katie and Leo sacrifice everything to help their country. But some things aren't as they seem. Is it time to go home and start fresh, or can something good come out of this terrible situation?

In The October Fall World

In the blink of an eye, an EMP changed everything for Lauren and her family. Now they are in a fight for survival, trying to keep their loved ones alive as society collapses around them. Their once peaceful town of Cody, Wyoming has turned into a powder keg. And with law enforcement a thing of the past, evil lurks around every corner.

Nonfiction Books

Millie has penned seven nonfiction, traditional food focused books, sharing how, with a little creativity, anyone can transition to a real foods diet without overwhelming their food budget. Many of her books also include preparedness and food storage tips.

Find these titles at:
MillieCopper.com

Acknowledgments

Thanks to:

Ameryn Tucker, my editor, beta reader, and daughter wrapped in one. I had a story I wanted to tell, and Ameryn encouraged me and helped me bring it to life.

Dee from Dauntless Cover Design.

My husband, who gave me the time and space I needed to complete this dream and was very patient as I'd tell him the same plot ideas over and over and over.

Three more adult daughters and a young son, who willingly listen to me drone on and on about storylines and ideas while encouraging me to "keep going."

My amazing Beta Readers! Thanks to Barbara, Christine, Christy, Ilona, Jim, Linda, Melonie, Tammy, and Tracy for your help in creating the final story. Your insights and abilities to see the things I miss are very much appreciated!

And also, a special thank you to Tim, a specialist in all things that go boom, for always answering my questions and pointing out things I wouldn't even think about.

And to you, my readers, for spending your time on our new Star Bright adventure. If you have five minutes, you'd make this writer very happy if you could leave a review. I appreciate you!

About the Author

Millie Copper, writer of Cozy Apocalyptic Fiction and preparedness mentor, was born in Nebraska but never lived there. Her parents fully embraced wanderlust and moved regularly, giving her an advantage of being from nowhere and everywhere.

Millie Copper lives in the wilds of Wyoming with her husband and young son, tending chickens and attempting a food forest on their small homestead. After living off the grid for several years, they've recently gone back on the grid. Four adult daughters, three sons-in-law, and six grandchildren round out the family.

Since 2009, Millie has authored articles on traditional foods, alternative health, homesteading, and preparedness-many times all within the same piece. Millie has penned seven nonfiction, traditional food focused books, sharing how, with a little creativity, anyone can transition to a real foods diet without overwhelming their food budget.

The *Havoc in Wyoming, Montana Mayhem, Dakota Destruction, Wyoming Fall, and Yellowstone County Fall* Christian Post-Apocalyptic fiction series use her homesteading, off-the-grid, and preparedness lifestyle as a guide. The adventures continue with the *Lights of the Collapse* series.

Find Millie at www.MillieCopper.com
Facebook: www.facebook.com/MillieCopperAuthor/
Amazon: www.amazon.com/author/milliecopper

BookBub: https://www.bookbub.com/authors/millie-copper
Instagram: https://www.instagram.com/cozyapoc
YouTube: https://milliecopper.com/Youtube

www.ingramcontent.com/pod-product-compliance
Lightning Source LLC
Chambersburg PA
CBHW061637190726
48289CB00006B/1637